NOT SUITABLE
FOR WORK

ANTI-BELLE BOOK I

SKYE MCDONALD

Susan!
Happy Reading!
xoxo,
Skye McDonald

Anti-Belle Books

For L'Orso
As promised.

1

The smell of professional cleaner and furniture polish hit my nose as soon as I pushed open the heavy glass door. I breathed deep and smiled at the whir of a copier in the distance. *Finally.*

"Good morning, Ms. Greene," the receptionist called from behind her high-countered desk. She set aside a copy of *The Nashville Scene* and smiled up at me.

"Good morning, Sarah. Mr. Rollings said to be here by nine." I knew that it was precisely 8:54, because I'd been checking the time every few minutes since I woke up.

Sarah—or Say-ruh, as she drawled last Thursday when I arrived for my interview—nodded and looked at her computer. "It's a bit of a Monday, if you know what I mean. Mr. Rollings said to tell you he's running behind. He asked you to go up to the third floor and settle in. He'll meet you there."

"Which office do I go to?"

"We just acquired that floor, and so there's renovation tarps on one side. You'll see the door on the left as soon as you're off the elevator."

As long as this wasn't a dream, and I really was about to begin my first day of work after a miserable eternity, Mr. Rollings could ask me to go anywhere he damn well pleased. I flashed the girl a tight smile and punched the elevator call button.

My phone vibrated. A quick glance left me completely unsurprised at the sender.

Mom: Good luck on your 1st day!!

I dropped the phone back in my bag and made a mental note to thank her later. I didn't have the head space to chat with my cheering squad, especially not as the doors slid open and deposited me on the third floor—the floor I was to report to every day, rebuild my career doing what I loved, and earn a respectable paycheck again after over a year of rock-bottom living. *I'm going to own this floor. No mistakes this time. No misunderstandings.*

I puffed out a breath to scatter the dark thoughts that threatened to resurface. The office door was a few feet away, and my hand already reached for the knob. *It's time to begin again.*

The door sprang open before I could touch it. My hand stayed suspended in midair as I faced someone who was definitely not Mr. Rollings. This man was taller and much younger than my boss. My chin tipped up slightly so I could meet his curious gaze. *God, he's—*

"Sorry if I scared you."

I dropped my hand and stepped inside. "You didn't scare me. I just didn't expect..."

Words died as I took in the scene. Beige walls, navy carpet, a line of windows overlooking the street, and a kitchenette in the corner were all perfectly normal and adequate. But where I'd expected desks, maybe cubicles or rows of tables, the room was almost totally empty. There were no filing cabinets, no plants, none of the usuals for an office. Only two desks, tall enough that you could stand if you wanted, faced each other in the center of the room, each with a computer mounted and ready.

I looked around again and noticed a poster in a frame on the wall opposite. A generic image of sand dunes and blue sky underscored the words:

There is no substitute for accurate knowledge. Know yourself, know your business, know your men. —Lee Iacocca

"Oh, god, Comic Sans? Seriously?" My eyes traveled over the chubby curves of the letters. The desert landscape made me thirsty, but the words sent a weird tingle of premonition through my gut. Heinous font aside, in my old life, I would've rolled my eyes and considered the statement obvious, but that was *before*.

Before, when my office was an exposed-brick loft in Manhattan. Before, when, at 26 years old, I had a client list that most web designers dream of their whole lives. Before the day I took an early lunch and went uptown to a different office, this one chrome and glass, and threw my career away on an interview—a promise—that I thought was a sure thing. Before I went home and—

"I know. Couldn't be more random."

I spun around at my companion's words. He nodded to the poster. "This is a marketing firm, and that's the visual aesthetic you bothered to put up?" His wry tone made me smirk; when I did, he flashed a quick smile. "You must be another sucker. Hi, I'm—"

"Morning, folks!"

My knotted stomach leapt into my throat when the door banged open and Mr. Rollings strode into the room. He shook our hands like a politician at a rally, all toothy smiles and pleasantries, but *sucker* rattled in my head and made everything else background noise.

Rollings finished saying something about sports to the man, then clapped his hands together and looked between us. "How are my interns this morning?"

I looked around, as if somehow I'd missed the team of people I'd pictured when Rollings had hired me for an "internship-to-hire" opportunity. Tenn Star was expanding their advertising and marketing business to include website construction. The entry-level paycheck was better than nothing, but the "to-hire" part mattered most. I didn't doubt that I could prove myself against any programmer a local business like this would recruit. Fantasies of single-handedly creating a website so stunning that Rollings would name me head of Tenn Star's Design department before the six weeks were up had played in my head ever since I'd left the interview last week.

That would, however, require a department to lead.

Both men's gazes were on me when I looked back at them. I bit my cheek to keep panic from my tone. "Sorry, Mr. Rollings, but I had the impression Tenn Star was creating an online department." *This isn't happening. There's no way I've been screwed over again.*

He nodded. "Indeed we are, Ms. Greene. We're excited to expand into web development and design, but we have to start small, thanks to budget. Oh, shoot, I didn't have all the little details nailed down when we met, did I?"

"You said it was an internship, that you'd hire and staff based on performance." I didn't even bother to try and smile anymore.

"And indeed I will. We have three current clients who need websites, and they've agreed to be our guinea pigs in this little challenge. You and Mr. Addison will each design a homepage and a specialty page based on their needs, and then submit proposals. We'll do the sites one at a time, two weeks for each project, a best-of-three situation, if you will. The clients will select the design they prefer. This way we'll see which of your styles is a better fit for Tenn Star."

The last of my optimism evaporated as I clenched my fists and jaw. A quick sideways glance turned into a traded look with my—competitor? Rival? *Enemy*?

His dry sarcasm from moments ago was gone. Now, his lip curled faintly with what looked like disgust. He glanced from me to Rollings and said, "You're only hiring one of us? On Friday you said you'd staff based on performance. I thought this would be collaborative, the start of a department."

Rollings's face bloomed. "I'm sorry you misunderstood, Mr. Addison. I've only got the funds for one position until January, but I like what both of you bring to the job. Would your rather not accept the internship?"

When Mr. Addison looked at me this time, the irritation in his gaze made my eyes narrow. *You think you're pissed? Get in line. My make-or-break opportunity just got turned into a reality-TV competition.*

He eyed me another moment, then exhaled loudly and nodded to Rollings. "I'm in."

"Excellent." Rollings's shoulders dropped about six inches. "And you're still on board, right Ms. Greene?"

"Definitely."

"Great, great. Well, y'all go on and get settled."

Mr. Addison and I walked in step to the desks and claimed them. Like reflections in a mirror, we each pulled out a drawer, dropped our personal effects inside, and then reached to power on the computers. They hummed to life; we frowned at each other.

Rollings cleared his throat. "Sorry to leave y'all alone up here, but we don't have space on the lower floors. Now, you both met with Janet in HR last week. Do you have any questions about the intranet or design platforms you'll be using?" We shook our heads. With another subtle cough, our boss clapped his hands together. "Once I get to my computer, I'll send you an outline of the first job and get an initial meeting set up for this afternoon. Okay, you two, good luck!"

Silence settled when he exited. I gazed blankly as a cold, distant memory crept in and changed the scene.

Not a desk, but a table stretched in front of me in my mind's eye. *The table in our apartment, the one where we sat most nights, me on my computer or sketchpad and him reading or working late. The table where I thought we shared our life together.*

The table I set my purse on when I came home and learned that it was no mistake; the man I thought I loved sabotaged my career and betrayed me, all in an afternoon.

I pushed the memories away and stood from the desk to hurry to the bathroom. The light switch was still covered in plastic, and the air was dense with new-paint smell. I clawed the covering off and balled the cellophane in my fist. Staring at myself in the mirror, I watched hope crumble and my walls spring back up.

I moved home to Nashville six months ago for a fresh start, had waved the white flag and said goodbye to New York and all the fabulous and nauseating memories I'd made there. With my coding skills and résumé, moving had seemed like a good way to get life back on track, but that was six long, *poor*, months ago.

My auburn hair, blown and ironed to a sleek shine this morning, seemed to go limp in defeat. I looked down at my DVF wrap dress and beloved Prada boots. The outfit suddenly seemed like a huge waste of effort. Designer clothes used to be my indulgence. Yesterday, I'd been excited to take them out of the garment bags they'd lived in for over a year. Outfits I'd forgotten I owned—I'd forgotten what it was like to be able to afford—hung in the bathroom of my apartment, airing out.

Damn Rollings, didn't he realize my life wasn't a game? That I needed this job? Getting back on my feet and doing what I was good at were all that mattered. Did my desperation, my lack of interest in friends and fun—forget about love, no way was I fool enough to try that game again—didn't any of it translate to professional intensity when I'd interviewed with him?

Do you seriously think he cares?

I took another deep breath and lifted my chin. "There is no substitute for accurate knowledge. Know yourself. Know your business."

Maybe that little poster was a good sign after all.

Mr. Addison looked up when I emerged and strode around the space to mentally stake my claim. The air was stale, so I went to the windows and pushed a top pane open. It was a warm October day, and the breeze soothed my nerves. I took another deep breath and turned to meet his steady gaze.

"Needless to say, I didn't expect this." His voice made me think of a perfect cup of coffee, strong and dark, but with a faint drawl like a splash of cream.

The breeze's balm evaporated. "Yeah, well, get in line."

He grunted. "How do you want to handle this? What coding languages do you know? We could—"

I sliced the air, and he stopped. "Did you hear him? There's one job, and since there's one job, it will be mine. I'll ace the first two projects, and you can be on your way."

Wow, that was harsh. I bit my lip but didn't apologize. *So what if he thinks I'm cold? It's the truth, right?*

"Do you really want to play his game?" He seemed unfazed by my biting tone.

"I want the job. If you don't want to 'play,' then, please, go tell him now."

He cocked his head. "I'll play if you do."

Before I could reply, ask what the hell that meant, he turned to his computer and made it clear he meant to pay me no further attention. I waited a beat to be sure, then sat down and opened Rollings's email, determined to lose myself in planning.

The videoconference with our first client was held in the early afternoon, and the details he gave us put my ideas from the morning into the garbage disposal. Mr. Garret's company was a wholesale distributor of office products. He wanted a website for online orders, in-house inventory tracking, and revenue analysis. Light on frills, heavy on data.

Back at my desk, I stared at my notes and twirled my necklace so tightly around my finger that the tip turned purple.

"Doing okay over there?" Addison's question broke my trance.

"Fantastic." He didn't need to know that my experience was in commercial sites aimed at mass appeal. I wouldn't mind name-dropping some of the international companies formerly on my client list, but no way was I going to even hint that this job was outside my wheelhouse.

And no way was that going to stop me.

Hours slipped by. At six, Rollings popped in. "Quitting time! How did it go?" We both muttered affirmatives. "Good, good. Glad to hear. Well, we close up at six most nights. Y'all won't have keys to the building as interns, so be sure you don't forget anything. If Sarah's already left for the day, you won't be able to get back in until she opens up the next morning." He grinned. "See you tomorrow!"

Addison and I looked at each other. This was a test, I was sure. Would I call it a day before him? The hell I would, hourly paycheck be damned. I turned back to the computer, prepared to stay all night if need be. An extra hard click on my mouse made my intention known, but Addison pushed away from his desk a minute later. I froze, fingers hovering over the keyboard, determined not to look up while he went for the exit.

"Goodnight." He shut the door.

Great. Now I was stuck. My focus was broken, but if I encountered him in the parking lot, things would be even more awkward. I fidgeted in my chair and felt another prickle of guilt for being so cold with him. *It's for the best, I guess.*

And how long do I have to sit here?

I rubbed my forehead and reached for my phone.

"Well?" Mom greeted on the second ring, so I filled her in on the situation. She was quiet. "That's weird. Sounds like a TV show."

"I know, right?" I cried, but it was a relief. Count on Mom to be realistic. "Rollings liked my portfolio, said my client list was 'impressive,' and now this. I didn't even cringe when he called me sweetheart."

Her laugh made me smile, even after this long day. "Your client list is indeed impressive, and I have no doubt your talents will see you through this, *sweetheart*." I groaned, and she laughed again. "So, this boss of yours. How would you describe him? Is he like the executives in all the books your Aunt Jen reads? Tailored suits, brooding, handsome as—"

"*Stop.*" I almost fell off the seat. "The man has pictures of his children all over his office, and is clearly in a committed relationship with both his desk chair and pastries."

Oh, it felt good to laugh. "Fine, fine," she said when our giggles subsided. "Come to dinner soon and fill us in."

I ended the call and sat in silence another minute. The idea of Tenn Star's CEO as a character in a romance novel was too funny. A moment later, though, a shiver ran through me when words spoken by someone who looked the part flashed in my mind.

I'll play if you do.

My gaze came into focus on Addison's chair. With a hard shake of my head, I shouldered my bag and headed home.

BEN

I jumped into my car and reached for the stereo. Eight hours of tense, nearly uninterrupted silence rang in my head. I cranked the volume, not giving a damn what was playing as long as my ears were full, and sank into the seat as I mentally reviewed this clusterfuck day.

That doofus Rollings hadn't said a word about a one-on-one contest at my interview last week. He'd explained the internship and warned me about, "A gal from New York with a hell of a former client list and some serious skill." I'd taken the message to mean she was my biggest threat for the head position, not my *only* challenge.

This morning, Sarah, the receptionist, told me I was the first new hire to arrive—again, no indication that I equaled half of the roster—and sent me upstairs to wait. I'd barely had time to wonder why there were only two desks in the room before I heard the elevator ding from the hall. Opening the office door, I expected to see Rollings and a crew of programming kids, probably recent college grads. What I got was much, much better.

Sea glass. Emeralds. *Holy shit.*

Her hand was outstretched to the doorknob, but all I noticed were those brilliant green eyes. *Rollings, you corny bastard, I love you.* The thought flickered while I watched her walk around the room, watched her confusion mount and connect to mine. But when our boss arrived and told us his plan, my little bromance turned into, *Rollings, you asshole, I hate you.* As the day went on, the sentiment intensified.

My thoughts scattered when light spilled from the building's entrance. I sat up and hooked my wrists on the steering wheel as Ms. Greene stepped out and looked around. Seeming to find the coast clear, she strode toward a sedan a few yards away. I turned down the radio—sure enough, I could hear those sexy boots clipping across the pavement.

I grinned. *I thought you were working late, Ms. Greene. That sharp click on your mouse was supposed to tell me you didn't mind working overtime for free, wasn't it?*

Never had I met a woman as guarded, as walled-off as she was. She'd been ready to eat me for lunch and toss the carcass from the moment Rollings left us alone, but her lifted chin and snippy tone went too far. It told me somehow that her walls weren't for me, they were for the world. Ms. Greene had something to prove.

Interesting. What are you hiding from? And who are you, really?

And why don't we talk about it over dinner tomorrow? My place, eight o'clock?

Her taillights faded, and so did my smile. I rubbed my eyes hard and glanced at the stereo. David Bowie's "Life on Mars" was playing.

How appropriate.

Her story doesn't matter to you. You've had enough trouble this year of your own. Keep your damn head down and do the job.

I fired the engine and went the hell home.

2

"Assistant? I thought you needed someone to head the department."

Mr. Rollings smiled. "Oh, no, Ms. Greene. That job has been filled for three months. I was surprised that you wanted an assistant position, especially since your firm spoke so highly of you, but Mr. Addison will be glad to have your help."

"You called my firm?" My non-compete clause leapt to mind and twisted my gut.

"Of course."

I sat up in bed, fists clenched in the cool satin sheets, and looked around. Pale daylight filtered through the plastic blinds that covered my little window; the beautiful blue quilt my grandmother made was twisted at the foot of the bed.

I fell back against the pillows with a huff. *Just a nightmare.*

Of course it was. Because of course it wasn't Mr. Rollings who had said those words to me. Despite the huge curve my new boss threw yesterday, *he* wasn't the one who made the phone call that unraveled my career.

And it certainly wasn't Tenn Star's posting on an employment website that made me ignore the non-compete clause and interview with a competitor for a job I thought was a sure thing. Nope, that kind of risk was based on trust —on love, or so I'd thought.

Look where that got me.

Yeah, but you learned your lesson. Now, go prove what you can do.

The workday resumed exactly as we'd left off. Deep concentration and zero conversation seemed to be the agreed-upon "rules" to our game. At first, I expected him to break and start up with chitchat or questions, but the silence held, and the longer it did, the more I appreciated it. The task was tough, and I had enough to focus on.

Besides, even without saying a word, Addison's presence was distracting. Anytime he yawned or moved, my attention wanted to flit across the desks. I itched to peek over his shoulder and see what his plans looked like. When he left Tuesday evening, I leaned back in the chair and exhaled like I'd held my breath all day. I was ready to leap up and leave, but remembered as I reached for my bag to wait ten minutes again. As soon as the timer went off, I was gone.

Keyboard clatter and mouse clicks filled my ears Wednesday morning, shattered around noon by one word: "Lunch." I jumped out of my skin at Addison's quiet declaration, but he was up and out.

Wonder what he does on his lunch hour? Is he vegan, eating sprouts in his car and listening to reggae music? I snorted; seemed unlikely. *Maybe he meets someone.*

Maybe he isn't your business.

A text notification chimed as I picked up my bag, and I scrambled for my phone. It was almost certainly Mom, but I still hoped it might be Amy or Kandra, my best friends in New York. We'd started to lose touch long before I moved home, but I'd texted them about my new job over the weekend, so maybe they'd finally gotten back to me.

The screen showed only the time and my frown in the reflection. Another chime sounded, and I noticed Addison's phone glowing by his keyboard. Three text bubbles crowded the screen.

Not your business.

My gaze slid sideways to the door.

Isn't your business.

I tiptoed around the desks and touched his phone. "So not your damn business," I whispered as I read.

Liv: Work SUX. Faking enthusiasm is so hard. #ThatsWhatSheSaid.

Jack: You'll be there on Saturday, right? Need your input on a new project.

James: I didn't ask if she was nice. I asked if she was HOT.

A car alarm blared from the open window and made me jump so hard I bit my tongue. *That's what you get for being nosy.* I scurried out of the office and tried to erase the memory of what I'd read as I pushed open the stairwell door.

After that first ride up, I'd taken the stairs daily for exercise, but no one else seemed to. Between that and my adrenaline, I almost fell down the top flight when the first-floor door banged open and footsteps pounded my way. I gripped the rail and locked my knees. My other hand groped in my purse for the mace I always carried.

Addison rounded the landing and stumbled to a stop

when he saw me at the top of the staircase. He was a little winded, and his lips parted as I stared down at him. My gaze dipped to his mouth and lingered there. By the time I met his eyes again, there was a wicked glint in his look that kicked my pulse even higher.

It wasn't my intention to speak first, but neither of us seemed in a hurry to break the moment. "This time, you scared me a little."

He climbed three steps and nodded. "Sorry, I forgot my—"

"Phone. It's on your desk." I refused the guilty reflex to cut my eyes away.

"Thanks. Are you going out?" I nodded at his question. "Where?"

"Just, um, to..." My words died when he ascended two more steps. Without thinking, I dropped down one, bringing us eye-to-eye.

"Out where?" he repeated, but I couldn't answer.

What is wrong with you? Did he scare you that badly?

If only it were as simple as fear. Addison's eyes were the color of pewter, gray like I'd never seen before. His black-brown hair kissed his forehead with just enough length to be stylish, and its contrasting darkness made his gaze even more striking. A strong jaw and cheekbones completed the dashing look.

Worse still was the trace of smile he wore. From this proximity, I could no longer ignore the other part of why he distracted me so easily. The thought that had started to form in the first moment I saw him, before the mess of this contest landed on us, hit me in the sternum. *God, he's good-looking.*

No, not good-looking. Addison was gorgeous.

When I'd gaped at him for far too long, he tilted his

head and cleared his throat. "Are we going to spend the hour staring at each other?"

"Oh, sorry, I'm in the way." I plastered myself against the wall.

He stepped up level, forcing me to cut my eyes up to see him. "Do you always take the stairs?"

"Yeah. It's only three flights."

The right corner of his mouth curled, and a mortifying heat swept over me. "Of course you do."

"Of course I do." The airy tone I was going for sounded more like a nervous trill. I closed my eyes.

"Later, Greene." He continued on, and my ears vaguely registered that he hummed a little tune under his breath as he went.

Cheeks burning, I hurried to the refuge of my car.

Rollings was leaning on my desk, chatting with Addison, when I returned. "There she is," Rollings greeted me. "Got an update from Jimmy just now. He wants to add a promotions page to the proposal. Can we make that happen?"

Addison and I exchanged a glance. Less than a day to finish what I'd started *and* add a page?

I put on a smile. "Sure thing, Mr. Rollings." *Guess there's no point in asking about overtime on an intern's salary, huh?* Good thing I didn't have plans that night—or ever. Addison nodded, and Rollings did his thing where he clapped his hands and "left us to it."

"You might as well sleep here," Addison said once I'd settled at my desk.

"What?" I snapped. *When did you become someone who snapped at people?*

"You've been working so late, I assume it'll be doubly so tonight, right?"

"Oh. Right. Well, um, best get to it."

"Indeed."

We were deep in the project when Rollings appeared again at six. "About ready to take off?"

"No, sir. I'll be here awhile." *Like you don't know that.*

"Me too."

My stomach clenched. *Of course he'll stay. He won't have a choice either. Dammit, why did you have to make such a fool of yourself on the stairs?*

Rollings frowned. "Y'all know I can't pay you extra, right? You're under no obligation to work late." We nodded at his question, under every obligation to do what was needed to impress the client. "Well, I hate to do it to you, but if you don't have a choice, I understand. Get home safe." He waved on his way out.

Addison and I traded another look before we went back to work. Right away, I realized I'd been silly to think this would be awkward. It was more of the same.

Close to 9:00, I found a stopping place. With a deep exhale, I shut down and leaned backward to arch my spine over the chair. My hair swung free while I stared at the ceiling and wall behind me, arms by my ears.

"Finished?"

For a moment, I'd forgotten about the man across the desk. Addison's question had me slinging forward, startled and inexplicably embarrassed. He watched me with a blank expression, but when my eyes met his, the smile that ghosted his lips somehow confirmed my embarrassment. "Yes," I whispered.

"Yes?"

"Yes, I'm finished."

He shifted in his chair and reached for the power button. "Then let's get out of here."

On the way down, I asked, "Did you finish?"

"Yeah, I wrapped up about ten minutes ago."

"Why didn't you leave?"

He glanced over his shoulder as we rounded the final landing. "I wasn't leaving you alone here this late."

Stubborn independence flared in my chest. "You haven't had a problem every other night."

He smiled, eyes lit with amusement, and the flare turned again into that terrible *heat* from earlier. "Ten minutes isn't the same as three hours. I took a call in the car before I left last night and saw you come out."

Heat was forgotten as my jaw clenched so hard I worried I might break a tooth. "I'm working my ass off on this project," I hissed, angry with myself for being caught.

"Sure, but the pretense of long hours definitely adds to your mystique."

How dare you, you... you... dammit! When I didn't reply, he nodded at my tongue-tied glare and turned away.

My pride was too bruised. I couldn't let it go, even while I shuffled to my car and tried to dismiss the sting of humiliation. With my keys clutched so hard they dug into my palm, I spun around and ran after him, boots clipping on the pavement. "Listen." He turned and leaned against the door of a black CR-V with a zero-interest attitude. "Listen," I repeated, throat tight. "I don't need to work late to do my job, and I don't have to explain to you when I choose to come and go."

"No one said you did." His sly tone goaded my anger. "No one said you had to stay a second after six. You're the one who—"

"I'm the one who finishes when I'm ready."

"Come on, Greene," he laughed. "It's for show. Like I said, it adds to the mystique. Don't worry so much."

"You're making fun of me, you son of a—"

"That's my mother you're talking about," he countered, still with that too-casual amusement. He was studying his nails, for crying out loud.

I bit my lip until I winced. "You have no idea what I can do. I'm good, and I'm dead serious about this job. You don't get to question that."

He dropped his shoulders and the attitude. "I don't question it."

I didn't doubt his sincerity. My thundering emotions started to simmer down—until he took a single step toward me.

"I don't," he repeated.

"Good. So, goodnight." I waited too long before turning away; when I did, he spoke again and brought me back.

"Hey, Greene? What's your name?"

My eyes widened. "Wow, how did we never—it's Celeste."

Another half-smile flickered as he gestured to himself. "Benjamin. Ben if you like."

Benjamin. "Oh. I see." *I see? What the hell kind of thing is that to say?*

"Goodnight, Ms. Greene."

The quiet humor in his voice made me all but run to my car. I dropped into the seat and sighed. "Know your business, Celeste. He's not it."

BEN

I already knew her name. I just wanted her to say it.

This morning, after I'd been so entertained to see her exit the building minutes behind me for a second night in a row, I leaned on Sarah's desk and whispered, "I've got an awkward question." Her eyes went round with curiosity, so I scratched my head and added sheepishly, "Figured you must know everything around here."

She turned pink. "Not everything. What can I help you with, Mr. Addison?"

"Start by calling me Ben." I smiled as her cheeks went from pink to red. Sarah was too sweet for her own good—I wasn't even *trying* to make her blush.

"What's up, Ben?"

I looked around to reinforce the secrecy. "I never got Ms. Greene's name, and I feel like an idiot sitting up there and not knowing it."

I thought I sold it well, but Sarah's eyes said a lot. What they said was, *nice try, boy*.

A dimple dotted her left cheek when she grinned. "Her

name's Celeste," she whispered—and then *winked* at me. I arched my brows, but she laughed. "You're welcome, Ben."

So, yes. I knew her name. But I didn't have it until she gave it to me.

Celeste nearly broke into a sprint to get to her car, and I leaned against my bumper and finally let myself laugh about our absurd situation. I laughed longer and harder than made sense, but dammit all, what else could I do?

I'd been good and stayed firm in my resolve to keep silent like she wanted. If it hadn't been for that little encounter in the stairwell today, maybe I could've ignored my lovely, stubborn counterpart indefinitely.

My laughter faded at the thought.

What had you so tongue-tied and breathless, Celeste? Did you feel the energy snap between us? I sure as hell did.

I shook my head and got in the car. My brother called as I drove home, so I tapped the Bluetooth to life. "What's up?"

"You never answered my text."

"Because I'm not dignifying that with a response. You asked about the job and my competition. I told you, she's determined."

"I reiterate: I asked if she was *hot*."

Fucking right, she's hot. I groaned. "She's got an attitude that would shrivel most guys' dicks, okay?"

James laughed. "Knowing you, that answers my question with a resounding yes."

I had to admit, he had a point. We both laughed, but his next words were serious. "Be careful, dude. No bullshit, you're my little brother. I don't want you to—"

"Not remotely the same thing," I hurried to assure him. "This is a competition, and she's no joke. Work is going to kick my ass. That's all I need to worry about."

He grumbled. "Okay. I'll see you Saturday."

I smiled as the line went dead. After three days of tension and silence, it was nice to know my people were thinking of me.

Who thinks of you, Celeste? Who's got your back?

3

Friday morning was a whirl. Our draft meetings with Garret were scheduled back-to-back after lunch. I was quintuple-checking every detail at midday when Sarah knocked on our office door. We looked up at our first visitor besides Rollings all week.

"Hey, you two!" Sarah grinned when we turned to face her. She was charming and friendly, and I'd started to enjoy her morning banter about the weather and entertainment news more each day. "I wanted to let you know that we do drinks at The Flipside after work on Fridays. You might be all alone up here, but you're still part of our team. You should totally come!"

Before either of us could respond, she bounded back out the door. Addison—*Ben? Benjamin? No, Addison is safer*—faced me. "Is she old enough to get into a bar?" he asked, and I agreed with a small smile. "Are you going?"

Was I going? Out? With people? "I don't know. I don't have plans, but... Are you?"

"It depends."

"On?"

"On if you're going."

I scowled. "Seriously? It'll kill you to sit at a table with me? Am I that horrible?"

"What are you talking about?"

"You just said—"

He waved a hand to cut me off. "Not that I'm surprised, but you completely misunderstood me. I didn't mean I'd go if you didn't. What I meant was," he leaned into his forearms and cocked his head. "I'll go if you do."

I didn't miss the way his inflection mirrored his dare from the first day. *I'll play if you do. Why the hell would you want to play with me? I'm nothing but an ice queen on a mission to kick your ass.* I bit my lip and glanced up at him. "Oh," was the only thing I could think to say.

His lips twitched, but he hid it fast. "Mm-hmm. Later." He pushed back from the desks, humming as he made his way to the door.

I slumped in my chair. *Good god, every conversation with that man is a test of nerves.*

Mr. Garret nodded at my draft, promised to have requests for changes in my inbox Monday, and that was it. I spent the hour of Addison's meeting making notes and cleaning my keyboard. When he returned, we traded a stoic glance that clearly said, *no questions asked.*

"Rollings says we can take off," he reported.

I'd worn a navy plaid pencil skirt, white ruffled top, and blue ballet slipper pumps that day, so my look was preppy but spiffy enough. All I needed to be Friday-night ready was a touchup of my favorite Urban Decay lipstick, so I rummaged in my bag and twisted the tube.

Addison cleared his throat, and I looked up. He stood behind his chair, one arm through his jacket, watching me intently.

I rolled my lips. "Ready?"

"What?"

"Drinks, right?"

"Yeah." He didn't move, his attention fixated on my mouth.

For a second, I itched to lean forward, smile, and ask what he was thinking. Just as quickly, reality smacked me straight. *Ice queen. Rivals. Know yourself.* "Then let's go."

Sarah looked up and clapped her fingertips together when we stepped into the lobby. "Yay, you're coming! I can tell 'cause you've got your lips on again, Celeste." I smiled back.

Addison laughed. "You can tell she's going out simply because of her lips?" His tone was lighter than usual, but a warm stone sank in my belly at the way his voice caught on the word lips. He narrowed his eyes and stepped closer to peer at my mouth, a wicked gleam in his eye.

Sarah's laugh made him turn—and let me take a breath. "Of course! A girl won't put on more makeup to go home on a Friday night."

"Unless she really has something to go home to, I suppose." He grinned and leaned on her desk, and I marveled at how relaxed he was with her, how friendly. *Because she's not you, duh. Why wouldn't people be friendly to a sweet girl like her?*

Sarah blushed and waved us away. "Y'all head on and get a table, okay? I'm about twenty minutes behind you."

Table, double whiskey, and a cold shower. Sure thing, Sarah. I hustled out the door, Addison close behind. "You know how to get there?" he asked.

Still foolishly rattled, I nodded but didn't look up.

BEN

The only way not to lose your mind in Nashville traffic is to know the back roads. The Flipside wasn't far, and a few shortcuts later I nailed a parking spot on the street out front. I twisted the rearview mirror to check my hair—then cringed at myself for being such a sap. Didn't stop me from doing a quick finger-comb before I hurried up the restaurant's porch to wait by the door.

Celeste pulled into the lot across the street minutes later. She paid the machine and hurried toward me. *Don't grin. She'll freak out after you teased her in front of Sarah.* That thought alone made me want to laugh, but I swallowed it down and held the door open for her.

The Flipside was decorated like a retro diner with high-backed booths and plenty of chrome. Chicken sizzled and perfumed the air, but the place was still fairly empty. We staked a long table in the back and took chairs opposite each other.

A waitress sauntered over. "What are y'all drinkin'?" she asked, so I nodded for Celeste to order first.

"Jameson. Also, could I get an IPA? Thanks."

Well, damn. I'd figured a "New York gal" like her, with her sharp fashion sense and haughty streak as wide as the Mississippi River, would've been all about the Cosmopolitans. "Sounds good. I'll have the same," I said to the server.

While we waited, I sat back and watched Celeste do everything she could to avoid eye contact. She studied her hands, the table, and the bar to our left, but her gaze flicked to me every few seconds. I suppressed another smile.

Come on, Celeste. Look at me. We're at a bar. We can chat a little, right?

I searched for a conversation starter, but nothing seemed safe enough. *What's your story? Why is a woman like you fighting for a position like this? Hmm, too invasive. How long have you been in programming? No, might sound like I'm fishing for info.*

Did you know how thirsty I was while I stared at your mouth? Do you have any idea how beautiful you are, how often I look at you during the day? Why do you seem so sad?

Is there someone who makes you happy? Is there someone who can make you come so hard that you forget all your troubles?

"What is wrong with you?"

"Sorry, what?" Celeste's brows knitted curiously.

Shit! Recover, quick! "What, ah, what's wrong with—"

"Two Jamesons, two IPAs."

I could've kissed that waitress for her timing. Celeste grabbed her whiskey the moment it was in front of her, but I lifted mine and said, "What should we toast? We don't have much to celebrate."

"Then let's drink to a week of work. And to the fact that, for tonight, we don't have to compete with each other."

I grinned, and her shoulders lowered. "Be careful, Ms. Greene. I can get competitive about Jameson." To prove the point, I tossed back the shot in a single gulp.

She watched me, and then belted hers, too. *Nicely done. God, I wish you'd been a Cosmo sipper.* The idea of sharing a bottle of whiskey—maybe under a blanket, in front of a fire—sounded too damn appealing.

Sarah arrived with five vaguely familiar people from the office in tow. We hadn't been introduced to them, so handshakes and hellos commenced. Drinks, food, and conversation filled the next hour and gave me somewhere else to put my attention.

From the corner of my eye, I noticed Celeste cradling her beer while she listened to the group talk about college football. She twisted her head to look around the room, and I abandoned subtlety and watched her until her gaze landed on me.

Her mouth softened into a tiny smile, just a flash, but it was enough. *Here we go.* I took another swallow of beer and stood up, rounding the table to the vacant chair beside her. My sleeve brushed against her silky white shirt. She sat up straighter, knees angled toward me.

"Why did you come out tonight?" she asked abruptly, saving me from asking the same thing.

"Because I wanted to." *Because I wanted this moment right here. Because I've been dying to talk to you.*

Her chin lifted, a saucy little move, almost playful. "You said you wanted to come if I did. So, don't you mean because *I* wanted to?"

"No, I said I'd go if you did." I chuckled. "It seemed right to see if you could compete with me on a different playing field." *What the fuck am I talking about?*

Celeste flipped her hair and went with my nonsense. "I can compete with you with one hand tied behind my back."

My blood began to pound at the host of filthy images that statement conjured. I let my gaze travel over her face, down to where one lock of hair rested against her collar. It looked dark brown in the dim bar, but I knew her hair was a rich auburn that blazed when the light caught it.

I met her eyes again. "I'm sure you can, Ms. Greene. Now, ask me a different question."

"Why would I do that, Benjamin?" she asked, her voice all throaty.

I swallowed a groan, but her brows twitched and told me she knew how much I liked hearing her say my name. To return the favor, I damn near hissed hers when I said, "Because that's what people do when they're having a conversation, Celeste."

She squirmed. *Aww, what's the matter? Feeling a little tense? Want me to make it better—or worse?*

"Which do you go by, Benjamin or Ben?"

"Either is fine, but my friends call me Ben."

"Your turn, *Benjamin*." She tipped her glass toward me.

I smirked at the implication and bypassed pleasantries. "Do you hate me?"

She startled. "Honestly? A little, yeah."

"Seems unfair. Why do you hate me a little?" I used her words to tease her and keep us from getting too serious.

"You're another roadblock in my life. I hate fighting for a job I know I can do very well. Plus, you're a jerk."

I itched to ask for elaboration on that roadblock comment but knew better. Instead, I widened my eyes put a hand on my heart. "I'm a jerk? Ouch. Maybe I could say the same thing about you."

She didn't smile. In fact, she looked away, lips parted to take in a breath. "I know. I'm good with that."

"Yeah?"

"Yeah. I don't care what you think of me."

Bullshit. "No, you want me to think you're a jerk. The real question is why?"

The flush of alcohol that had begun to tinge her cheeks morphed into an angry blush. "Next question, please," I said before she could shut this down.

It worked. Her pinched forehead smoothed as her color ebbed. "Are you glad you're here, Benjamin?"

I reached for my beer, suddenly thirsty again. Once I'd drank, I looked into her expectant eyes and gave her the God's honest truth. "Definitely."

"What do you think, Addison? Do the Vols have a chance this year?"

I didn't want to look away, mostly because I knew the guy who'd spoken—Joe, I think his name was—had been eyeing Celeste across the table all night. His loud, pointed question was clearly a way to butt into our conversation.

But these were our colleagues, and I knew impressions mattered. I grimaced a smile and looked over. "They always have a chance," I said, and then recited what I'd read about the University of Tennessee's new quarterback and this year's recruiting class. They gave me a boisterous agreement, and I grinned and returned to Celeste.

But the music swelled before we could speak, and Sarah interrupted us again. "Come on, y'all!" she called while our colleagues made for the dance floor.

"You want to?" I asked Celeste, unsure if dancing with her would be hot as hell or a terrible mistake. *Both. Definitely.*

She shook her head, an exaggerated motion clearly aided by the drinks she'd consumed. "Dance? Oh, god no, not me."

I frowned at the finality in her tone. "Why do you say it like that?"

She started to object, but bit her lip instead. *Let your guard down. I dare you.*

I laid a hand on the table and bent to her ear. Her flowery scent filled my head as I whispered, "Suit yourself, but it's not a crime to let go and dance, Celeste." I lingered for another deep inhale, then pulled back.

Her dazed expression had me triumphant, but then she shook her head. "Time to go home." She was up before I could object. I rose to follow, not surprised at all when she put her fist on her hip. "I don't need you to escort me."

"Yeah, well, I'm going to. Contrary to popular opinion I'm not actually a jerk." I gestured her on despite the scowl she flashed.

She weaved a path to the door. Outside on the patio, I closed my hand around her elbow when she rummaged for her keys. "Put those away. You need a cab. You staggered all the way out here. No way are you driving."

I ignored her spluttered protests and ordered an Uber. "A car will be here in ten. I'll wait with you." *I'd drive you, but offering would probably be way out of bounds.*

"You're not my father." Her scowl intensified, but I refused to engage in a debate. "I don't need someone to—I mean, I've been on my own since—shit." She rubbed her forehead and sighed. "That's probably a good idea. Thanks."

"No worries." We leaned together on the patio rail. "Tell me one more thing," I said to break the silence.

She looked at me. "Like what?"

"I don't know. Tell me something you wouldn't if you were sober. Give me a truth."

"I'm not *that* drunk." Her laugh let me relax. I watched her expression grow distant, thoughtful, before, "You know that little poster on the wall at work?" I nodded. "Would you say that you know yourself, Benjamin?"

Interesting. "I'd say so. I like to think so."

"Well, I learned to know myself the hard way. I learned that who I thought I was wasn't close to what people saw in me. I learned—I didn't know—how empty I am." She closed her eyes and drew a long breath, then attempted a smile. "Not an easy thing to know about yourself," she whispered just as the car pulled up with a beep.

Holy shit. Her walls were down, and that fucking driver was going to take her away and ruin everything. "Wait, don't go, I—" I reached for her without considering what I was doing.

She stepped away and curtseyed mockingly, eyes cast down. "Burn that statement from the record."

Her ride honked again. All I could say was, "Goodnight."

Once more, her gaze hit me hard. "Goodnight, *Benjamin*."

~

I didn't go back inside, just grabbed my keys and got the hell out of there. When I fell facedown in bed awhile later, I had to acknowledge my own truth.

Celeste Greene wasn't an idle curiosity or a cute girl at work. She was something much more, much deeper than I'd anticipated.

I didn't need this distraction. Hell, except for my friends, I hardly trusted women anymore beyond a casual encounter. On top of that, our situation was a terrible setup for any sort of personal connection.

But connection was precisely what I felt. And I would very willingly explore how deep it could go, if only she'd say the word.

4

With no place to be and not much reason to get up, I slept late the next day and spent the morning in bed. No brunch dates, no extra spending money, nothing to do but let my thoughts drift. I didn't want to think about last night, about how fuzzy my head had really been or how my stupid mouth had felt free to run to the person who was essentially my enemy, but it was hard to avoid. Harder still was pushing away the memory of how he'd whispered in my ear with that damn tempting smirk on his lips.

A long-dormant itch tingled in my fingertips. I rolled to my feet and hurried to the single shelf of books beneath the TV in the living room. A sketchpad was sandwiched between its twin and a novel I didn't remember buying. Running my fingertip over the top to wipe away the dust, I plucked the pencil from the spiral bind and wandered back to bed. The book was only about a third full, but all the images were dark and gloomy. My favorite was an hourglass where the sand poured out of a crack, filling the bottom of the page with shadow.

Darkness wasn't in my head that morning. I sprawled on

my stomach across the bed, feet in the air like I was twelve years old again. The warm autumn sun kept the tingle of embarrassment away as I drew the only thing I could picture:

Lips.

Lips—smiling, laughing, frowning, women's, and men's —filled my page. Drawing was my favorite hobby since I could hold a pencil. I'd almost forgotten how soothing it could be, how my thoughts quieted as I took an idea from my head to the page.

When I finished, my own lips were curled in a smile. "You've got your lips on again," I whispered at the paper, then closed the book and went to start my day.

Mom was more than happy to support the choice not to drive home the night before. Once she and I retrieved my Toyota, I went to the gym, and afterward reported to my parents' house for dinner. A feast of salmon, wild rice, and broccoli was a welcome break from the potatoes and salad that dominated my grocery budget. My mother had "hired" me to run her patisserie's website when I moved home, but all that meant was she paid half the rent on my apartment. Good thing they'd taught me to save my money since I started working, or else I'd be living with them, or in a cardboard box, by now.

"How's the job going, Twink?" My father's blue eyes sparkled whenever he worked my childhood nickname into a conversation.

"Well, Sam, the project is a challenge, and the contest is an added headache," I returned, triumphant at the eye-roll from both of them. Attempts to insinuate that "Mom and Dad" were passé had fallen on deaf ears throughout my adolescence. Now, it was just a running joke.

"What's the other guy's story?" Mom asked.

His name is Benjamin, and he's too handsome for words. He's quiet, but I think he likes to laugh—maybe at me. He makes me warm. I like it.

The response flashed and stunned me so badly that I paused, the water glass halfway to my lips, and then took a long draught. My parents traded a glance while I drained the whole thing.

The glass thumped on the table a little harder than I intended. "I don't know his story, and I don't need to." A pair of lowered chins and curious stares met my declaration, so I hurried to ask after the eccentric neighbors and take the focus off my situation.

It worked until Mom started to clear the table. "Do you have plans tonight?"

I looked up at her overly casual question. "I thought this was my plan."

Her green eyes sparkled. They were the same shade as mine, but hers always seemed brighter, especially with her blonde hair and the smile she usually wore. "Oh, good, because I've got a surprise. Nick's sitting in with a group he knows, and we thought you'd..." Mom's words and mirth died when I set my jaw and crossed my arms. She tried again. "You won't have to chat with anyone, since it's a show. Nick's good, did you know that?" I shrugged. "You two were best friends growing up. Have you called him since you came home?"

"No, mother, I've not called my cousin. I haven't called anyone, and you know it." I took a steadying breath and softened my tone. "I'm not ready."

"You've been home for *six months*. It's your family, honey."

"It's people who don't know me anymore."

"Celeste! How can you say that?"

I shook my head. "I can't do it, Mom. I can't take the questions. Am I glad to be home? Do I miss the big city? How's work? And, let's not forget the inevitable: what happened to that guy I was seeing? Derrick, wasn't that his name? He seemed so nice and—" I broke off, unable to continue the rant over the bitterness in my throat. "Excuse me." I threw my napkin on the table and stalked out to the patio.

Yellow light sliced the darkness several minutes later. Dad dropped into the chair beside me without a word. "I didn't mean to flip out," I whispered, but he only hummed and studied the moon. As usual, his thoughtful silence got me to talk. "It's just, they don't know anything about me and I... I'm not ready to explain." I sighed. "I don't have a story worth telling."

"You're absolutely right. They don't know you. They know the girl you used to be, not the woman that you are. And, no, your life these days isn't something I'd want to chat about over a casserole, either." We both chuckled. "None of that changes how they're there for you, how much they love you. Time and circumstance don't damage bonds like those. I really hope you feel the truth of that someday."

I looked down at my shoes. How do you tell your father the *woman you are* is a cold-hearted shrew who can't keep friends or a lover? The thought of the people I adored as a child seeing who I'd become was unbearable. Mom and Dad knew I'd lost my job and had a rough breakup, but no one knew all the details. *No one.*

The screen door creaked again. Mom appeared, one hand on her hip, a gentle glare fixed on me. "So are you coming, or what?"

"No." I stood and looked between them. "I'll head home. You guys have fun."

The pain in her gaze startled me almost as much as the ferocity of her hug. She gripped my arms and looked me in the eye. "What happened to you, baby?"

I bit my lip and shrugged. "I learned my lesson."

She squeezed. "It was an honest mistake. You thought the job would be a good—" My expression stopped her again, and I wanted to hide from her assessing stare. "What lesson did you learn, Celeste?" she asked, soft and slow.

I gripped her wrists, imagined for a moment that I was drowning and she was a life raft, and then shook that image free and lifted her hands from my arms. Without the stupid Jameson in my system like last night, I knew to keep that terrible word, *empty*, in my mouth. "I'm going home." I tried to smile. "You guys have fun at Nick's show."

My father's frown cut a sharp gash in his normally open face. He didn't move when I hugged him quickly; neither of them did much more than murmur goodbye as I hurried to my car. A text chimed on the drive. When I parked and looked, I groaned.

Mom: I want you to see a therapist. Let me make an appointment.

Me: I'll think about it, promise. xoxo

I stashed the phone and hurried upstairs, already prepared to hear the usual.

"Evening, sweetie."

My apartment complex was, at best, clean and outfitted with strong deadbolts. However, it also came with two dudes in trucker caps who lived at the top of the stairwell to the 2nd floor. My unit was around the corner, but whenever the weather was fair, these guys parked themselves in folding chairs on the balcony and smoked, and they *always* liked to say hello.

I gave them my usual, "Hey," sans eye contact, and didn't

stop walking. Inside, I flipped the lock and left the lights off while I sank onto the couch. Lights or no, there wasn't much to look at in this little shoebox. Nothing decorated the walls, and most of the furniture had come with the rental. Very little of my personality was on display besides the bookshelf where my sketchpad rested—but then, very little of my personality was on display anywhere these days.

I heaved a sigh and pushed off the cushion, shuffling blind down the hall to brush my teeth. It was only 9:00, but exhaustion and the look on my mother's face haunted me. I crawled into the sheets, where ideas and questions tumbled around in my head in a jumbled mess.

Give me a truth... I'm fine. Once this job sorts itself out, life can begin again. I'm not hiding, I'm... playing to my strengths. I'm better alone. I can focus. Know yourself. Your business is you.

But, as always, my thoughts turned back to That Day. The day I blew it, the day Derrick taught me the hardest truths of my life.

I was in the lobby after the disastrous interview when my boss called, reminded me of the non-compete clause in my contract, and fired me on the spot. Outside on the sidewalk in the gorgeous May sunshine, businesspeople and tourists swirled all around. Not one of them stopped when I leaned into the nearest potted plant and heaved up the smoothie I'd drunk for lunch.

An assistant position with an established, international corporation like Miller & Watts is still an honor, Celeste. You've barely been out of school for three years. I couldn't stake my reputation by suggesting my girlfriend head the online department, not when I'm up for promotion next quarter. You were so hell-bent to upgrade your job. I figured you wouldn't mind starting small and working your way up. That's how business works.

Derrick's explanation of why he let me sabotage my

career came as I sat in a heap on the living room floor. By then, it hardly mattered, because it came *after*. After the train ride home, staring dully at my reflection in the window and not giving a damn about my streaked mascara or the pink smoothie puke stains on my white silk shirt. After I stumbled into our apartment with the sole purpose of crawling into bed, only to find that Derrick was home... and our bed was occupied.

Stop. Don't. Don't think about it. Don't go there again. I gripped my arm tight and braced against the memories I couldn't control, could never forget.

The moan. No, the moans. The stilettos. The pink fuzzy handcuffs. My partner, my supposed love, with *two* women over him.

Something new. Think of something, anything else. My nails dug into my skin as I searched my mind and landed on...

Benjamin.

Wonder where he is tonight, what he's doing? Is he drinking Jameson? Is he thinking of me? Definitely not, but still. What if he was?

And why are you holding your elbow so damn tight?

My grip slacked, and blood began to flow again. It had been such a nothing move, only a means to stop me from driving home, but the memory of his hand wrapped around my arm made my skin tingle.

Give me a truth.

In the dark, alone, the truth was this: I wanted him to touch me again.

5

Drunken conversations and late-night truths changed nothing about reality, and Monday morning had me queasy with nerves. *Keep your mouth shut. Mind your own business.* I barely remembered to crook a smile at Sarah as I hurried upstairs.

"Morning." Benjamin—*No, it's Mr. Addison, dammit*—was already at his desk, a cup of coffee in hand.

"Morning," I replied once I settled in.

I waited, but Addison didn't say more. Instead, he set his coffee down and reached for the keyboard. My lungs started to burn, so I exhaled as subtly as I could and peeked to see him focused on the monitor. Of course he would honor our code of silence.

Of course? You've known him a week, and you can predict his behavior?

Apparently I could.

"What did you do this weekend?"

I almost looked around to find the bastard impersonating me. No way had I said that aloud.

He startled and looked at me blankly for a second before

a slow smile broke on his face. I set my jaw to hide a shiver, unsure if it was embarrassment or pleasure that curled my toes. "The usual, I guess. You?"

"Same. The usual. I guess." Good god, I sounded *wooden.*

He leaned on his forearms and cocked his head. "Yeah? What's the usual? Raves? Krav Maga? Line dancing?"

Play along. "Voodoo."

His smile deepened. "That's why my knee's killing me." He rubbed his leg, and I bit my lip to keep from laughing.

"Get to work, Mr. Addison," I whispered.

"Yes, Ms. Greene."

I spent the next hour terrified that I'd broken the rules before I realized he was working intently and I'd barely read Garret's email. That got me back on track fast. The changes were minimal but enough to keep me busy for the rest of the day.

Tuesday, I got a surprise email from Sarah: "Some of the girls are going to lunch. Want to come?"

I typed back an immediate yes, more excited than I cared to admit to be included in a lunch date for the first time in forever.

At noon, Sarah, Janet from HR, Allison from marketing, and I walked to Panera in the strip mall across from the office. The three of them had a heavy gossip agenda that began steps out the door, and yet again I was rocked with nostalgia. In the old days, lunch was prime time to catch up with my colleagues. Even though I focused on my food and had little to contribute now, the routine was immensely comforting.

I glanced up from my soup when Sarah put her elbows on the table and smiled at me. "Spill it, Celeste. What's it like working alone with Ben all day?"

"Oh yes, do tell," Janet said while Allison grinned.

Ben. The way she said his name so casually caught me off guard. Leave it to me to over-analyze what I even called the man. Most people were perfectly capable of accepting someone's name and using it, not worrying that any slip in formality might be a sign of weakness.

Ben. I looked around at my companions and cleared my throat. "What do you mean?"

Sarah snorted. "You know what they say about the ugly tree? Well, Ben Addison fell out of the sexy tree and hit *every* branch on the way down. How can you get anything done? I'd be too busy staring at him!"

I coughed so hard I had to drain half my tea while the other women giggled delightedly. Before I could stutter out any attempt at a response, Sarah switched topics. "Oh, guess what! Joe is setting me up with his brother."

Janet and Allison squealed, and I smiled. "But what about 'Mr Addison'?" Allison asked, hooking her fingers in air quotes. "Bet you could get a date with him if you wanted."

Sarah blushed and shook her head. "No thanks."

"Why?" I asked.

"Mm, he's too good-looking for me." Her blush deepened as all three of us protested. She fluttered her hand. "Hush. I like sweet guys. Ben is nice, but he overwhelms me."

You're telling me. Funny, a little intense, quiet but quick-witted. I understood what she meant too well.

Allison redirected the conversation. "Come on, Celeste. What's he like?"

"Quiet. We don't really talk." It seemed the safest answer.

"Hmm, he talked to you Friday night." Janet nudged me,

and the others laughed. "He seemed *very* interested in what you had to say then."

"Friday? No, um, we—"

They laughed harder at my stuttered denial, and Janet patted my shoulder. "Aw, honey, you're so serious. We're just teasing you."

I still needed to explain. "Mr. Addison-um, Ben-and I don't work together. We work *against* each other. It's not like that."

Allison nodded. "That's true. Y'all are rivals."

I smiled, a silent thank-you to her for understanding, but she had already turned to ask for more details of Sarah's upcoming date. By the time we were back at work, the ladies had chosen her outfit, her hairstyle, and possibly the names of her future children. I smiled at their chatter and breathed easier without attention on my weird situation.

"How's it going?" Rollings burst through the door for his evening check-in.

I jumped and scowled at the shattered silence. My neck-lace chain dropped from my lips—a habit I was barely even aware of anymore—before I could scrape together a welcoming smile. "Going great, Mr. Rollings."

"I sure am pleased to hear you say that, Ms. Greene. Got a call from Jimmy just now. Told me he met with his management team, and they've got a couple more revisions on both proposals. Can you work them in before the presentations Friday if they email you first thing tomorrow?"

I rubbed my neck where a nerve had begun to ache. "Of course," was the only thing to say. Addison nodded.

"Great! Well, y'all get on home, get some rest okay?"

Y'all, y'all, y'all. Rollings said practically the same thing every night. His dogged, unwarranted cheerfulness chafed in the face of the "contest" he'd thrust me into. God forbid he let us work in peace.

"I saw that," Addison said when the door closed.

"What?" I yelped.

"You rolled your eyes. I saw you. Don't like our regular night-nights with the boss?"

Dammit, busted again. "I—I don't know what you're—I mean, I wasn't," I faltered, unable to look anywhere but at him. *Fell out of the sexy tree... Stop that!*

His brows lifted. "Come on, confess. It breaks your heart to see him go, doesn't it? I bet you wish he'd tuck you in at night."

"*What?*" I gasped, too horrified to appreciate the glint in his eye.

"You can tell me. It'll feel good to say it out loud, get it off your chest."

"When did you become a comedian?" *There you go, snapping again.* I huffed a deep breath—and caught him when his gaze flicked to the top button of my blouse as my lungs expanded. He winced and looked away almost immediately, but my pulse exploded. *Get it off my chest, hmm?*

I licked my lips and took the edge from my tone, leaving my voice soft and daring. "Don't deflect your fantasies of being Rollings's bottom spoon onto me, Mr. Addison."

His attention jerked back to me, a quiet laugh following quick. "Well played, Ms. Greene."

I pulled on my jacket and smirked. "You're right; that did feel good to say aloud."

We walked out together that night like colleagues, but jokes were forgotten first thing the next morning. The ache in my neck began to throb thanks to the laundry list of requests in Mr. Garret's latest email.

"A *couple* changes, my ass," Mr. Addison grumbled, and I looked over with wide eyes. We nodded at each other, no words needed to know we were in the same place.

The day flew by, both of us so busy that we lunched at our desks. Rollings popped in, but only to apologize for the long hours before he disappeared again. Once he was gone, Addison said, "If he had said, 'y'all have a good night now,' I might have thrown my mouse at him."

A laugh erupted before I could stop myself, so I covered my mouth to muffle it. He gave me a sardonic look, and I laughed again and dropped my hand. "I'd have blamed it on you," he added.

"Oh, yeah? You think he'd believe that?"

"I can be very convincing." His wink killed my laughter, but my smile lingered. "You have an arresting laugh, Ms. Greene. Think that's the first time I've heard it."

I inhaled sharply, but he didn't flinch. "What does it arrest?"

"My concentration, for one thing." He waved at the monitor.

Part of me wanted to keep up this back-and-forth, but I couldn't ignore the need to work. I nodded and studied my notes.

He resumed typing. Over the clicks, my ears registered that he was humming again. The tune was familiar, but in a general way that I couldn't place. My ears strained to recognize it until finally, I grunted in frustration. "Do you realize you hum?"

The room went silent. "Do I?"

"Sometimes."

"When?"

I thought about it, startled to realize the answer was *after we talk*. "Sometimes," I repeated. "What are you humming?"

"My favorite song."

I glared at the obvious bait. "Which is?"

"What's yours?" he countered. I shrugged, and his brow furrowed. "You don't know? How can you not know your favorite song? Music is life."

Of course I knew my favorite song, but it was my turn to play it cool. "Whatever you say." I went back to my screen.

He was silent for less than a minute. "At least answer this: Beatles or Elvis?"

"Who?"

He threw his hands up with a groan. "Oh, my god, Greene. The Beatles or Elvis Pres—" His eyes narrowed when I cleared my throat to hide a laugh, but his grin began to grow. "Damn, well played. You had me going for a second."

"What do you hum, Addison?"

"It changes every time."

"Beatles. I like The Beatles better than Elvis."

He held my gaze and clicked his mouse, and "A Hard Day's Night" began to play. We nodded at each other and refocused. The classic rock playlist lightened my mood a lot and made the long hours more bearable. I started to groove while I worked, silently singing along when I knew the words.

I stood up to stretch when the opening crash of "Born to Run" began. "Can you turn this up?" I asked. Bruce Springsteen had been a staple on the tape deck in my father's car when I was young. I rolled my shoulders in time to the beat, the familiar lyrics in my mouth while I went to open a window.

"Are you dancing?" Addison asked.

"Nope." The cool night breeze gusted my face while I whispered lyrics into the wind.

"And singing, too?"

"I can't sing." The second verse began, and I turned around.

Addison upped the volume and leaned back in his chair. "I bet you can. Go for it."

Why did I take his dare? Why did the last verse burst out of me, and why didn't my fluttering stomach stop me before the final line? *Who are you suddenly?*

Addison applauded and laughed. "Bravo, bravo. That was great."

"Shut your mouth, Addison," I barked, pissed that I'd humiliated myself with that little performance.

"Or what, *Greene*? You'll shut me up?" He yawned and rose to wander around the empty space on his half of the room.

My venom had zero effect on him, and that made everything worse. Determined to save face, I stalked over and stamped my foot. "We are not friends." *Very mature, Celeste.*

He snorted and turned to me. "I caught that, thanks."

"Exactly my point, but you keep teasing me. You—"
Oops.

The light caught his eyes as his pupils grew larger. He dragged his teeth over his lower lip with a long breath, and every nerve in my body tingled. "You think I'm teasing? You don't get teased often, do you?"

His words rolled over me and settled low in my abdomen. I was still embarrassed, but part of me gave that up in favor of wishing he would say *tease* again, it was so hot. "What does that mean?"

"If you think I'm teasing you, then you clearly don't have a lot of experience in being teased. All we've done is talk, but believe me, if you want to be teased, I can do that, too."

"You think you could tease me?" I thrilled to whisper the tempting word myself.

He smirked, slow and deliberate, his look telling me I'd asked the world's dumbest question. "Who's teasing now?"

Tension sizzled between us, undeniable, unprofessional, and exciting. The desire to touch him made me dig my nails into my palms. "Don't you get it? I'm a jerk, like you said." I wanted it to be a defense, but the wobble in my voice undermined me.

A low chuckle rumbled in his throat. "I get it. It's pretty funny." My brows knitted, and he stepped closer. "There's no way you're this much of a jerk by default. You work to make me hate you. Must be exhausting."

I rubbed my neck. "It'd be a lot less so if you'd get the hint."

His eyes flicked between mine intently. "I like making you work hard. I think you like working hard, Ms. Greene."

"I'll work as hard as I have to."

"I'm sure you will."

Dark as espresso and completely raw, the *tease* in his words made heat break between my legs. I stared at him and forgot to blink, much less speak.

Benjamin smiled again. "You know what I see when I look at you? Walls."

"As well you should." A decent recovery, given that my tongue was a knot.

He bent to my ear. "I bet behind those walls, you're not nearly the asshole you pretend to be." He inhaled deeply, and I nearly fell over, just like when he'd pulled that move at the bar last week. "I'm not afraid of you, Ms. Greene, no matter how hard you bite."

Good god, I wanted to bite, to twist my head and sink my teeth deep into his bottom lip, to hear him groan when I did, but I clenched my teeth and kept my sanity. Eyes narrowed in what I hoped was an icy glare, I spun around and put several paces between us as I gripped my aching shoulders and dropped my head.

"Are you in pain?"

"That's not your business," I grumbled.

His shoes appeared in my line of sight. "Your neck, Celeste. I'm asking if it hurts. You've been rubbing it the last two days."

I glanced up. Benjamin wore a neutral expression, but he twitched his brow. "Maybe you'd be less of a jerk if you took care of it."

"Maybe." I hesitated, unsure if I was crazy to hear the unspoken implication behind his words. "But I tried working it out last night. It still hurts."

"Hmm. Hold up your hand." I did, and he mirrored me. "Yeah, see, your hand is small. You probably need someone stronger to do it for you."

His expression sparked with unveiled amusement, his tone overly concerned, clearly enjoying this game. Meanwhile, my pulse pounded with what felt a lot like fear. *We can't do this.* "Are you offering, Benjamin?"

Amusement darkened into something far more potent. He walked behind me. "Only if you're asking, Celeste."

My nerves were strung out. I worried I couldn't speak, or that I'd convulse the moment he made contact, but, good god, I didn't care.

"It hurts. Can you help?"

Warm, strong hands came to rest on my shoulders. He brushed my hair aside, and I stilled from brain to toes. Nerves and the knots of tension dissolved as his thumbs rubbed circles along my spine. His fingers worked into my shoulders with the perfect amount of strength—the kind of strength and pressure that made it impossible not to think about what else those fingers could do.

"You are melting," he murmured. "And it is *hot*."

Behind my eyelids, a memory flashed of my hands—on Derrick's shoulders.

He'd come home late, and he'd slept at the office the night before. "Hey, can we talk?" I asked, so he leaned on the couch and waited. "I was wondering where we are on the web designer position with your firm?" He liked it when I called it "his firm," even though he was a junior relator.

"I'll let you know soon, okay?"

I put my hands on his shoulders, but he tensed. "What's wrong?" I asked.

He sighed and rubbed his eyes. "Just tired, I guess."

My fingers kneaded into his muscles, and I crooked a smile. "When my dad touches Mom like this, she always melts. Did I inherit any of his magic?" He twisted his lips, so I continued to massage and said, "When I'm running Miller and Watts's website, and you're selling multimillion-dollar properties all day long, do you think we'll—"

"God, do you always have to talk about work?"

The memory of his harsh voice made me shudder. I curled into myself and backed straight into Benjamin's chest. I think he laughed and said something like, "Oh, okay, if that's what you—" but I shuddered again and jumped away.

"Celeste?" Concern laced his voice now.

I shook my head, hurried around the desks, and grabbed my purse with shaking hands. "I've got to go."

I clattered down the stairs, careless of my heels and his shout behind me to wait. He tailed me to the parking lot, but I didn't stop.

"Wait a minute. I'm sorry, dammit," he huffed.

I paused with my hand on the car door. "I've got to go. We can't. This is *work*."

"I know, but what if we—I know." He sighed and shoved a hand through his hair, nodding once in farewell.

In the cool silence of my car, tears slipped down my cheeks. The sweet sensation of Benjamin's touch was long gone, and memories sucked me deep into the muck. *I should've seen it coming. That was March; how long did Derrick hate me? How many nights at the office were lies?*

I reached for my phone. Mom answered on the second ring. "I'll talk to a therapist."

She took a quick breath. "I'll call Monica and get you an appointment tomorrow."

"Make it at lunch," I said dully. "I'll have to work late."

BEN

In the silent haven of my car, I watched Celeste drive away and reached for my phone.

Liv answered fast. "Hey, you. What's up?"

I rubbed my eyes. "Am I an idiot?" She laughed, but I went on. "I'm serious, Olivia. Am I a total fool?"

"Of course not, Ben. What's wrong?" she asked gently.

I'm crazy about the wrong girl. I just fucked up big-time. I thought I'd already fucked up this year, but now I've gone and invented a new way to do it.

"Come over."

My blurted request hung between us, and I cringed. Those two words were a terrible thing to say to one of your best friends who happened to be your ex-girlfriend.

Worse still was the fact that I didn't mean it. I knew damn well that no one and nothing would distract me from Celeste's murmured sighs, from the way she turned to butter under my hands.

From the haunted look on her face just before she ran out.

I rubbed my eyes again. "For a drink. We can play a little *Call of Duty*. That's all I meant."

Liv chuckled. "Good, because anything else *would* be foolish," she said, a lesson we'd learned long ago. "I would, but I'm watching my niece tonight. How about I take you out to lunch tomorrow? My treat."

I smiled. "Sounds great."

6

At lunch the next day, I sat down on a brown suede couch and faced the therapist, my necklace already wound around my fingertip. "Hi, Dr. Zeller. I only have thirty minutes."

Her brows knitted. "Yes, I was told your time was limited. That's unfortunate, but we'll do what we can. But first, Celeste, call me April."

My gaze shifted to the door to hide a wince. Why the hell had I become so formal with everyone lately? Did I think using last names somehow kept a wall between them and me?

Bingo.

"Um, is Monica here?"

April smiled. "She's on lunch, but I'll let her know you said hello. Your aunt, correct?"

I nodded and didn't bother to elaborate that Monica was technically my mother's best friend. It didn't matter; what mattered was the connection had gotten me this appointment in less than 24 hours.

She gazed at me over her cat-eye glasses, an obvious prompt for me to speak. I dropped the necklace and hid my hands in my jacket. There was no reason to take it off since I'd only be there a few minutes. *This is a waste of time.* "What should I say?"

"Say whatever you like. What brought you here today?"

"I've been under a lot of stress. Mom thought I should talk to someone."

She nodded. "Mm-hmm. But what brought you here *today*?"

My fingers knotted around the sleeve. "I don't know. Last night I freaked out a little, but it was one of those things where I woke up this morning and knew I'd overreacted." *Where I woke up and knew I made a fool of myself.*

She nodded for me to go on, but I had to think hard. How could I explain the job and arrive at a logical point where my rival gave me a freaking back massage without telling her everything?

"Celeste. You don't need to filter with me."

I sighed hard and sat forward. "I don't think this is going to work. Sorry."

"You've been here fifteen minutes. Isn't that a little early to decide?" I didn't answer. "Okay, but can you answer a few questions first?"

"I'm not on drugs, and I'm not in danger of self-harm, don't worry. I'm just trying to come to terms with myself. I'm not who I thought I was."

"Who did you think you were?" I didn't respond, so she tried again. "Who are you now?" I looked into her eyes and twisted my lips. She frowned, but nodded. "Celeste? Can I leave you with this? You are who you want to be. No one but you can define that."

I stood up and zipped my jacket with a tremor in my fingers. Her words bounced hard off my frozen heart and left reverberations through my chest that I knew would linger. "Thanks."

"Come back anytime."

I made it back to the office with five minutes to spare and dove straight back into the project. It would be a late night for sure, but I'd made good gains over the morning. With Dr. Zeller's—no need for familiarity with someone I'd likely not see again—with her words tucked neatly on a mental shelf, I committed to the zone for the afternoon.

My focus was shattered when Benjamin returned, 30 minutes late and on the phone. Neither of us had said a word all morning, but now I heard: "Yeah, yeah, I know, but I've got to stay late and finish this project. Shut up, don't go there, I'm already back at the office... Tomorrow? Sure. Later." He caught me peeking and flashed a grin as he dropped into his chair.

I arched a brow at his loose posture. "You seem relaxed."

"Compared to you, I'm a sloth in a bucket."

My cheeks heated, but his phone rang before I could reply. He answered with his gaze on me. "Kira! What are you —aw, thanks. Yeah, Liv bought me lunch. You'll be there Saturday, right? My place. Great. See you then." He ended the call and nodded. "You were saying?"

"What'd you do, drink your lunch?"

I meant it as an insult, but he laughed. "A little bit, actually."

"Was that your girlfriend?" I asked, and then mentally stapled my stupid mouth shut.

Gray eyes widened. "Who? Kira, or Liv?"

"Either."

"Both," he said. I startled, and he laughed again. "I'm kidding. They're my friends."

I watched him stroll to the kitchen and pour a glass of

water. Work seemed paused for both of us, and I found it hard to care. Playful Benjamin fascinated me; even at the bar, he hadn't been this open.

He sat back down. "Anything else you want to ask? If you do it without rolling your eyes, I might answer honestly."

I practically glued my eyes to the ceiling. "Get back to work, Mr. Addison."

Another laugh rumbled in my ears. "You know what I like about you, Ms. Greene?"

His smirk was too tempting to ignore. "What?" I whispered and tried not to hold my breath.

"I'm not sure," he murmured, but his soft, thoughtful tone made it sound very far from an insult.

I spent the afternoon waffling between intense concentration on my pitch and curiosity about Benjamin Addison. Would day drinking affect his productivity, somehow give me an advantage? Were those women really not his girlfriends? Could a man as hot as him have female friends without benefits? How did he know them? What *did* he like about me, and should I be concerned for his sanity if there was an answer beyond *nothing*?

It took several hours past Rollings's evening drop-in to finish, but I kept my head down and got it all done. Just as I did a final save and sat back with a sigh, Benjamin's phone chimed. He jogged for the door, only to return minutes later with a pizza box in hand.

The gorgeous smell of bread and cheese hit my nose, and my stomach growled like a demon lion. I coughed to hide the noise, but Benjamin was on his way to the table in the kitchen and didn't seem to notice. "I'm starving," he said. "Want some?"

"Does it have anchovies or olives on it?" I wrinkled my

nose. He shook his head, and hunger won out. I slithered off my chair and hurried to follow him.

Good god, I hadn't had pizza this delicious in ages. I stopped short of groaning or licking my fingers, but my slice disappeared in seconds. Benjamin waved at the open box. "Have as much as you want."

"I'll pay you for half." I lifted another triangle.

He snorted and rolled his eyes. "Oh, please. Let it be my treat. Call it a birthday gift."

"It's not my birthday."

"Too bad. Give that slice back, then."

I paused mid-chew, made a face at his cheeky smirk, and kept eating.

My ears filled with another softly murmured melody. The low, under-his-breath subtlety made the habit far from annoying—if anything, my brain whirred to guess the song.

So, Benjamin, what's the tune of the day?... Don't ask questions. You're not friends. You... are who you want to be.

Dr. Zeller's words interrupted my thoughts, and I frowned. *Do I even know what that means anymore?*

"What are you humming now?" Apparently, I wanted to be nosy.

My question stopped the tune. "I was wondering how long it'd take you to ask."

"Were you testing me?" He nodded at my question, so I rolled my eyes. "Whatever. I don't care."

"It's not a song you'd know. No one knows it yet." My mouth full of pizza, I knitted my brows in confusion. Benjamin ignored me and changed subjects. "Show me your pitch."

I dropped the slice. "Are you crazy?"

"Come on. I'm not going to steal your ideas—not that I could at this point."

I huffed and went back to eating. When I was done, though, I threw the napkin down and groaned. "Fine. Come see."

He stood behind my chair while I called up the file. "You're a commercial designer," he said as I flipped through the samples.

"No, I'm a damn good designer." *Fantastic, he can tell this isn't in my wheelhouse.* I hesitated, then admitted, "But with so many different pages, I just wanted to keep it consistent."

Benjamin hummed. He watched while I finished the presentation, but his silence gave too much validity to my concerns. I needed something else to think about, so I closed the program and spun to him. "Show me yours."

As soon as the file opened, I groaned inwardly at how skilled he was. Even though I knew I was in trouble, I admired his style. A dozen questions about his approach popped in my head. I knew I wasn't allowed to ask, would never answer if the tables were turned, so I bit my tongue and kept quiet.

I laid my hand on the back of his chair when he opened the promotions page, but he moved on faster than I wanted. "Wait, whoa. Go back a second." He obliged, and I leaned in closer and hissed. "Fuck me, that's sharp."

It was only because he turned to look at me with wide eyes that I realized I'd spoken aloud. It was only when he turned that I think either of us realized we were practically nose-to-nose. And it was only the way his lips parted and my stomach flipped that it occurred to me that I had just said *fuck me* to Benjamin Addison.

"Sorry."

"Don't be."

My lungs constricted and turned my voice into a whisper. "What does that mean?" *Should I not be sorry I just requested you fuck me?*

His breath grazed my cheek, but he didn't answer.

I couldn't move. I couldn't even form the thought that I *should* move. All I could do was look at him and sip uneven breaths of air. That, too, was forgotten when he did what the sane part of me dreaded.

He leaned in.

A thin gasp escaped me, but my lips softened at the warm tickle of his skin on mine. "It means," he said against my mouth, "don't be sorry, Celeste."

"I am." Okay, maybe I hummed the *m* a little longer than needed. And *maybe* I enunciated just to feel him when I added, "so sorry," on an exhale. But I definitely had to have been out of my mind in the next moment, because I parted my lips and pressed a delicate kiss on his. It was so feather-soft and hesitant that it barely happened.

Except it sent my heart into free-fall and ignited my blood like a wildfire.

I jerked away and covered my burning mouth as his eyes slowly blinked open. "Oh, shit, this is bad."

"Very bad," he agreed, but his rumble made *bad* sound like the best thing in the world.

I backed away and shook my head. "This nonsense is over right now, understood? Stop distracting me."

"*I'm* distracting *you?* Give me a break. My own focus is enough of a concern with you around."

My face was hot, but I held my ground. "Whatever. It's done. *Now*," I repeated, in case either of us was unclear on the timeline.

We traded another wary look and went to clean up dinner. I kept my head down and hid behind the auburn curtain of my hair while I replayed the last few minutes in my head. *What is wrong with you? This guy is not an option. And what the hell does he think you do that's so distracting? You're not the one humming and smiling and—*

"Oof." In my quest to avoid eye contact, I managed to crash into him when I turned around. My hands flew up in a reflexive block and landed on the broad expanse of his chest. *Good god.* Under that dress shirt, he was warm skin and hard muscles, and my body ignited all over again.

He steadied me, but then backed up. "Sorry," he grumbled, already headed to fetch his jacket.

I wanted to lighten the mood and ease the tension. I *needed* to forget the lingering burn on my lips and palms. So, as I followed him downstairs and outside, I said, "If you want somewhere to focus, maybe you should know that the ladies downstairs have crushes on you."

Benjamin paused, his head cocked. "Who?"

"A few of them. You have options."

His gaze flickered over me once more. "Happy birthday, Ms. Greene," he said quietly.

I pursed my lips. "It's not my birthday, *Mr. Addison*."

That grin flashed again, and there was no way to ignore the way my heart fluttered. "I know. It's mine. And you have made me very happy." Before I could wish him well, he turned for his car.

You made him happy. He can talk to Sarah or Allison—I think Janet's married, but I'm sure there are others—but you *made him happy.* I started the car and sighed. *You've got to stop thinking about him this way.*

7

Friday morning was my first major presentation in almost two years. I dressed for power in a black BOSS suit that I fondly remembered buying at Bloomingdale's. With it, I paired an ivory blouse and three-inch nude heels to give me a classic look. Still, as I pinned my hair back and did a final examination, the nagging feeling that I was going to lose remained.

I wanted to review my presentation before the 10a.m. meeting. The office was empty when I arrived, which let me read my notes twice before my concentration was wrecked.

Brooding, handsome, oh Benjamin Addison, you are sin in a suit today.

Mom's words on my first day pinged through my head as I tried not to stare at the eye candy across the desk. His usual dress shirt and tie were upgraded to crisp white and plum-colored silk under a perfectly fitted charcoal gray suit. Even his hair was styled different, combed back to give him a devastatingly suave effect.

Ugh, give it a rest. He's hot, you know he's hot, now move on. Even if he's got smoke coming off that jacket from his hotness, it's not your business. You have ass to kick. I stole one more glance. *Hot, well-dressed ass to kick.*

I cleared the fog off my brain, gave him a nod, and gathered my files.

The meeting went fine. Jimmy Garret was a friend of Rollings, cut from the same kind of good-old-boy cloth. With him, I was "sweetheart" *and* "little lady." It was clear he appreciated my work, but his patronizing made me tense. I'm terrible at playing up attention like that, and I'm defensive about my skills in a male-dominated field. Add that to how tight I knew my competition was, and, yes, things went fine. But "fine" and "nailed it" were hardly the same, and I knew it.

After we shook hands, I slunk back up to the third floor and went straight to the kitchen to avoid my opponent's—my rival's, my enemy's, *you have to remember that*—quizzical gaze. When he left for his presentation, I buried my face in my hands and swallowed the desire to scream out loud.

Lunch floated away. Too nervous to eat, I passed the hour with YouTube videos of Corgis enjoying teatime, then switched to shopping for furniture for my dream house. Benjamin returned when the hour was up, but the way he slouched and clicked his mouse idly told me he was doing the same thing as me: keeping one eye on the clock and awaiting our results.

At two, Rollings stepped into the room, his phone held aloft. "The big news is in. Let's see what Jimmy says." Addison and I both got to our feet while Rollings tapped his phone. Our awkward stances reinforced the game-show vibe of the situation.

Rollings read a moment, and then looked up. "Congratulations, Mr. Addison, Jimmy has chosen your proposal. Ms. Greene, he liked your work, but this one goes to Addison."

His expression made it clear he hoped for a reaction, but neither of us moved.

Benjamin finally spoke. "Thank you. Please pass along my appreciation, and let Mr. Garret know I'll be happy to do any additional pages they might need."

Rollings smiled, but no more conversation came from either of us. He took a step toward the exit. "Well, why don't y'all take the afternoon off? We'll start again Monday."

The click of the door brought me back to life, and suddenly I could barely hold myself together. I'd lost—failed—again. Facing it in front of *him* was about the last thing I wanted to do, so I snatched up my bag and shoved my arms into my jacket.

"Listen," he said.

I glared over my shoulder with pure loathing, but if it was for him or for me, I'm not sure. Far more sharply than I'd like to admit, I barked, "We have nothing to say to each other. I'll be back on Monday, and I will hand you your ass on the next project, understand?"

His brows lowered into a scowl. I froze when he rounded the desk and stalked to me. "Take it out of bitch mode for a second and—"

Even an ice queen can blaze with fury. "Don't *ever* call me a bitch, you—"

"Careful how you finish that thought, lest you look like a hypocrite. And, for the record, I said to take it out of bitch *mode*." His lips curled in a sneer.

He was so close, I could see the details of his long eyelashes framing his gray eyes. I stamped my foot, and he laughed. "Go *away*. I hate you, I hate Nashville, I hate this stupid contest. Just go away." I knew sounded like a frustrated child, but dammit, why did everything have to be so hard? Why couldn't he just let me snap at him and storm out?

Another laugh lashed my ears and blinded me with rage. Without thinking, I opened my palm and swung for his face. He grabbed my wrist well before I made contact. I screeched and used my left hand to shove his chest, but he caught that one, too.

Benjamin cuffed my wrists. I flailed, and he let me, all the while holding on. "Dammit, Addison," I grunted.

"Dammit, *Greene*. You can't hit me, for god's sake."

That made me pause. My jaw softened, eyes wide. Good god, I'd actually tried to strike him.

Shame and self-loathing kept me short of breath. I waved my fists in both a struggle to be freed and a gesture of defiance. This time, he tightened his hold. The bind stopped my arms and made my blood pound a new tempo. My spine pressed into the desk when I took half a step back; he followed.

"Are you through, or—" Benjamin's tone was soft, but he didn't get to finish.

I don't know what possessed me to thrash again, to test him, but I did. I twisted my shoulders and jerked my arms—and got exactly what I wanted. Benjamin gripped me hard, immobilizing me quick. I bucked against his vise-grip, the burn in my biceps a weirdly satisfying outlet for my roiling emotions.

"What are you doing?" he half-grunted, half-laughed.

"I don't know!"

I gave up and slammed my hands down on the desk, and Benjamin's covered the backs of mine. His fingertips stroked the crevices of my fingers, so I spread them wide and let him lace our hands together. *Oh, my, that's nice, too.*

"Are you through?" he repeated after a pause.

"Just warming up."

He arched a brow. "How warm do you intend to get?"

We breathed onto each other's faces in ragged gasps. Despite the tempest in my heart, his presence soothed me. *Come closer, Mr. Addison. No one makes me warm like you do.*

I heaved a sigh, just for the pleasure of the rise of my breasts against his chest. He didn't flinch, but when I did it again, he smirked.

"I know what you're doing. Inappropriate, Ms. Greene."

"Since when is breathing inappropriate?"

"Since it felt like *that*."

I took another deep inhale, and this time let my whole body arch.

Oops.

Benjamin groaned when my pelvis pressed into his erection, but he recovered fast and drove my ass against the desk with a sharp thrust.

A wicked smile curved my lips. "Speaking of warm," I taunted and flexed against him again. He grunted and pushed back. "Shame on you, Benjamin, getting all worked up from fighting with me."

His gray eyes were glassy, but he bent his head, lips almost on mine, and teased me right back. "I'm not the only one. If Rollings walked in now, how could you explain yourself? How could you explain why you want me to restrain you, and what would you tell him about why you're bright red?"

"Easy. I'm pissed at you," I huffed.

He laughed, literally in my face. "Come on, Celeste. Shame on me? Look me in the eye and tell me you're not worked up. Say with a straight face that the reason your eyes are so bright has nothing to do with wanting me to find out how *warm* you are."

I inhaled sharply. *Warm* was the least of my problems. *Can underwear dissolve? Because I think mine just did.* "I admit nothing."

"You don't have to—I can see it. You're hot as hell, and you're wondering how much hotter I can make you."

My tongue stuck in my throat. I wanted to be fearless, but *dammit* he'd stolen all my reason with that rumbled dare. I took a breath and licked my lips. "I need us to be enemies," I whispered.

"Mm-hmm. It's not working."

"We don't have a choice."

Benjamin tilted his head. "There's always a choice."

I nodded slowly. "True. I can choose to file a complaint against you. Unsuitable office behavior."

He grinned when my lips twitched. His neat backcomb had fallen with our tussle, and now his hair splintered over his forehead, stiff from the gel. Coat rumpled, tie askew, a flush of exertion high on his cheekbones—he was absolutely beautiful. The sexy tree *wished* it could compete with him.

"I can do the same. Assault in the workplace." His smile dimmed and turned thoughtful as his gaze cut to our hands. He stroked his thumb across my knuckle, and then released me. Gently, he pushed the hair in my eyes off my forehead and tucked it behind my ear. "Is that the choice we want to make? Or should we explore other options?"

His question took a long, sultry slide from my ears to my core. *God, he can make anything sound sexy.* I gazed at him and tried to keep my eyelids from drooping. I wanted to kiss him more than I'd ever wanted to kiss someone in my life. I wanted his lips and tongue, his hands, my hands in his hair. I wanted his cock, his body, my legs around his back, my back on the desk. I wanted him to make me laugh again. I wanted to laugh like I used to, before I was this version of me.

I waited for the fallout, for the sound of Derrick's voice to drag me back into the dark, but the only sound was our rhythmic breath.

Benjamin assessed my expression and wet his lips. "Come with me tonight, Celeste. Screw the job; I promise it's the right choice." He bent a little closer and laughed softly. "We can explore all the options you want."

Every part of my being wanted to take that offer. Every part—except the part that knew enough to know better. I shook my head, and the moment was over. The heat in his expression ebbed. He inched backward and lifted his hands from mine, taking all that warmth with him.

"We're in trouble." I sighed.

"No kidding." He raked his hair and straightened his jacket.

We eyed each other with plenty of space between us now. "I'm sorry I freaked out," I said at last. "It was unacceptable for me to swing at you."

He nodded. "I apologize, too. I hope I wasn't too rough."

Rough took the same journey through my body as his earlier question, but I smoothed my hair and lifted my chin. "I'm fine." He nodded again but didn't speak, so I edged toward the exit. "Well, um, have a good weekend, Mr. Addison."

"Ms. Greene."

The rednecks on my floor gave me their usual greeting when I got home. I don't even think I mumbled a reply as I trudged past. Inside, I kicked off my heels, peeled off my pants, and left both on the floor. After a detour to the kitchen for a bottle of wine, I shuffled straight to bed.

My favorite thing in my basic little apartment was the

sleigh bed that belonged to my great-grandmother. She made the quilt, too, and I'd splurged on lovely satin sheets to complete the experience. Burrowed deep in the covers, I sipped straight from the bottle to shut off my brain for a while.

The room was dark when I woke with a jolt, unaware I'd dozed off. Night had fallen, and I reached clumsily for the wine or the light; whichever I encountered would be fine. My hand closed around the bottle. I took a long draught, barely bothering to ensure it didn't spill when I set it on the floor by the bed. With a sigh, I sagged against the pillows.

The alcohol warmed my cheeks and heated my blood until I tingled all over, a lovely glow emanating from my pelvis. I pressed my thighs together and began to unfasten buttons on my shirt, tracing my fingers across my belly. My lips pulled into what must've been a sloppy smile. I sank my head deeper into the squishy pillow and lifted my chest off the mattress. Even though it barely mattered in the darkness, my eyes closed when my legs fell open to my own touch.

I imagined the bedroom door opening, a silhouette in the light from the hallway, and that voice like strong coffee. "*Don't be sorry, Celeste.*"

Oh no, I wasn't sorry. Not here, not now. I was very far from sorry as I petted myself and imagined those lips, warm and soft, and how they'd feel on me—all over me. My breath quickened, and I imagined him over me, dark hair dusting his forehead, gray eyes burning.

"Yes. Okay, yes, I'm sorry, I'm sorry," I panted, a mantra to the day and to myself for everything that had gotten me here.

"*You are melting. And it is* hot."

My climax claimed me. I shuddered and arched higher

off the mattress before I collapsed, exhausted and unable to get him out of my mind.

Not the job. Not my past. Him. Only *him*.

I stared at the orange flames popping and crackling in the bowl. Mom and Dad were snuggled in a two-seater chair opposite the fire on their patio. No one spoke while the larger logs began to burn. The wine in my hand was more of a prop, since I'd had my fill the night before, but it was nice to have something to sip.

"Sorry about the project," Mom said at last. "If I know you, you started planning the next one before you got home last night."

Glad for the flames to hide my heated face, I nodded but didn't answer. *No, actually, I drank alone and masturbated to the thought of the man who stands in my way. Then I woke up this morning and spent an hour drawing his eyes to minute detail.*

I'd even drawn the crinkle on the right side that denoted his smirk, all the while acknowledging that I might have completely abandoned my sanity. Celeste Greene never lost her head over a guy, certainly not one who was the definition of a terrible idea.

The dancing flames took me back to the party where I met Derrick. Then, the fire had been on TV, that Netflix Yule log program that let apartment-dwellers simulate cozy. He and I had chatted about the value of such a sham. He'd left with my number, and from there, we'd had drinks, then dinner, then sex, until it was a given that we were a couple. Moving in with him had been the natural next step. We both worked long hours, and it was easier than trying to arrange dates.

Power couple, that's what we were. Climbing in our careers, hanging out with our friends, living the life. We made the right moves, went to the right shows, rented a cabin upstate to get away then rushed back to the madness of the city as soon as possible. Passion wasn't part of the package. He was cool, charming when necessary, but he never stopped my heart with a look or a smile, and I'm sure he felt the same about me. He was a good choice, a smart idea.

Dating in the city was always daunting. My two college relationships had been solid, but neither of them were about building a life together. By the time I got to Derrick, I thought the life we were building *was* the relationship. I didn't know he was so dissatisfied.

Spoken like a true ice queen.

I pulled my shawl around my shoulders and took another drink. Mom looked over, so I put on a smile. "How was Nick's show last weekend?"

She shook her head. "We weren't in the mood to go without you, but Jen said it was great."

I had to laugh. "Like Aunt Jen would ever critique her son—or anyone."

Mom and Dad both chuckled their agreement, and the chilly memories dissipated. My orgasm last night—my first since before Derrick and I broke up—must've done me well, because the knots in my soul seemed a bit looser. Admitting my obsession with Benjamin Addison, even to myself, was a mortifying relief. I'd named it, drawn it, and now I could leave it. He and I agreed that our mischief was trouble, and he knew about the office ladies' interest. Monday would be a reset.

See? You didn't need that therapist. Tomorrow you'll clean the apartment and go to the gym. You need to buy groceries and make your lunch. Then, on Monday, you'll go in there and crush the new project.

Where did he want to take me?

It wasn't the first time I'd wondered it, and it wouldn't be the last before I got to work again. In my mind, I heard his coffee-dark voice again. *Come with me tonight. Screw the job.* The possibilities were fascinating, a declined opportunity I'd always regret and never question.

BEN

The whiskey tumbler slipped in my hand. I sat up a little straighter from my slouch and remembered to tighten my grip. Around me droned a hum of voices and the occasional twang of a guitar.

"This is the dullest-ass birthday party we've ever thrown," Liv announced. "It's Saturday night; let's turn it up. Someone take off their shirt. I'm ready to do a body shot. Come on, Field, strip for me." She grinned.

"If you insist." My friend laughed and reached to tug his shirt off, but the rest of us drowned him out with a collective groan, waving for him to sit back down.

"It's Ben's party," Kira spoke up and looked my way. "What do you want to do?"

I shrugged and sipped the whiskey. "I'm happy here. I've had a couple drinks, and I don't feel like cabbing it to a bar. Sorry, guys. This job's wearing me out."

Liv snorted. "What a weird fucking deal. Competition— how do you not know who you want to hire? Just pick one, geez."

Her comment earned nods from everyone, including

me. I'd filled her in on the situation over lunch as a nifty way to skirt the real reason for my call the night before. After a night's sleep, I knew it was smart to keep mentions of my rival vague and purely work-related. It was advice I should've heeded myself a thousand times over.

"How's that going anyway?" James asked.

"It's going," I murmured, zero interest in sharing that I'd "won" the first round. Silence answered me, and I glanced up to see my six closest friends clearly awaiting more details. "It's fine. It's—fuck it. Let's do those body shots."

That earned a good laugh. Kira yelped and covered her eyes when Liv and James started to lift their shirts as if to comply, which kept the humor going. My little drama was forgotten, and conversation and music filled the room once more. Liv broke out a deck of cards, so I joined the circle for a wicked round of "Bullshit" that soon became a drinking game. By the time everyone said goodnight a couple hours later, we'd laughed ourselves hoarse and agreed the party had been salvaged after all.

When the door closed and silence settled, I poured another Jameson and raised it in silent salute to the girl I couldn't get off my mind. Staring at the amber liquid in my glass, all I saw was emerald green.

The temptation in her eyes Thursday night, fear and want battling hard in the moment before she kissed me.

The ocean of pain when Rollings gave us "the big news" yesterday.

The dark flame of lust that sparked long before she quit fighting me—long before she shorted my senses with her body pressed against mine.

We're in so much trouble.

I lifted the glass again. "Then here's to trouble."

8

The specs for the second project came in first thing Monday, and they were a dream. Threads was a boutique clothing store that was about to expand into a regional chain. They wanted a chic website to cater to the "New Nashville" style. Know my business? This was it.

Benjamin and I both lost ourselves in work again. It might've been my imagination, but there was an ease in our silence that wasn't there before. Between that and the inspiring project, I finally felt like the universe was letting me catch my breath. Even the text from Mom on Tuesday didn't knot me up too badly.

Mom: April says she'll see you @ lunch tmrw for therapy. You must've forgotten to reschedule.

I pursed my lips at the phone, doubtless she knew I hadn't "forgotten," but didn't argue. Maybe a second visit on a week this productive would prove that I really didn't need her services.

I broke for lunch five minutes early Wednesday and hurried downstairs. Allison and Sarah stood in the lobby chatting, but they looked up when I appeared from the stairwell exit.

"Oh, hey, Celeste," Sarah said. "Did you change your mind about lunch?"

"No, sorry, I've got to be somewhere." Sarah had emailed me another invite this morning.

Allison grinned. "Ben is joining us today," she said as a few others, men and women, began to trickle in from the hall behind Sarah's desk.

You're deep in the project, there's no weirdness between you, and Allison is clearly interested. Everyone's happy. "Awesome. See you later." I held my smile and moved toward the door.

Everywhere in Nashville takes ten to fifteen minutes to get to, so long as traffic is kind. I sat down on the brown suede couch right on time and nodded once at the therapist.

"Thanks for coming. I was surprised to see you scheduled," April said. No sense in clinging to formality when I was doing so well, and Dr. Zeller was a mouthful anyway.

I snorted. "Yeah, me too. You told Monica about our session?"

Her voice was suddenly firm. "I never disclose details to anyone, Celeste. That's the first rule of therapy: everything you say is between us. Monica asked if we'd had a good session. I told her I didn't expect you to return. That's *all.*"

I smirked. "That's enough for Aunt Mon. She filled in the rest."

She mirrored my expression. "Her exact response was, 'Celeste is just like her mother.'"

"I wish I was as strong as Mom," I muttered under my breath. Her brows rose, but I shook my head. "Anyway, I'm doing fine. Better than last week. Things are fine."

"Mm-hmm. What's improved?"

"A new project is going well. Plus, I have this colleague.

No, he's more of a—forget it. Point is, we came to an understanding."

"Does he have a name?"

"Benjamin." When I heard myself, how softly I spoke, I cringed.

April's brows twitched. "Benjamin, hmm?"

Benjamin. Oh, god, Benjamin. I clamped my teeth on my lips and nodded. My pulse quickened, and I hoped desperately that it didn't equate to a blush.

"Is this a personal or professional understanding?" Her tone was gentle, coaxing, but the question cooled me down.

I cleared my throat. "Professional. I don't do personal relationships."

She frowned. "With coworkers, you mean?" My nod took too long, and she made a note on the pad in her lap. "Okay. Well—"

"I should go." I reached for my bag and stood up, surprised to see that we had almost filled the half hour this time.

April looked at the clock and rose to face me. "Can we try again next week?"

"Sure. It'll make my family happy." We shook hands.

I ate a Luna bar alone in the office before Benjamin returned. "Good lunch?" I asked when he sat down.

"It was okay."

"Told you you had options."

"So you did."

I thought therapy was supposed to make you feel better. The knots that had been loose all week were undeniably tighter as I worked through the afternoon.

∽

Thursday was back to normal, and I raced to meet my deadline by quitting time. Just before Rollings popped in, I sat back and had to remember not to squeal in triumph. The pitch was ready, and it might've been my best work ever. Hopefully when I met with Ms. Fowler, the CEO, tomorrow, she'd agree and green light me to start design with minimal changes. *Know yourself. This is what you need to focus on.*

Takeout sushi for dinner was a fitting reward. I drew a hot bath and finally bothered to shave for the first time since Monday. Pampered and stuffed with eel avocado roll, I dropped into a deliciously exhausted sleep.

The next morning, I dressed in black trousers and a cowl-neck black sweater similar to one of Threads' featured pieces. My Prada boots finished the look, and I'll admit I had a bit of swagger in my step as I walked to my desk.

Benjamin noticed. He eyed my model-stomp with a brow up. When I met his gaze and cocked my jaw, he smiled. "You've been a machine this week."

"Inspired, I guess." I shrugged.

"You're going to hand me my ass on this project, aren't you?"

I couldn't hide a smile. "I can't say that."

"Sure you can. You already did."

"Get to work, Mr. Addison."

"If you say so, Ms. Greene."

My proposal was perfect, but I still checked it over twice. Just before lunch, Sarah appeared. "Hey you two," she chirped, and we both greeted her with a smile. "Hope you're free. We're going *out* tonight."

"Trick-or-treating?" Benjamin asked.

"Ha, more like dinner and dancing, silly. I'm bringing Joe's brother. We went out last weekend and really hit it off." Sarah toyed with a strand of her long hair, a pleased blush on her cheeks. "Anyway, tonight a bunch of us are going to party. Go home and change, and we'll meet at Cabana at seven-thirty. Are y'all in?"

"Sure."

"Yeah," Benjamin said, an echo to my agreement.

"Good! Oh, um, Celeste?" Sarah turned her attention to me. "I bought a new dress at Kohl's I thought I'd wear. Can I show you?" She scurried across the room, thumbing her phone, and showed me a photo of a cute printed dress. Her aqua-colored eyes looked to me hopefully. "You have such great style. Is this okay?"

"It's adorable." I smiled, and she beamed at me.

"What should I wear, Sarah? The tails, or just a suit?" Benjamin teased with a grin that drew both our attention.

Suit. Wear the suit again.

Sarah giggled and shook her head. "It's so much easier for guys. You can wear whatever you want."

I held up a hand, ready to add to the banter. "Hold on. Whatever he wants is a slippery slope. What if he wants to wear denim cutoffs and a bowtie?"

Gray eyes widened in obvious surprise, but Benjamin was quick. "That's my go-to weekend uniform. What's wrong with it?"

"Nothing, as long as you have the right shoes."

"Cowboy boots, of course."

I tried to nod seriously, but both of us wound up joining Sarah's laughter. He tossed me a look that made my heart flip as she headed back to the door.

"Fine, wear whatever you want *within reason*, and I'll see you later." Sarah vanished with a wave.

Neither of us returned to our work. We just sat, reclining in our chairs and chuckling now and then until I cleared my throat. "Um, stupid question, but is today Halloween?"

"You didn't realize?"

"I guess I lost track of the date. Will it be safe to go out tonight?" How did Nashville do this strange holiday?

"Where we're going will be fine, nothing too crazy. But if you're going alone, I could give you a ride—if you want."

Since last Friday's antics, I'd been hell-bent on the idea that Benjamin Addison and I had decided to let drop whatever energy had popped between us on those late nights. Save Wednesday's lunch hour, I'd done pretty well convincing myself that I'd held up my end of the agreement.

But the offer of a ride, phrased casually though it was, had warnings blaring in my head all over again. It was completely inappropriate, but it was also kind and considerate.

Stop over thinking, and admit you'd feel safer with someone than going alone.

"Are you sure you don't mind?"

His expression didn't alter. "It's no problem, just give me your address. Maybe your number, too." He typed the info into his phone as I recited, only then letting his lips curve up. "Cool. I'll pick you up at seven."

That smile made me flutter with panic. "If you're sure."

My panic grew in direct correlation to his grin. "Oh, I'm very sure, Ms. Greene." A laugh slipped out, and he shook his head. "Are you?"

I wet my lips and kept my spine straight. "I'd really appreciate the ride, Mr. Addison." That wooden hollowness had come back to my tone.

He nodded and strolled for the door, phone at his ear. "Hey. Yeah, no, I'm busy tonight. I'll call you tomorrow, okay? Tell Jack we're on for next weekend."

Alone, I went to the kitchen and fetched another home-made lunch from the fridge. *I'd kill for some really good ramen right now.* My phone chimed, and the message was the next best thing to a wish granted—for a moment.

Kandra: OMG, I cannot believe Amy! She JUST told me.

I choked on my salad and scrambled to answer.

Me: What??! What's up?

Kandra: Her & D! R U kidding me?

"Are *you* kidding *me*?" I asked the phone just as it lit up with a call from Amy herself.

"Hey, lady," she squealed in greeting, but I was already holding my breath. "How's life?"

We chatted. Amy caught me up on life in the city. A tsunami of nostalgia crashed over me as she reported on the latest concert she'd been to, the apple picking adventure the girls had gone on, etc., etc. The whole time, I kept my fist clenched in my lap, the letter D from Kandra's text in my head, until the moment she said, "So I called because I need to tell you something." She sighed. "Celeste, you know you're my friend, and I'll always be there for you. I never really knew all the details about you and Derrick—"

"You know he cheated."

"Yeah, but you never gave me the whole story of why you guys fell apart. But, um, Derrick and I are dating. We ran into each other at a party in May and started talking—god, I swear I never even looked at him when you guys were together—but now it's serious. We're um," she laughed, "in love. Like, we might get engaged."

"Seriously?"

"It's different with us. I know you guys didn't work out, but people change. We're really good together."

The door clicked open and shut. "I don't know what to say," I whispered.

"It's okay. I know it's weird, but I swear it's not a diss to you. We just happened. I knew you wouldn't love it, but I needed you to know."

"Yeah, uh, thanks for that. I guess. Listen, I should go."

"Sure thing, girl. Love you!"

I ended the call. My cheek ached where I bit down on it, but Benjamin was on his way to the kitchen, and I'd be damned if he saw me vulnerable. *Ice. You are ice. New York is over. Keep it together.*

"My meeting's in ten, but I'll go blind if I look over the pitch again." His casual tone matched the way he dropped into the chair, legs stretched long while he drank a glass of water. I kept my breath shallow, my gaze fixed on the empty salad container in front of me. He sat forward, elbows on the table, and I glanced up. "What's up? You look like you want to punch something."

"You could say that," I gritted through my teeth.

He rose from his chair. "In that case, I better clear out. Last thing I need is a black eye to face a client. A little advice before I go?" He tucked a folder under his arm. "There's no one here for the next hour. You can sing and dance all over this room, and no one will ever know."

"Don't be ridiculous.".

But when he was gone and I'd reviewed my work yet again, I stood behind my desk and logged into my parents' Spotify account on my computer, glad they didn't mind sharing with me. Alanis Morissette's "You Oughta Know" began to play. With a quick, cautious look around, I took a breath—and belted that damn song with all I had. Up next was "Shake it Off," and if it was good enough advice for Taylor Swift, it was good enough for me.

With five minutes to spare before I needed to be in the conference room, I reapplied my lipstick and combed my hair, then grabbed my files and strode down to the 2nd floor.

I could only hope that the flush on my cheeks translated as excitement about my pitch to the client.

I'm pretty sure Benjamin's smirk as we passed in the hall meant he knew it was from dancing, though.

Derrick and Amy were forgotten by the time I returned upstairs. The CEO of Threads had clearly been excited about my ideas, and the meeting went better than expected. With a little luck, *she* wouldn't be emailing laundry lists of changes and add-ons, like Garret had done.

Benjamin looked up when I came in, so I straightened my expression. "Rollings says have a good weekend."

His eyes narrowed playfully. "Did he say have a good weekend, or did he say, 'y'all have a good one'?"

I smiled at his twangy impersonation of our boss. "I think you know the answer to that."

We walked out together. In the stairwell, he said, "Glad you took my advice."

"I don't know what you're talking about." *Be cool. Be. Cool.*

"One word: webcam."

I stumbled off the stair and nearly fell into him. "*What*?"

Benjamin turned around, took one look at my blood-drained face, and laughed harder than I'd heard him yet. "Jesus Christ, I'm *joking*."

I put my palms to my cheeks as they began to blaze. "God, I hate you, Addison."

He wiped his eyes, but they still sparkled. "I know. You told me already. But only a little, right?"

"Try a hell of a lot. You nearly gave me a stroke."

"And you gave yourself away."

I opened my mouth to argue, but he was right. He laughed again and leaned against the wall. "Do you hate me enough to change your mind about tonight? Can you and those boots kick enough ass on your own?"

I hesitated. *He offered you a ride, coached you through that nightmare at lunch, and what do you do? You snarl at him again. Good job, Frosty the Snow-woman.*

My footsteps echoed on the tile, but it was a shuffling sound, not the usual staccato clip. I walked toward him and the exit. "You offered. Are you backing out?"

He stood up straight and turned for the door. "Not a chance."

Sarah gave us both a curious look when we stepped into the lobby, but we tossed her quick waves and promised to see her soon.

BEN

Celeste opened the door wearing a silk robe...red, maybe—no, black. I arched a brow. "You don't look ready. I thought you said seven."

"Oh, I'm ready." She crooked her finger, and I strode inside, not stopping until she was backed against the wall. Her pink lips parted, tongue flicking out to lick them and torment me. "Are you ready, Benjamin?" she teased.

I bent my head and let her taste my answer.

I killed the engine and rubbed my eyes. How had I driven over here so deep in that stupid fantasy? "A fucking grip. Get one," I grumbled. To cool down, I tried tapping a drumbeat on the steering wheel—until I realized "Sex on Fire" was the song in my head. "Laundry, groceries, clean the bathroom..." I whispered a mental chore list as I crossed the parking lot. By the time I got to her door, things were under control.

My phone chimed just as I rang her bell.

James: Was gonna come over. Busy?

Me: Yeah, I'm out tonight w/ coworkers.

James: And by coworkers, you mean HER. And by out, you mean inside of. Right?

I chuckled and shook my head. I'd made the mistake of letting a little more slip to him at the gym on Sunday. James had given me hell, but once I'd sworn about eight times that this situation wasn't remotely similar to the shitstorm I wound up in earlier this year, he'd quit the protective vibe and commenced with the ribbing.

Me: I'm giving her a ride.

James: ATTA BOY! Make it the ride of her life for me. Remember to make breakfast!

The door opened, and I forgot all about the phone. Hot had a new definition that even my fantasies couldn't compete with.

I might not survive the night.

9

When the doorbell issued its barely-functional ding-dong right after seven, I was ready. I wiped my sweaty palms and did a last check in the mirror, told myself again that it was just a ride, and went to peek through the peephole.

"God, he's—" My breath condensed on the paint; I didn't need to finish the thought. Benjamin waited with his head bent to his phone, cheek creased in a smile while he shifted his stance. *How long can I get away with just watching him?*

I forced myself to open the door.

Benjamin's head lifted, but his lids lowered as he gazed at me. My heart started to pound. Neither of us moved while his eyes traveled down my body and back up again. "Uhm," he grumbled. "Uhm."

His phone chimed, startling us both. It fell out of his hand and clattered to the ground. He cursed under his breath and bent to retrieve it.

"Is it broken?" I toyed with the lock to keep from fidgeting when he fixed that mesmerized stare on me again. *Did you drop that because of me?*

"Nah." He didn't glance at the screen, just pocketed the phone and looked away.

"Good. So, do you want to come in, or should we—"

"We should go if you're ready."

"I'm ready. Do you think this is okay?" I'd dug deep in my closet to put together a decent Halloween outfit. The black leather pants had been an impulse buy ages ago, but they still wrapped around my hips like second skin. The burgundy chiffon tank top took the edge off with sweet ruffles and thin straps that crisscrossed my shoulder blades in the back. Ankle boots, a smoky eye, and dark red lipstick finished the look. It was far bolder than usual for me, hopefully vampy, not trampy.

"It's fine. Get your coat." He turned away and looked out over the balcony rail, so I ducked inside and grabbed my black pea coat from the hook. *It's just a ride. It is just a ride.*

But it wasn't just a ride. It was an offer of support, an offer to look out for me. It was a gesture of kindness that I hadn't expected and had grown very used to living without. For a year and a half, I'd lived deep in my head. Friends had fallen by the wayside as I struggled to survive with no job and a shattered soul. Hours of self-analysis never got me closer to the moment I should've seen it coming. I always wound up at the beginning of the mess, that terrible afternoon with Derrick in his boxers, explaining in no uncertain terms why my inexperience made me unfit for the job I thought he'd recommended me for—and how my lack of attention to *him* made him seek affection elsewhere.

"Benjamin?"

He'd avoided eye contact all the way down the stairs, had ignored my whispered thanks when he opened the passenger-side door of his CR-V, but he paused with the key in the ignition when I spoke.

"Yeah?"

I hesitated, then reached out and laid a hand on his arm. "Thank you."

"What for?"

"For the ride. For the suggestion this afternoon that got me out of my head." I withdrew my hand and twisted my necklace. *For smiling when I'm a monster. For laughing at me. For making me feel seen.*

God, he made me feel seen. I knew it was my imagination, a combination of wishful thinking, loneliness, and the fact that he was so damn sexy. I mean, come on. Those steel-colored eyes could make any girl feel special. I still couldn't shake the idea that he *got* me, and what he got was worth getting. That what he saw in me was very different from what Derrick had spelled out as I'd sat in a heap on our apartment floor. Benjamin didn't even know me; how could he understand me like I sensed he did?

He flicked his gaze over me once, lips curling slowly. Then, he fired the engine and threw the car into reverse. "No problem."

The radio played, but I could hear him humming under his breath. Tonight, his fingers joined in and tapped a rhythm on the steering wheel.

He must've noticed my stare because he paused and cleared his throat once we were on the interstate. "So, how long have you lived in Nashville?"

"What?"

"I've worked with a lot of expatriate New Yorkers. How long have you been down here? Are you from Manhattan or a different borough? Seems like everyone's from Brooklyn."

I fell back against the seat. "How did you know I'd moved here?"

"Sarah knows everything."

The way he said it made me wonder what all he'd gotten from her, but I wasn't sure I was allowed to ask. "I'm not from there. I grew up here, but I lived in Manhattan."

"I'm sorry you dislike Nashville so much. Besides the traffic, most people love it."

We were inching toward the skyline, a perfect illustration of his point. I almost asked if Sarah had told him that, too, but remembered screeching the sentiment last week during our argument. "It's not the place, it's the circumstances," I said, surprised that I did. Benjamin had the grace not to press the issue, but my mouth kept spilling. "It wasn't my choice to move home. Now that I have, I want to find something I can call normal. I love working, and I liked going out last time. I'm sure our coworkers think I'm weird —obviously our situation is weird—but I like being out. It feels more like a normal life. Much better than sitting alone in a crummy apartment and contemplating how everything has changed."

Benjamin parked while I spoke. He faced me, an attentive tilt to his head that I startled to recognize as his most focused expression. I pursed my lips. "Or did Sarah tell you all that already?"

He grinned and reached for his wallet in the console. "No. I was just thinking that those were the most words I might've heard you say that didn't feature some kind of warning."

I bit my lip. "I'll try not to ramble."

"No, please do. Sarah will love the gossip," he teased, and I rolled my eyes. "All we could get on you with a Google search was your killer portfolio from your website."

My heart skipped several beats. "You *Googled* me?"

"Of course. Not much to find, though. Your thumbnail photo was cute. You look young."

"I haven't touched that site in years. That photo's about four years old." I smoothed my hair and sighed, not bothering to add that I'd suspended all social media after my life fell apart. "I can't believe you guys stalked me."

"It's pretty common. I figured you'd have a dossier on me —your enemy's weaknesses, all in one folder."

"I hadn't thought of it," I admitted, surprised at the disappointment that flashed in his eyes. "Now I wish I had, and I can't without looking like an idiot. Thanks."

The momentary cloud lifted, replaced by amusement. "You could ask. I already told you I'd answer, so long as you don't roll your eyes."

We need to go inside. I put my hand on the door, but then whipped back to him. "What would be the first hit if I Googled you?"

God, his smile could blind me. "Probably something about music."

"What, you enter professional humming competitions?"

That made him laugh. "Yeah. I'm the world champion. Come on, we've got to go—or skip dinner and cause a scandal."

Option B. I have more questions. I rolled my eyes at my inner voice. Benjamin took it as the end of our conversation and opened his door. "You look nice," I blurted.

He paused and looked at me, a deadly hot fire in his eyes. "You think?" His voice had that bit of growl that gave me chills. He wore black dress jeans and a dark navy shirt with a black silk tie. The Puma sneakers were a cool touch of casual.

"Well, I was curious about the cowboy boots and cutoffs, but this works, too," I said. He laughed in the same low pitch, but didn't say more while we crossed the parking lot.

Inside, we spotted Sarah right away. She waved us over

to a much bigger party than the last one. "Sit here, Ben," Allison called, pointing to an empty seat between her and a dark-haired woman I didn't know.

"Celeste, this seat's for you." Sarah indicated a place on her end of the long table. Frustration rashed over me, but Sarah welcomed me into her corner, and the feeling died fast. She and her date, Allen, were on my left. Joe-from-HR rounded us out to my right, and we fell into easy banter about the idea of a light rail in downtown Nashville.

The brothers were nice. Both had sandy hair, friendly brown eyes, and the kind of jaw that gave them an open, approachable vibe. Allen, the younger brother, seemed to know he could use that vibe to command attention. He threw around a lot of facts about carbon emissions that were clearly meant to impress Sarah. She nodded attentively, but her eyes kept darting to me, a secret smile flickering. I didn't get why until the waitress arrived.

Joe touched my hand. "What can I get you?"

Sarah bit her lips in a line, and I almost laughed aloud.

I let him buy me a beer. After that, everything I said about traffic jams or the weather seemed to be the most interesting thing he'd ever heard. He was nice, but the looks that crossed Sarah's face were far more entertaining than the conversation. More than once, I had to swallow a fit of giggles and the desire to drag her to the bathroom so she could tell me what the hell she was thinking, like I would've with girlfriends in my old life.

When the waitress came with our food, I allowed myself a look down the table. Allison and her friend flanked Benjamin. Each woman had an elbow propped on the table, tits aimed straight at him. He spoke, and they threw their heads back in raucous laughter that threatened my gag reflex.

I snuck one more glance to find Benjamin's gaze on me. By the look in his eyes, he had definitely noticed my cringe. He raised a brow, so I mirrored the expression and pursed my lips.

"I saw that," he mouthed.

"Who, me?" I mouthed back with a hand on my heart.

Benjamin winked, and my heart tripped again. Allison tossed her hair and began to speak at the same time I realized Joe had been calling my name, so we returned to our dinner companions. Sarah squinted at the smile that ghosted my lips, but I shook my head.

Once plates were cleared and checks were paid, Sarah rose and declared our next stop was a dance club. She gave the address while people searched it on their phones.

Joe fell into step with me on our way past the hostess stand. "Do you need a ride? My Lexus is right out front."

"I'm good, thanks." I chose to ignore the name-drop on his car.

He held the door open. "Think I'd be lucky enough to get you to dance with me?"

"Oh, well, maybe."

Joe chuckled. I'd already gotten the impression he took my lack of reaction to his compliments as shyness. "Don't worry, my dancing's nothing special. We'll just have fun. Sure you don't—"

I shook my head and flashed a smile. He nodded, and I hurried to the CR-V. *It is way too cold to stand out here talking, Joe.*

Benjamin was leaning against the front bumper, his eyes on his phone. "Riding with me?"

I frowned at his overly bored tone. "I thought so. Is that still okay?"

He pocketed the phone and looked up with a shrug, but

I didn't miss the glint in his eye. "Well, yeah, that's why I'm still here. Waiting on you to stop flirting with Joe."

Despite the cold, embarrassment flamed in my chest. "I was not—"

Benjamin stepped toward me, derailing my declaration. "Yeah, you were. He was drooling over you. You could've ridden with him. Or just ridden him, depending on your preference."

I shrugged. "Could've. Didn't. Thanks for waiting. Quick question though." He tailed me to the passenger side and opened the door. "Is there enough room for me in the car with your fan club?" I turned wide eyes up to him.

My innocent face dissolved at the laugh that burst from him. "Yeah, I made sure they saved shotgun for you," he said. I harrumphed, and we traded another smile.

Pleased that my teasing had worked, I continued on the drive. "Be careful. It takes a certain kind of man to handle two women at once."

Oh, my god, did I really just say that?

Benjamin laughed again, but my stomach dropped to my toes. I fought back a wave of nausea as That Day flashed through my mind for the millionth time. *A certain kind of man? More like a certain kind of bastard.* I didn't care that I was generalizing like crazy. I crossed my arms and pulled my coat tight, but it wasn't the October chill that had me so cold now.

He was merging, preoccupied with double-checking his side-view, and didn't notice my changed mood. "Yeah, I'm sure you'd know all about it, huh?" I didn't answer. I felt his glance at a red light. "Hello?"

"Uh." I cleared my throat and my thoughts. "Uh, I'd... I-I mean..."

"Holy shit, you've had a—"

"I—"

"I didn't expect it of you—god, that's hot, though."

"No! I mean, no, not me. I just—hot?" I mentally slapped myself for acknowledging that, and added another for good measure for the way my stomach flipped when I repeated it. "Come on, Benjamin. I'm not the sort. But if you are, then godspeed and good luck."

"Hmm, thanks." He seemed to finally sense my unease and let the matter drop.

It occurred to me that Benjamin very well might want to explore his options with Allison and her pal. He'd mentioned those lady friends last week; maybe this was a regular thing for him. It wasn't my business. Why should I care? "If you want, I can get a cab home," I whispered, unsure if he heard.

We parked in front of the club. Sarah and Allen were already at the entrance, an orange plastic bag in Sarah's hand. When the group was assembled, she grinned and rummaged in the bag.

"In the spirit of the night, I got us costumes." She displayed two stacks of black plastic masks. They were the simple, cheap kind that covered your eyes and nose, but it was a cute idea. The ladies' had a cat-like shape, while the men's were plain and rounded.

Sarah took Allen's arm and led the party past the bouncer. Once we were all inside, she handed out the masks and guided us into a Halloween-themed lounge. Mist hissed from the corner, the waitresses were dressed as devils, witches, and Playboy bunnies, and the DJ played a dance mix of *The Twilight Zone* theme. We settled into a booth and ordered a round, but people quickly made for the floor.

"Come dance, Ben," Allison's friend purred before he'd

gotten his drink. He held up both hands to protest, but they each grabbed an arm and dragged him away.

Only Joe and I remained in the booth. "Hey, can I ask you a question?" His tone was too casual to sell the disinterest. "I hope this isn't out of bounds, but, um, you and Ben?"

I turned to him, frost in my voice. "Where was the question in that?"

"I—oh. I wondered if you were—never mind. It was nothing."

"It sounds like nothing to me," I agreed, and he squirmed and tugged his collar. *Serves him right, trying to pry, suggesting—gah!*

"You're a little intimidating, you know?" he mumbled. I curved my mouth down, even though I knew he was right. My frown made him sit up straighter and turn on a smile. "I'm sorry, I didn't mean to be rude. You're real nice. Beautiful, too, but I bet you do know that."

"Hmm, I bet you say that to all the girls." This was boring. It reminded me too much of nights out long ago, enduring pickup lines while Kandra flirted with her boy of the evening.

Huh. For the first time, memories of my old life didn't come with a twist of longing.

Joe laughed. "Well, for you, it's definitely true. So, I asked earlier if you'd be up for a dance. How about it?"

I looked around at the empty seats, suddenly sick of being on the sidelines of life. "Let's do it."

10

Joe and I grooved for two songs before I thanked him and returned to the table. I settled in with my Jameson and pushed the mask up on my head for a better view. Joe had found a new partner already, and I spied a few more of our party here and there in the throng of dancers. The DJ played pop hits with classic Halloween tunes sprinkled in, which made for a hot dance floor. I snuggled against the bench, happy to take it all in.

As soon as I spotted Benjamin, I knew I'd been looking for him all along. He was in a group with Sarah, Allen and, of course, his fan club. Allison and her friend were working hard for his attention, grinding on each other like crazy, but I barely gave them a look. How could I, when I could watch *him*? I twisted my necklace and took in his shirt stretched across his broad shoulders, the jeans that hugged his narrow hips, and the dark denim that highlighted curve of his ass. *Good lord, girl, get a grip.* My body pulsed with the music and the memory of how he'd loomed over me against the desk, so warm and so very, very hard.

Benjamin drew back from his dance partners at the start

of a new song. The brunette reached to drape her arms around his neck, but he removed them with an apologetic smile and a shake of his head.

So much for spying. I sat up straight when he strolled back to the table and slid into the booth beside me.

"Critiquing my moves?" He pulled off the mask and looked around.

"Were you dancing? I hadn't noticed. Figured you'd be in the middle of an orgy by now." I put my hand on my cheek in an attempt at a bored slouch, but had to bite my tongue when he chuckled and shook his head. "Enjoying your options tonight, Benjamin?"

He angled to face me. "What do you mean?"

"Isn't it obvious?" I waved at the dance floor. Allison's friend was currently twerking, while Allison shrieked with laughter.

He smirked. "I'd think it was terribly obvious by now."

The words hung between us, too tempting for me to begin to trust the implication I thought I heard. I shivered and looked away.

"I can't believe you're sitting here, your necklace on your finger, all aloof at a club. Would it kill you to dance, *Ms. Greene*?"

I paused in the middle of a sip of Jameson and glanced sideways at him; I'd dropped the chain when he walked over. It did not escape me that he noticed my habit. "I did, *Mr. Addison*. Joe and I danced to two songs."

"You call that dancing? My sister and I have better moves than what you two did out there."

"Oh, you're of those families, hmm?" He laughed at my reply, and I had to battle a giddy grin. "If you're bored, you can go back to your friends. I don't need you to sit here and bully me."

Dark brows went up. "I *bully* you?"

I nodded. "Making me show you my work. Making me sing that night. The humming mind games. Trying to get me to dance."

Okay, I admit it was a lame attempt to flirt. I was so far out of practice at flirting, I suspected it sounded more like a litany of complaints, but I tried. He made me want to try. He made me *want*.

"I'm offended, Ms. Greene. That's not bullying, that's suggesting you do what you knew you wanted to all along."

"What makes you think you know what I want?" Just saying it made the ache between my legs throb. *Yeah, you probably know exactly what I want, don't you?*

He drew in a slow breath and leaned toward me. "Now that," he murmured in his black-coffee voice, "is an excellent question."

The space between us electrified, but we both held our stare. His hand covered mine on the bench. Again, his fingers skimmed over my knuckles, asking for entrance. Again, I opened to let him lace our hands together.

My lungs tightened. "What do you suggest we do now, Mr. Addison?"

"It's time to dance, *Celeste*. Consider yourself bullied into it if you like."

He stood. I stared at our entwined fingers, but he gave a little tug and beckoned me with his free hand, so I rose and trotted along to keep up with his long strides to the dance floor.

On the edge of the crowd in a dark corner, Benjamin turned to face me. He smirked and lowered his mask, crossed his arms, and took a step backwards.

Alarms wailed in my head. *"It's time to dance."* He's not *dancing* with *me? Am I seriously doing this alone?*

I debated my options. An indignant stomp back to the table would've been smart. It would've declared that I didn't need any of this. That I meant what I said about us being enemies. It would've affirmed the distance we needed.

Yep, an indignant stop it will be. I'm out of—oh, god.

I made the mistake of looking at him again. If I hadn't looked, I could have done it. If he hadn't been staring at me through that mask, *seeing* me through that mask, walking away would've been easy.

So much for options.

The bass pounded; I positioned the mask on my face and took a deep breath. Starting slowly at first, the beat dripped into my shoulders and trickled down through my hips and feet, and then I began to dance like I hadn't in a long time. Benjamin didn't move from his corner. I couldn't see him well anyway, so I let go and accepted the fact that I was dancing for him. Adrenaline buzzed through my veins and made me hot all over, but the high only emboldened my moves. *Is this what you wanted? Do you feel anything like I do right now?*

The more I danced, the more I wanted to be touched, and there was only me to do it. I swiveled my hips, ran my hands down my body, and pretended they were his. Eyes closed, my fingers splayed over my breasts before I caressed down, down my abdomen to my pelvis in time to my writhing body. *Go ahead, watch me. You know what I'm thinking, what I want.*

The lights flashed over our corner, and I looked up when he stepped closer. The mask couldn't disguise his eyes glued to my hands. My breath hitched, and I skimmed my body again, just to see his gaze follow.

Beyond any good judgment, I reached out, grabbed his wrists, and slid within inches of his tall, broad frame. He allowed me to lay his palms on my waist; I shimmied, but it was really a shiver. With another swish of my hips, his fingers contracted, pressed into my sides so hard they pinched. *God, yes.* I draped my arms around his neck and leaned backwards as the song ended.

"Satisfied?" I couldn't care about the strangled rattle in my voice.

He released me, far too slowly to be subtle. "Hardly."

Fearless Celeste was on a roll today. I pushed my bottom lip out and cocked an eyebrow. "What? You don't like my moves?" I feigned hurt, but his open-mouthed stare and complete lack of reply had me triumphant.

"Okay, boys and girls, let's shake like Winona in *Beetlejuice!*"

The DJ's announcement made us both turn. The new number was a hot mashup of Harry Belafonte's "Jump in the Line" and Pitbull's "Shake Senora."

"This is your song, Benjamin. Let's see those moves." I gave a decisive nod.

"Gosh, okay, I guess." In a grand display of nervousness, he bit his lip, adjusted his collar, and bowed to me. Benjamin began to do an old man dance, swiveling one leg and pumping his fists from side to side. I covered my mouth, chest tight with smothered laughter. When he scooted around in a little circle, I couldn't take it anymore.

"What? What's wrong with my dancing?" he asked when I doubled over in giggles. He laid a hand on his heart and bowed his head. "You're laughing at me? I'm crushed."

"No, no, it was good, p-uh-promise," I stuttered through my mirth, but another bout of laughter bubbled up.

Before I could compose myself, his hands were on my waist again. Mine landed on his chest as we locked eyes. "Then show me how it's done," he dared.

Old man my ass. Instantly, we were in step together, far more fluid and skilled than Joe's moves had been. His palms flirted with my sides while he encouraged me to work my body. I let him guide my feet. My hips rolled, my arms in the air as he spread one hand across the small of my back and stepped closer. His thigh pressed between my legs, and I tipped my head backward to hide a moan at our perfect sync.

The tighter he held me, the slower we moved until my arms were around his neck and we had completely lost the beat. At every point of contact, I burned with beautiful electricity. Everything else blurred into a pulsing background.

Benjamin lifted one hand from my waist to brush my cheek and lift my mask. Such a simple gesture, but somehow so intimate, like I was being revealed. I moved a little slower, my head a little fuzzier, and glanced down to escape the moment. When I did, he leaned in closer. "Look at me," he commanded softly. My eyes flew back up. He nodded and then spun me around.

He drew my ass close to his hips, and the shaky, tingling sensation that radiated from between my legs spread out to the tips of my fingers. I got back into the beat, but my face was on fire as I swayed down until my fingers grazed the ground, then slid up and turned to face him.

Benjamin's jaw was set hard, his face as red as I imagined mine to be. When the song closed out, he grabbed my hand and returned to the booth, where we both collapsed on the bench. I gulped half a glass of water while Benjamin drained his whiskey beside me.

BEN

Jesus Christ.

I was definitely not going to survive the night.

11

I looked up when the group descended on the table, and chatter hit us from all sides. Allison put her head on Benjamin's shoulder when she slid into the booth. I inched away.

Sarah stood over everyone and waved her phone. "Guess what! I called The Patterson House. They said we could have a table in about an hour and a half. We should go now, though, because you never know when something will open up."

I smiled; the girl knew how to run a party.

"Can we wait at the bar?" Allison asked, draped over Benjamin. He shifted but didn't push her away. *Not your business, Celeste.*

"No, the bar is part of the seating. But this place is super cool and always packed," Sarah explained.

"You can't have a drink while you wait?" I frowned. "That's crazy."

"Celll-essste, this place is awesome. It'll be worth it." Sarah's playful whine made me smile again. "Let's go, y'all!" She pointed to the exit.

Benjamin stayed silent through this exchange. Once Allison removed her arms from his shoulders, he stood up and threw on his coat. The brunette reached for his hand, but he quickly waved his arm for them to lead on. Outside, while the group collected on the curb to discuss carpooling, Benjamin stepped away from the huddle and said, "Sorry guys, but I think I'll call it a night."

No one missed the stricken looks on Allison and her friend's faces. "No, you can't," they cried in harmony. Even Sarah pouted.

"I've had a long week. I'll embarrass everyone by falling asleep in the corner."

"We'll keep you up!"

Jesus Allison, blow him right here, why don't you?

He shook his head. "Y'all have fun. Drink one for me."

"Hate to see you go, Benjamin. We'll tell you all about it on Monday," Sarah said.

"Awesome. Great party, Sarah." He flashed her a smile and turned away.

Sarah giggled and twirled her hair at the compliment. She noticed me watching her and blinked. "Are you staying with us, Celeste?"

My ride was halfway to his car when I whirled to his retreating form. "Hello?" I called.

He turned back. "Yeah?"

"Are you leaving me?"

"Oh, I didn't know if you—" he gestured to the others while they dispersed.

"I'll drive you home, Celeste." Joe appeared at my elbow, but I looked at Benjamin. *Suddenly you can't see me? What happened?*

But that didn't feel right, either, because he *was* looking at me, and it was a different kind of casual than his usual bored affect. This one had something beneath the surface that I couldn't put my finger on.

Benjamin slid a quick look at Joe, and I had to wonder when I'd become so attuned to this man that I could notice the split-second glare in those gray eyes. "Did you want to go home now?" he said to me.

"Do you mind? I'm pretty tired, too."

"No, it's fine. I wasn't thinking. Come on."

I turned to Joe. "Thanks anyway, Joe. It's been fun. I'll see you around."

He gave me a tight, clearly defeated smile and a hug goodnight, but I didn't give him a backward glance. I marched to the car and opened the damn door myself. Benjamin was behind me fast enough to shut it, though, and I couldn't hate the consideration in that gesture.

"I didn't mean to be a dick," he said when he started the engine and I sat with my arms crossed.

"Didn't you?"

"No! I just didn't think it was right to assume you would want to leave."

"But you're my ride. You could've asked what I wanted."

"But if I'd done that, I'd have sounded like your *date*."

I glanced over, but he was focused on the road. "Oh. I see your point."

"About time," he snorted.

I scowled but let it drop, staring up at the moon while we drove through the night. I was tired, overheated but cold, wired but sleepy—the usual for a night of partying. "This was fun," I whispered at last.

He pulled into my complex and parked. I scanned the balconies and then turned my attention into the car. Benjamin rested his head against the seat, eyes closed. "Yeah, it was great."

"I thought Allison was going to climb into your lap at the club," I teased, glad he didn't seem rushed to leave.

He inhaled. "Her hand was already there."

I gasped, delighted by his wicked smile. "I can't believe you bailed on the party to go home. They were a done deal."

"Oh? And what about your Joe? He was very ready to take you home."

"Maybe the three of them can get into some trouble together. I hope so. It'd be a good ego boost for him, after I turned out to be so disappointing."

We fell quiet until Benjamin faced me. "Truth time."

"I'm not drunk." I held up a hand in warning.

"Does truth require alcohol?"

"Ask a question. We'll see."

With withering side-eye, he said, "Do you *really* hate me?"

"Do you care?"

"Yes." The bottom dropped out of his voice on that one syllable and turned my reply into a whisper.

"No, I don't hate you. And," I bit my tongue.

"And?"

"And I like that you care."

His face creased with a lazy smile. "Another truth?" he asked after a few moments. "Why are you still in my car?"

"Wow, okay then, goodnight. I thought Southerners had manners." I reached for the door as embarrassment crept to my cheeks.

He interrupted me with a soft laugh and his hand on my arm. Like at The Flipside, I froze at the gentle restraint. "You should recognize by now when I'm *teasing* you."

Ooh, that word again.

"Not teasing, bullying. All night, just like always."

"Oh, really? Bullying you all night? How so?"

I rolled my eyes, unable to keep the smile from my lips. "Um, let's see. Start with the whole Googling me thing, then move on to tormenting me about Joe."

"Aw, humblest apologies." His drawl sounded very far from apologetic, and it egged me on.

"Jesus, Ben, you made me dance by myself, you ass. Text-book bullying."

He blinked, interrupting the banter. "That's the first time you called me Ben."

"Sorry," I said, unsure how else to answer.

The lazy smirk returned. "No, I like it. And, for the record, I suggested you dance."

I lifted my chin. "I'll leave now. Sorry to keep you. I was just waiting for those guys on the second floor to finish their smoke."

He peered out the front window. "Why?"

"They always say something to me. Since it's late, I'd rather they were inside when I go up."

"They bother you? What do they say?" His brows drew together as he gazed up at the building.

"'Hey baby, you're so beautiful. Got a boyfriend?' Your usual redneck pickup lines."

Benjamin nodded and shut off the engine. "Let's go."

Before I could even think of objecting, he had my door open. We crossed the parking lot and climbed the stairs, his arm circling my waist as we emerged from the stairwell.

"Evenin' gorgeous," came the greeting on cue. My neighbor looked hard at Benjamin. "On a date huh? Good for you, sweetheart." His drunken slur and deep country accent made him barely intelligible, but both men laughed.

"Y'all take care now. Don't get into anything too spooky with that masked man," his buddy called after us.

Ben kept a firm hold on me until we rounded the corner

to my side of the complex. When we reached my door, he let go and leaned against the rail, and I had to swallow my pride. For all the times I'd navigated life on my own and been just fine, there was something lovely about having another person look out for me.

"Thank you. I'm sure you know I hate the idea of needing someone to protect me, but thank you."

He shrugged. There was tension in his posture that made me edgy. I adjusted my coat and asked the first thing that came to mind. "Do you want to come in for a drink?"

"No."

"Do you want to come in to talk?"

"No."

"Seriously? That's all you're going to say?"

He stirred, a faint smile flickering. "You say seriously a lot." I wrinkled my nose, and he shook his head. "Sorry, no, I probably shouldn't come in. It's just kind of hard to walk away." He smiled wryly.

"Yeah, the palatial surroundings are seri—uh, very compelling." I leaned beside him on the balcony railing and nodded toward his face. "I'll stand out here a few minutes if you want, but that has to go."

"I'd forgotten about it." He pulled the mask off, running a hand through his rumpled hair. "Better?"

I had to stifle a groan and remember to nod. *Yeah, better —try perfect.* I swear, even wild hair and the orange light of the streetlamp made him look amazing.

We chatted a little about work, and then about dinner and the club. I was commending the DJ when he interrupted. "You're shivering. Are you okay?"

Not until he said it did I notice that my teeth chattered. "It's pretty cold out here."

"You could go inside."

"What was that you said about it being hard to walk away?" The question got no reply, so after a beat I said, "Anyway, it's late and you're tired. You should probably go home."

"You sound like my mother. She's always worried about me getting enough rest."

I shook my head at the detail. "Sorry, I meant to say don't let me keep you anymore. Feel free to do exactly what you want the rest of your night."

Out of the corner of my eye, I saw his posture stiffen and his head turn. "Say that again."

12

Something in his tone made my heart pick up speed. "I said you should do what you want. If you want to go home and cut your toenails, I don't need to know. Or maybe go see if the group is still at the bar. Maybe Allison and her friend will..." I trailed off when he moved so we were face to face.

He cocked his jaw. "Why would I be interested in two women I barely know?"

I gestured helplessly. "I told you about the office ladies having crushes on you. You said I made you happy. Your birthday, remember?"

"You didn't *seriously* think I meant your office gossip made me happy, did you? You have to know I meant spending the evening with you."

"But-but we just worked all night." Without the buffer of work or alcohol, the energy between us tightened my lungs and knotted my tongue.

Everything about his posture had intensified. "Wrong. We worked. Then we ate pizza. *Then* you kissed me."

"I— it was a—mistake." Words failed me as he stepped closer. "I didn't—"

"Yes, you did." He gripped the railing and bent so we were eye-to-eye. "You definitely kissed me. I tasted you for the rest of the night."

"Damn garlic."

He laughed, but even that was too sexy, a deep rumble in his chest. It was difficult to hear his next works over my pounding pulse. "How is it not obvious what I want to do, Celeste? Did you believe me when I said I was tired?" His eye crinkled. "I'm *not* tired. I have nowhere better to be. And I want nothing from this night as badly as I want to kiss your mouth."

Who talks like that? I meant to exhale; a dreamy sigh came out instead. He was *on* me. His spicy, masculine scent, mingled with a hint of sweat from a night of dancing, hit my nose. Warmth pooled between my legs, and the tingling numbness spreading over me wasn't from the cold.

I lifted my face so our foreheads touched, and he traced my jaw with his finger. "I don't believe you," I mumbled when he nuzzled my nose. His lips glanced off my cheek, and I gripped his jacket to stay upright.

He pulled back enough to meet my gaze. His pupils eclipsed the gray of his irises, but his brow creased in confusion. "How the hell can you—"

I silenced him by pushing to my tiptoes. My mouth brushed over his, and I delighted in the sigh he emitted. His lips were cold, the faint hint of whiskey still on his breath— a perfect combination for a fall night. I wanted to lick until I was drunk on the flavor, but I held back to keep control of the moment.

My tongue flicked out for a quick taste while my hand pressed to his heart. I lowered off my toes, and he followed eagerly. Another lick, a flutter of his lashes, and I skimmed my touch down his coat to the outline of his erection. "I don't believe a kiss is *all* you want," I teased.

His groan was my victory, a sound of contained pleasure that told me how right I was. Before I could consider the next move, Benjamin had my head in his hands. He bent to me, and so much for control.

His lips touched mine lightly once—just once—before our kiss exploded. My insides glowed as he explored my mouth, deep and hot, lips pulling hard in answer to me. I clung to his jacket, breathless and unsteady and fully aware that this was the most electric kiss of my life.

He nipped along my jaw, and my head lolled. "Do you still want to invite me in?" He punctuated the question with his teeth on my earlobe, then pulled away and waited.

I straightened my coat, wiped his saliva from my lips with my pinkie finger, and willed my knees to have the fortitude to hold me up if I tried to walk. The keys were almost in my hand when I paused. Taking him inside would be so dangerous, so stupid. How could we compete against each other afterward? *How will you compete against him after that kiss?* This was nothing but trouble.

So play it safe. Tell him what you both know: that you can't do this, that it's too risky. Thank him for the ride. Say goodnight. Or be reckless and... Even my inner voice stumbled. *Open the door, take him inside, and let him use your body any way he likes. Touch him. Be touched until you can't think of anything else. Oh, god, I—*

I glanced at him. His shoulders were tense, but he waited patiently, one hand on the rail.

Dark hair a mess.

Features shadowed in the moonlight, but still so handsome.

Hello, trouble. Make yourself at home.

I reached for his coat and strode the six feet from railing to door with him right behind. His laugh tickled my ear while I fished the keys from my bag. He blew gently on the back of my neck just as I found the right one. "Do you mind?" I snipped with a smile. "I'm trying to concentrate."

"So am I. Here, let me help." He reached around to cover my right hand with his and guide us to the lock. I jumped as his left hand skimmed down my back and hitched up the hem of my jacket. He squeezed my ass until I swayed and fell against his chest with a moan.

The lock was forgotten. I turned my head for his mouth and pushed against his grip on my backside. His fingers slid between my legs, pressing up until I groaned and fell out of the kiss. A firm tap on the seam of my pants sent reverberations of pleasure through me, and I stepped apart a little wider. My arm snaked around his neck for support, eyes wide and fixed on him.

"I'm going to throw you against this fucking door if you don't open it right now." His voice was French roast with an espresso shot, but I didn't move until he grasped my wrist and guided me to the lock.

Inside, we reached for each other in the darkness. My hands connected with his waist; he held my arms. His breath brushed my cheek when he bent his head, seeking my lips. We froze before contact, breathing together for just a heartbeat.

I was the one who moved. I leaned the little bit it took to find his mouth, and he did the rest. He held me by the head again, angled me to his lips in another all-consuming kiss that only intensified the hunger to *feel* that had gnawed at me for weeks.

Touch him. I groped for the buttons on his coat and pushed it off. His breath hitched when it dropped to the floor. My own shoulders were bare a second later. Both of us grunted as we wrapped our arms around each other, our kiss even deeper than before.

One hand on his arm him to steady myself, still deep in the kiss, I reached down to remove my boots. The zip slid halfway down, then stuck. I tugged vainly until he broke away. "What's wrong?"

"Stupid boot," I mumbled.

"Allow me." Benjamin put his hands on my arms—and slid them down while he dropped to his knees. I gripped his shoulders, longing to squirm as his touch glided down my hips, thighs, and calves. At last, he opened the zipper with a sharp pull. When the other was undone too, I kicked them away.

Those hands took the same route up as they had down. They paused on my hips while he sat up higher on his knees and chuckled. "Huh."

"What?"

His answer was pure tease. His arms wound around me as he kissed his way over my pants and up my shirt. "You're so much shorter without those ass-kicking boots you always wear," he whispered when his lips finished the journey up to mine.

I huffed and tried to push him away. "Thanks a lot."

I'm not sure which was better, his laughter, or the way he refused my push and instead hugged me close. Before I could decide, he walked us back, leaned on the wall so I stood between his legs, and kissed me senseless. His lips were soft, his skin a little rough with stubble, and the pressure of his pull on my mouth—the varying intensity, from hair-gripping urgency to sweet little nips and caresses that gave me butterflies—had me out of my mind.

I don't remember when we stumbled out of the entryway, or when he sank onto the couch, or if he brought me down to straddle his lap or if I did it myself. I don't even remember how the light got turned on. All I remember was how he kissed me and how I wanted him to never stop.

The world beyond Benjamin's mouth slowly returned when I began to unknot his tie, then slid it off his neck and draped it over my shoulders. He leaned back and smiled, breath heavy, and held each end of the black silk to glide it over my skin. With a tug, he tipped me toward him again so our foreheads touched. His dark eyelashes swept down in a slow blink, and then widened to look up at me. Each word he spoke was punctuated by a kiss.

"You. Are. Delicious."

I shivered while he kissed across my cheek and down my neck. I shivered again when his hands slid under my shirt to stroke my back, but it was a different kind of chill. There was nothing pushy or rushed about his move, but something about this next step turned my thrill of pleasure into a jolt of reality. *This isn't you, remember?*

Jagged thoughts floated up yet again in Derrick's voice. *"You make it impossible to be close to you, Celeste. You're so cold."*

I didn't kiss him back this time, and he noticed immediately. "Everything okay?"

"Yeah, uh, do you want a drink? Wine or something?" I pulled my shirt down, and his touch retreated instantly.

Braced for a frown, what I got instead was a headshake and that damn sexy smirk that made me quiver. Benjamin slid the tie across my arms again. "No thanks. I'm pretty drunk on *you*."

I almost fell off his lap. My lips curved into a dopey smile. "You've seriously got a way with words, Ben Addison."

His grin went broad, but I drew back when he tried to

pull me forward again. As much as I loved what he said, worry still clung to me.

Benjamin frowned. "What's wrong?"

"Nothing. It's stupid. It's not you, I swear." *You're about to ruin this.*

"Obviously something's wrong. What—"

"I have trust issues. My last boyfr—uh, I have trust issues. And it's been a long time since I—" I fumbled, horrified to admit my truth.

All the wonderful heaviness, all the tingles, were gone. Now I sat, cold and miserable on this gorgeous man's lap—a man who had just called me delicious, for heaven's sake—waiting for him to ask me to move so he could get his coat.

His eyes softened from that steamy gaze that had been on me all night. "Someone hurt you?"

I studied my arms hugged across my ribs and breathed out more truth. "Yeah."

"What happened? No, I shouldn't ask." He stopped himself when I startled, then tried again. "You trusted him?" Nod. "And he lied to you." Nod, this time with tears at the corner of my eyes. *So cold. So pathetic.* Benjamin exhaled. "Damn, that sucks."

The silence was loud after all our breathy kisses. He laid his hands on my thighs, and I prepared to feel a gentle push to indicate I should stand. Instead, he ran his palms up and down my legs and began to speak, this time in the deliberately casual tone that had gotten my blood racing more than once.

"I hope you know, but I'll warn you anyway. You definitely shouldn't trust me."

His deliciously dark register negated the warning and made goosebumps run up my arms. I lifted my gaze to see the spark in his.

"Why?"

He leaned forward and spoke against my mouth. "Because I didn't come in for a drink, *Ms. Greene*. I'm here to explore my options with you, and not a damn one of them is suitable for work. I would very much like to *explore* all the ways I can make you lose your mind. I want you to blush when you think about me afterward. That part, you can trust. Okay?"

Memories were gone. I couldn't even remember what cold felt like. I nodded, unable to speak but agreeing to every syllable he'd uttered.

But he shook his head and withdrew an inch. "Is that an option that works for you? I want to hear your answer."

"God, yes." A little cry bubbled from my throat we met in another kiss.

Benjamin broke us apart. He shushed my protest and coasted his palms down to my waist, but I beat him to lifting my shirt up and off. His jaw clenched before his lips were on my cleavage, my fingers in his hair. The warm bite of his teeth on my soft flesh made me jolt and tug. I jolted again when he unzipped my pants and stroked down, over my underwear.

"Oh, god."

But the words in my head weren't said by me. Benjamin pushed further between my legs. He groaned again, and I flushed to realize how wet I was. The edges of my vision were already dark, a tickle of climax starting to condense. I lifted my hips and let my body beg for more.

He laughed. "Nah, I'm not done *teasing* you."

I whined. My eyelids were lead, tongue too focused on kisses to bother with words. Dammit, every one of our exchanges that had left me warm and flustered were in his arsenal.

And I *loved* it.

I squealed when Benjamin's thighs flexed as he lifted us off the couch. He lay me back on the carpet and knelt over me, one palm by my head as he skimmed his feather-soft touch up my abdomen, stopping just below my bra. He coasted over the satin; with two sharp pulls, the fabric was nothing but a shelf for my exposed breasts.

Benjamin smiled before he began to kiss down my throat. He licked a line of fire across my breasts before he sucked one tip into his mouth. I arched my spine, almost blacked out from the pleasure. It had been so long—so long since someone had touched me, yes, but so long now that I'd wanted *him* like this.

His tongue drew a circle, then flicked hard against my nipple while he reached down and tugged at my pants. I leaned into my palms behind me and raised my hips, and he sat on his heels and stripped the leather off my legs, raking a salacious stare from my toes up. "Fuck."

I glanced at the green plaid bikinis I sported and pursed my lips. "These aren't sexy."

He lunged forward and threw one knee over my hips. "Everything about you is sexy," he vowed while I began to unbutton his shirt. I wasn't done before his tongue was in my mouth, his hand on the back of my head. I fell hard against the carpet while he kissed and petted down my body, tickles and bites alternating to make my blood boil.

He licked the crease of my hip and ran his thumb between my legs. My breath stopped, but he hissed and flicked his gaze up to me. "Oh god, Ben," I mewled, so tight, so hot it hurt. "*Please*."

"Yes?" he drawled.

I grabbed his shoulders, demanded he meet my mouth, then pushed him back and looked him square in the eye.

"No more teasing. Make me come." In the back of my mind, I marveled at my boldness, but that was only a tiny part of me. The rest was consumed with the desire to have him fulfill my request.

I held my breath when he hooked the elastic of my underwear. We stared at each other until I nodded once, and he licked his lips. "Touch your breasts." I lay back and began to pet myself at his command. "*Fuck*," he whispered when one finger slipped inside of me and drew a circle. I gasped as a second finger joined the first.

I'm not sure if I could say that Benjamin's touch was better than I thought it would be, because I couldn't think at all. I was nothing but feeling, nothing but absolute bliss. The rhythmic pulse of his fingers set the tempo of my breath, and all of the fire in my blood turned into a singular ache when his thumb found my clit. My hips bucked, blood singing for the impending release. The last thing I heard was an *mm-hmm* from him, and then, with a cry of relief and ecstasy, my orgasm exploded. "Oh god," I moaned over and over, quaking with the force of it.

His hand disappeared when I got quiet. I lifted my head to look at him, and his brows rose, a silent question of what came next. "Come here."

In an instant he was on top of me, kissing my neck and unzipping his pants. I curled up to press my lips to his jaw, but the sound of his belt made me open my eyes.

"Wait."

He didn't have time to respond before I gently pushed him to sit up, clambered to my knees, and faced him. Still a bit shaky, I unbuttoned the rest of his shirt. At the last button, I licked my lips. "I want to touch you."

Benjamin's chin dropped to his chest on a deep breath. "God, yes," he exhaled.

I helped him out of the sleeves, and he tugged off his undershirt. My heartbeat was in my fingertips as my nails traveled over his broad shoulders to the curves of his sculpted arms, so warm and hard. Slowly, I wandered down his abs and followed the trail of hair below his navel; when I reached for his fly, his hands covered mine. I looked up while we removed his jeans together. My palm slid into his boxer-briefs and closed around his—*oh.*

My eyes widened, mouth dry as I slid my hand up and down his hot, smooth skin. Ben paused with his pants at his knees to give me another panty-soaking smirk, but it dissolved fast when I continued to stroke.

"Do you have protection?" I released my grip reluctantly, waiting.

"Of course." Benjamin kicked off his pants and grabbed his wallet from the pocket. He tore the foil wrapper, then rolled the condom on while I leaned back on my elbows again. We met in a long, lazy kiss until I was flat on the carpet and my legs were squeezing his hips. I reached for his cock, guided him down, and grinned at his moan when I teased him against my slick skin. Benjamin released my grip and kissed my palm before slowly inching into me.

It took my breath how tight I was, but damn was my body ready for this—ready for him. He sank down and stopped to give me a look that clearly sought approval to continue. I nodded, and he pulled out and slammed in hard, making me groan loud.

"Too much?" he asked, but his hips flexed already. I whispered no, and he began to really move. "It's just that you're so wet, I couldn't resist."

"You're not resisting much anymore, hmm?"

Benjamin flashed a brief grin. "You're one to talk, with your gorgeous tits in your hands, letting me finger-fuck you

—not a hint of resistance there." His words rumbled in my head while his hips continued a killer rhythm.

"Mm, yes," I huffed. "But I *tried* to resist."

"Oh, yeah? And just how long did that go on? Just how long did you *resist,*" he bit my ear, "while you were so very, very wet?"

I open my mouth to respond, but his cock inside me and his dirty words stole my thoughts. *Again? Already?* My fingers clawed down his back, and I pushed my hips against his rhythm. I was so full of him, and the way he moved lit me up along every nerve ending.

"Damn, are you ready to come again?" One look at me told him the answer. He stilled a moment and sucked on my nipples while I writhed helplessly, and then the rhythm resumed and my throbbing condensed. One more powerful thrust pushed me over the edge, and I bit my lips to swallow a loud groan in my throat as I fell apart. "Let me hear it next time, Celeste. I want to hear what I do to you. I—god, you're incredible."

He propped up on his elbows and upped the tempo of our bodies. I knew he was close from the sweat on his back and the shallow huffs of breath in my ear.

"Ben, I have a truth," I panted.

"Hmm?"

"You've had me wet all night." Even more heat swept over me when I gasped out my confession.

His palm struck the floor as he thrust hard with a groaned *yes*. I dug my nails into his shoulders, and he pulsed deep just before he collapsed on top of me. "*Yes,*" he sighed.

Yes. Yes, yes, yes.

13

I stared at the ceiling. For once, my mind was completely blank, and it was amazing.

Benjamin removed the condom and rolled onto his back beside me. "Holy shit," he breathed, and I nodded even though he didn't see.

I sat up after my pulse evened out. He looked over while I was fixing my bra, so I clutched the first article of clothing I found to my chest and got to my feet. "I'll be back."

I closed the bathroom door and flipped on the light. Dear lord, the face that greeted me in the mirror was the scariest Halloween harpy I'd ever seen. My lipstick was beyond gone, my eyeliner smudged to no end, and my hair, which I'd so carefully piled up earlier, swirled around my head in an auburn tumbleweed. *How the hell did this just get laid?* I grabbed the makeup remover.

And froze as the thought sank into my brain.

The bottle almost cracked in my hand as I struggled to breathe. Panic raised goosebumps on my arms. Adrenaline clashed with the orgasmic fatigue in my muscles. *What have we done?*

With trembling hands, I forced myself to wipe away the eyeliner, brush out my hair, and find fresh underwear. Damn my luck, why did this have to happen at my apartment? And why couldn't my bathroom have a window I could slither out, so I never had to see him again?

Well, until Monday, you mean.

"Dammit." I groaned and slammed the brush on the counter.

I'm quite sure anxiety could've kept me hidden in the bathroom forever. But when I grabbed what I thought was my blouse and discovered it was his undershirt, my rioting thoughts paused. After a brief hesitation, I pulled it on.

His scent washed over me and lit up my body all over again. I buried my nose in the collar and breathed deep, that dopey smile returning. *Oh, god, Ben, what are we going to do?*

If it were up to me, there would be only one answer tonight. *More.*

Just as my jitters started to ease, a new fear hit me when I stepped into the hallway. *Is he freaking out too? What if he's looking for his shirt so he can leave? What if he left already? It would be best if he did, I guess...*

Benjamin lounged on the couch, his knees spread wide, dressed in boxer briefs and his unbuttoned dress shirt. He looked quite the opposite of someone about to go anywhere. When he saw me, the smile that broke on his face had me leaning against the wall for support.

"There's my shirt."

"Uh, yeah. Do you want it?" I toyed with the hem.

"Yes. I need it back right now. It's urgent," he said seriously, but then crossed his hands behind his head and wiggled his brows. I startled when I realized what I'd offered, but Benjamin laughed.

I knew I wore a deer-in-headlights look, and it irked me.

You aren't shy. Stop letting him daze you, dummy. My brows lowered to their normal position. I rolled my eyes and flashed a little smile.

Benjamin leaned his elbows on his thighs. "Come here."

My pulse jumped, but I refused the reflex to sprint across the room and leap into his lap. I moseyed around instead, adjusted a lamp, and then bent to pick up the clothes on the floor, sure that he got a full view of my blue lace boyshorts in the process. His grunt of appreciation made me smile while I folded my pants and stacked them on the coffee table.

"Come *here*." He chuckled this time, and I went to stand in front of him.

"Would you like some water?" I tried to stay casual, but his eyes were darkening again, and it was hard to ignore the lust in his expression.

Benjamin stared at the hemline that barely covered my underwear. One finger traced up my leg and lifted the shirt to my bellybutton. He drew little circles on my stomach, gaze intent on my hip, and the memory of the circle he'd drawn *inside* me began to tickle. Before I could touch him, though, he pulled back. "Water sounds good, thanks."

Okay, this is good. Is that weird? Why aren't we awkward? Aren't we supposed to say—

"You let your hair down."

I whirled around with a squeak at his voice behind me. He blinked. "Was that a squeak?" he asked.

"You surprised me." I handed him the glass. We eyed each other as we drank. With a nervous swallow, I said, "Yeah, I brushed it in the bathroom. I looked horrible." I wrinkled my nose.

Confusion lifted into total, gorgeous smugness. "You didn't look horrible. You looked fucked."

I barely remembered what it was like to *not* have this ache between my legs, but I clenched my thighs and stayed stubborn. "Horrible. You weren't paying attention."

Benjamin set the glass down and stepped forward to run his fingers through my hair and tilt my chin. He hummed, a patiently condescending sound. "Have I been that subtle about how much my *attention* is on you?"

"Well, I mean, I got the hint out on the balcony."

His thumb skimmed my lip, so I opened up and sucked. "No, Celeste, not just tonight." He bent so his lips were against mine, thumb still in my mouth. "Every damn day," he breathed.

All the water in the world couldn't quench my thirst. I gazed at the mischievous fire in his eyes while he licked the corner of my lips. "Every day?" I mumbled around his thumb.

"Mm-hmm."

Ben scooped me up and set me on the counter. With my legs wrapped around his waist, I fisted his thick hair and deepened the kiss. His cock aligned with my sex through our underwear. I squeezed my knees, and together we let out a moan.

"Wait, wait." He lifted his head. "That was the only condom I had. Where can I get more?"

I leaned into my palms on the laminate. "I don't know, Benjamin, that's a lot of trouble."

He opened his mouth to object, but my lips twitched, and he glared. "Are you teasing me, Greene?" He buried his face between my breasts. I laughed when he nuzzled me. "No trouble, but it'll be agony if I don't have you again."

I bubbled another laugh. "There's a gas station with a market at the end of my block to the left. It's twenty-four hours. Take my house keys."

"Perfect."

In the living room, he stepped into his jeans and turned to me. "I'm afraid if I leave, you'll reconsider."

"I'm afraid if you leave, you won't come back." I looked down.

"I'll come back," he promised. "I have your keys."

"I'll be in my bedroom." I pointed down the hall, then spun and scurried away.

BEN

I stumbled out to my car and slammed the door. My head smashed against the headrest while I tried to breathe. *Holy shit, did that just happen?*

It didn't. It couldn't have. All these weeks I'd restrained myself from so much as looking at her too long. No way had a first kiss turned into sweaty, screaming sex on her living room floor.

My heart thudded hard. I lifted my hand off the steering wheel to rest two fingers under my nose. Sure enough, the faint but definite scent of her still lingered on my skin. I inhaled again and flashed over everything once more.

I hadn't let myself hope for more than a kiss tonight, but as the evening wore on and her walls lowered more and more, a taste of her had definitely been at the front of my mind. Her mouth—*dear god, her mouth.* I opened my eyes and smirked. *Her. All of her.* Body limp and quivering for every damn thing I did, hands in my hair, touching my chest, my back, until...

"No more teasing. Make me come."

I laughed and shook my head. Had anyone ever made me feel like a sex *god* before? My ego filled with helium. Make her come? I made her come *twice,*. Easily. And she wanted more.

She's waiting for more while you sit here, dumbass.

I fired the engine and didn't waste another second daydreaming when I could get back to her bed instead.

Condoms jammed in my coat pocket, I slipped into Celeste's apartment. The lights were dim, the place silent, but her clothes still sat neatly on the coffee table, boots scattered just inside the doorway. A soft yellow light glowed down the short hall.

After a moment of not-so-irrational panic—*She's going to tell you to leave, that you made a mistake*—I strode to the cracked door.

Auburn hair fanned out on a white pillowcase. One knee propped up on a navy quilt, exposing plenty of winter-pale thigh. Her hands rested on her heart and her stomach.

And her eyes were wide open, a tiny smile on her lips while she gazed at me.

I cleared my throat as adrenaline spiked. "Are you busy?"

She crooked a finger, just like in my stupid fantasy. "Very."

Holy shit.

I tossed the condom box to the bedside and climbed over her, bending to accept the kiss she lifted to my lips. Her arms circled my neck, and I surrendered to the need Celeste Greene fueled in me.

While we kissed, she started to hook her ankles around my legs, but I wanted her on top and in control. I rolled to my back and brought her to straddle my hips without breaking the kiss.

Celeste tensed for only a moment before her fingers flew to undo my shirt buttons. When she sat up and gazed down at me, her hooded, appreciative stare made me glad I worked out regularly. Fingertips skimmed my pecs and down my stomach to my jeans. *You know where that trail leads, Ms. Greene. Don't be shy.* Thinking of her as Ms. Greene in that moment made my blood rush. The knowledge that the woman on top of me was the same prim, haughty girl who'd told me to "get to work" so many times was *hot.*

My thoughts shattered when she rocked her hips, grinding against me as she flung herself forward. Her lips landed on my neck with a sharp pull, and I groaned and lifted my pelvis.

She stripped me slowly and kissed me everywhere. Her sweet, hot mouth nipped and licked my neck, my arms, and my fucking *ear* until I shivered. Patient hands removed any clothes that stood in her way.

I held her hips and let her play as long as I could stand, but when she sucked my ear again, I blurted, "I want you naked. Now."

She jumped hard, and I laughed and encouraged her to sit up. Celeste bit her lip and inched my t-shirt over her head, dropping it behind her. "Keep going," I said without moving my lips.

The bra joined the shirt, and I exhaled. "Fuck yeah."

"Fuck yeah?" she echoed.

Fuck yeah, she was perfect. I didn't want to blink, didn't want to miss a second of this woman's beautiful body, her soft skin and sweet curves, seated atop my lap. "Mm-hmm." I skimmed my hands up her thighs and fisted those little blue lace panties. "I want to tear these off you."

"Okay," had hardly left her mouth before I destroyed

those beauties with a satisfying rip. *Damn, that was fun.* She smiled down at me and fell forward for another hungry kiss. Her breasts filled my hands, my thumbs switching over the tight peaks until she shuddered and groaned.

I reached for the condoms and rolled one on blind. "Whenever you're ready, Celeste."

She shifted her hips, and my already-quick blood began to fucking *thunder*. I opened my eyes to take in the sight of Celeste Greene lowering herself onto my cock. Heat swept over my skin as my pulse went erratic. No woman had ever turned me on this badly; I could barely breathe while she squirmed and settled with a tiny sigh.

She looked at me, brows pinched. It took effort to ask, "Everything okay?"

"Yeah, just—*oh*," she moaned when she rocked her hips and jolted me with pleasure. Her eyes squeezed tight, but she rocked again, moaned again.

My body heard what she wasn't saying. I stroked her thighs and reached for her breasts, pinching lightly until she opened her eyes. "I see you holding back," I said in a voice so dark I didn't recognize myself. I caressed her again. "Don't fucking *dare*."

Her expression told me I'd read her right. She wet her lips and tipped her head backward.

And then, she rode the hell out of me. I had to brace my hands in the quilt to stabilize as she moved hard and fast over my pelvis, destroying me with her rhythm. I groaned as a hoarse cry spilled from her lips. She scrabbled for my wrists and planted my hands back on her breasts. "Hell yeah," I breathed, but she didn't hear.

I knew by the dark flush on her face and neck, not to mention the way her nipples puckered and responded to me, that she was ready to come quick. She kept changing angles just enough to prolong, and I wanted to promise to give her more if she'd just let...

Go.

"*Ben, please.*" Her shout bounced off the walls as her body quaked and jolted.

Yes, baby, yes. Whatever you please. Whenever. However. I'll give it to you.

I had her on her back as soon as she went still. "Scratch me," I rasped and drove into her with hard, steady thrusts. I needed to feel something to remind me this was real, to tell me this pleasure had a place in reality. Her nails dug tracks down my back and made my skin burn, exactly like I needed, and the sweet pain helped me find my own release fast.

"Holy shit *again,*" I huffed as I caught my breath on top of her.

Her fingers tickled over the lines she'd just made on my spine. "Mm-hmm," she murmured, and I grinned into the pillow.

After discarding the condom, I returned to her bed and rested my head on her heart, lightly tickling her belly. The longer we lay, the more exhaustion took hold. "What time is it?" I asked at last.

She turned to look at the clock. "Almost three."

"So late."

"Mm, shh. Too late to talk."

"How about to fuck?" I winked, mostly joking.

"Again? Seriously?"

I drew circles around my nipples and wiggled my brows.

Celeste swatted my hands. Her musical laugh, the one I'd only heard once before, made me grin hard. "You're terrible," she said, still smiling broadly.

"You're amazing."

Her cheeks colored. "Hush. Don't be so nice to me."

It was too late for her to put her walls back up. "Okay. I'll bully you in the morning."

Celeste yawned and hugged my neck. "Thanks."

14

On the "morning after," some people need a minute to remember what got them into the arms of another person. Not me. I woke knowing full well whose chest rose and fell peacefully against my back. I needed no time to remember exactly how we'd ended up here, and there was no jolt of shock or embarrassment about being stark naked in his presence. I *was* a little surprised at the soreness between my legs and the puffiness of my lips, but let's face it—it had been a long time since I'd been so, um, active.

Yeah, but it's morning now. And this situation is very, very complicated. You can't assume this means anything. You have to keep your wits. This isn't romance, this is a rivalry. Not that you know how to do romance anyway. Know yourself. Know your business. He's not your man.

The thought made me blanch, but it also got me out of bed. Time to get back to me.

Benjamin stirred when I sat on the vanity bench and laced my sneakers. "Mmm, hey. Uh, going somewhere?"

"I thought I'd go to the gym. I usually do on Saturday."

He rubbed his rumpled hair and sat up with a yawn.

"I'm not awake yet, so spell it out for me. Are you kicking me out, leaving me here, or something else?"

His sleepy confusion was too adorable. It took a lot not to jump back in bed, sneakers and all. "I'm not sure. I don't know what happens next." I dropped my elbows onto my knees.

Another yawn as he lay back against the pillows. "What should happen is you should get back in bed. Making plans is irrelevant in a bed this comfortable." He opened one eye. "It's also impossible to freak out," he said softly.

I toed out of my shoes and returned to sit on the edge. "Promise?"

"I would, but you won't trust me. See for yourself."

"I know what my bed feels like." What I didn't know was how many times I'd need to see Ben Addison *in* my bed wearing nothing but a lazy smile before my cardiac health stabilized.

He caught my fingers and tugged, so I tumbled over and let him fold me into his arms as he traced my mouth. A little kiss made me shiver; the tenderness only made it better. "Look at these swollen lips."

I kissed him again. "You're a little puffy too," I noted.

"That was a lot of kissing."

I returned his grin, absurdly pleased that we shared such a tangible marker of passion. We lay for several minutes, kissing intermittently, mostly quiet, definitely together.

"What gym do you use?" he asked after a stretch.

"The Y." *Thank you, sliding-scale membership rates.*

"Me, too. There's one in East Nashville, where I live. If you don't mind swinging by my place so I can change, we could work out together if you want."

Work out together? I smiled. "Sounds good."

I stayed in bed and stared at the ceiling while he dressed. Rivalries and what next questions shut up in my head. He was right. This bed did make everything a little easier.

"I'm ready." He broke my reverie with a hand on my hair. The familiarity of the gesture solidified my happiness a little more. I rolled to my feet and followed him out.

"Do you want to take both cars?" he asked on the way to the parking lot. He didn't look at me as he said it, but I heard the real question: did I want him back here?

I answered before I could think it over. "You can drive. Or, we can both—"

"No, I'll drive, no problem," he said quickly.

He wasn't humming this morning. The radio filled the silence between us on the ride, and I let my thoughts try to sort themselves out. Every moment we were together, we fell deeper into a tangled mess. This was crazy on levels, but it felt *right*. The obvious hazards of being with him couldn't keep a foothold in the face of that truth.

But still.

Was it weird how *not* weird this was? We were going to the gym together—spending time together, weekend time, personal time—and neither of us had batted an eye at the suggestion. The morning after had a routine, didn't it? He was supposed to get dressed, maybe kiss my cheek, and tell me... what? That he'd call? That it had been fun? That he'd see me at work?

None of those options made sense. Work was precisely why none of this should've happened in the first place. It was also why he wasn't going to call me. Why would he? To set up a date? Drinks, maybe? After eight hours of trying to poach each other's job, cocktails were an absurd idea. Besides, last night had been so much more than fun. How would a casual date compare to what had already happened between us?

Going to the gym together made no sense, but then again, neither did anything else.

I glanced at his profile and wondered what he was thinking. Was he worried about the complexity of our situation, too? Or was he just enjoying getting laid, content to let the rest work itself out? Did it matter to me? I wasn't sure.

Benjamin pulled into the driveway of a converted house. I admired the creative way the house had been sectioned into separate apartments, a bit jealous when I compared it to my own abode. His was the one on the left, and even his front door was nicer than mine, blue with detailing and a bright copper plate around the knob. Beyond the door was a small entryway with a private staircase; I followed him up to a living room, muttering under my breath about the cost of rent. He waved for me to sit on the couch. "I'll be quick," he promised.

I pulled my attention from the bookshelf as an insane idea raced from my heart to my head. "Ben?" He paused in the doorway. "What are you—I mean, what did you have planned this weekend?" I twisted my jacket sleeves.

He thrummed his fingers on the wall and shrugged. "Not much. Why?"

"I guess I was thinking that maybe you should get more than gym clothes. Like, if you wanted to stay a little longer or... something."

He didn't speak or move for a long moment. Then, with a "Yep" that hit me like a slap, he turned and disappeared.

I sat back against the couch, ready to shred this poor jacket at the seams with the way I tugged at it. What had I said? What did he *think* I'd said?

He was gone for about five minutes before we were off

again. When he parked at the Y, I couldn't keep all the thoughts in my head anymore. "Truth?" I blurted.

The engine went silent. He turned to me. "Yeah?"

I threw my hands in the air. "What does *yep* mean? What kind of thing is that to—"

The seatbelt clicked open. Benjamin leaned across the console, palmed my cheek, and turned my face for a kiss. "Yep means hell yes I'll stay with you—as long as I can."

"Oh."

"Yep."

The gym only served to make me more lightheaded and flustered than ever. By the time we were done, I was such a mess of hormones, fatigue, and hunger, I could barely stand. He met me at the entrance. I greeted him with a scowl, and he stopped walking.

"What's wrong?"

"Why do you look so refreshed? I'm shredded."

His medium-olive skin damn well glowed gold in the sunlight, a post-workout flush making his eyes sparkle. The shadow on his jaw was darker than I'd seen before. Added to his tousled, damp hair, his look bypassed unkempt and went straight to *hot*.

He arched an eyebrow at my snippy tone and tucked a strand of hair behind my ear. "You look stressed. What do you need to relax?"

"I never relax."

He quirked his lips and changed the subject. "Caffeine? We can go to a place down the road."

I stalked to the car with a grunt of agreement and rode in frustrated silence over to a place called Portland Brew.

Inside, David Bowie played on the speakers while baristas called hello to regulars and the smell of roasted coffee made me salivate.

We took a small booth in the back by a display of hand-crafted mugs for sale. He let me take two satisfying sips of my latte before speaking. "Why are you so upset?"

I sighed. "I don't know. This whole thing is weird for me."

"This isn't my usual weekend schedule, either."

"Yeah, but I've never done something like this. I don't even know what we're doing."

He tilted his head. "What do you mean?"

I sighed again. "I don't even know that. Sorry, I'm being difficult. I guess I'm trying to say I don't do flings or whatever. I know it's just sex, but—"

"Just sex?"

"Just—yeah. Sex."

"That's what you think this is?" He looked at the table.

"I'm certainly not asking you to make it more, don't worry—"

"That's not the same as—"

"But it's still complicated." I paused to realize he'd spoken. "What?"

Benjamin swirled his coffee around the mug. "You're right that it's complicated, but I disagree with..." He trailed off, still intent on the drink. When he looked up, my brows lifted. There was a lot going on in his expression, and I had no way to interpret it.

"I'm sorry you're so upset. You weren't worried last night," he said at last.

"There wasn't time for worry. Last night was crazy."

Steady patience evaporated from his posture. He set his cup on the table and pointed a finger at me. "Last night was incredible. And you thought so, too, because if you didn't, I wouldn't have a bag of clothes in my car right now. So say what you mean, please."

I bit my tongue and glared, but he waited me out until I caved to the truth. "Last night was incredible. I wasn't worried. I didn't care about anything but us. And it's stressful but, yeah, clearly I'm interested in more us."

Ben sat back, arms crossed. He didn't speak; his face said enough.

I raked my nails across my scalp. "Look, I'm sorry I'm stressed. This is a lot, and I'm tired and starving. Watching you work out didn't help, either."

"Excuse me?"

"You. At the gym. It was very distracting."

He almost spit out his coffee. "You watched me?"

I grabbed my drink and clenched my thighs. "How could I not? Someone had to critique your moves."

"Would you like to give me your notes?" His foot touched mine.

"Stop," I whispered, but his voice was already giving me goosebumps.

"Why?"

"Because."

"Do you know you're blushing?" I nodded, focused on the pattern in the wood tabletop. He leaned in closer. "You can hide your beautiful eyes all you like, Celeste, but that blush on your cheeks still gives me ideas."

I glanced up. "Ideas?"

"Ideas."

"Are they bad?"

"Mm, well, they were bad. But now you're giving me that wide-eyed look with your lips open, and every time I've seen *that* look over the last few weeks..."

"Yeah?" I breathed and didn't care that it was exactly what he wanted me to say.

"Let's just say that when you make that face, the ideas it gives me are definitely not suitable for work."

"Stop," I repeated, but failed to convince either of us that I meant it.

"No," he mimicked my tone, leaning closer still. "Should I tell you more?"

His expression left no doubt that he was thoroughly enjoying this, but so was I. My face was still hot, my heart was in my throat, and I was two seconds away from either bursting out laughing or kissing the smirk off those lips. We both knew it, didn't need to deny it.

"Confess, Mr. Addison." I smiled at the spark in his eyes.

Benjamin glanced around to ensure no one was near, and then motioned me closer. We were leaning across the little table so far that I could feel his breath when he spoke. "When you look at me like that, I want to make you come so hard you feel it all over your body—and I don't care if we're in public, in my car, or," he lifted a brow. "In the office stairwell."

"Benjamin, shut your mouth," I stuttered.

"Or what? You'll shut me up?"

"Damn right I will." I leaned the last inch it took to find his kiss.

He licked his lips and grinned. "There's the answer I wanted the first time."

We ordered more coffee and sandwiches. They were delicious, but I was so hungry by then that I could've eaten the table. It had been a long, eventful time since dinner last night. Finally full, we headed back to my place. "I want to be clean," I announced as we climbed the stairs.

"I like you dirty," Benjamin said, and I shoved his shoulder.

He followed me inside. As soon as the door clicked, his duffel bag hit the floor. I squealed and threw my arms around his neck when he pulled me close. "At the gym," he said between kisses, "all I could think about was taking you... on the mat... on the bench... I couldn't look at you. Gym shorts are terrible at concealing erections."

I laughed, but it died when his tongue slid between my lips.

"I was serious at the coffee shop. You make me think *crazy* dirty things with the looks you give me sometimes." He nipped along my jaw. "I wanted to put my hand down your pants in that booth."

"I wanted you to bend me over the weight rack at the gym." I clawed his shirt off. Mine hit the floor next. Somehow, we got to the bedroom in the midst of all this.

Benjamin stripped off my sports bra and shook his head with a *tsk*. "Such dirty thoughts, Ms. Greene." He grabbed my waist and practically tossed me to the bed.

I landed with a bounce and a giggle that faded fast when he crawled over me, eyes dark and breath ragged. He'd suited up with a condom, and now he kissed me, dragging my bottom lip between his teeth. "I never thought you'd be that filthy," he scolded.

"What are you going to do about it?"

"Exactly what you want, just without the weight rack. Get on your knees, *Celeste*."

Oh, he made my name sound so sexy when he hissed it like that, all sharp Ss and soft Es. I took a long breath and ran my hands down his chest. His damp skin smelled of sweat and sex in the best kind of way.

My knees trembled when he turned me to face the

vanity mirror. I stared, captivated by our reflection. His hair dusted my neck as he kissed down my shoulder. Strong arms were wrapped around my abdomen, but otherwise my body was on display. My hair tumbled out of its ponytail from where he'd gripped it, and I could see the redness of my mouth even from the distance. It was like staring at a fictional version of myself, a Celeste who knew how to be wild and reckless. A Celeste who knew how to dare and tease and please someone. This Celeste was beautiful, thrilling, and so very different. I watched my lips part when he began to trace the curves of my breasts. He kissed my ear, and my reflection smiled and tilted her head to give him better access. Her shoulders arched back when his fingers drifted down to find how wet she—*I*—was. His reflection smiled.

God, it was sexy.

Ben looked up and met my gaze in the mirror. "Are you watching me touch you?" I nodded, refusing to look away. "Do you like what you see?" Nod again. He studied the scene a moment, coasting his hand up and down my body. His lips moved against my temple. "Then see how you look now."

A blush swept over my cheeks and neck. I moaned when he pushed two fingers inside me, flattened his palm, and pressed up. I reached for his hair and pulled his mouth down to my shoulder. He sank his teeth into my flesh before breathing in my ear, "Can you see how much you like it? Because I can definitely feel it."

His voice, his touch, and our reflection were a triple threat I could barely handle. I already burned for release, but I wanted him inside of me to get there. His cock pressed against my ass while he fingered me at a torturously slow pace. The other hand caressed my breasts one at a time.

Reflection me groaned, her hips lifted for more of what he gave.

He breathed deep. "Do you have any idea how in-fuck-ing-toxicating you are, how beautiful you are? Do you have any idea what you're doing to me?"

Distracted from the scene in the mirror by the intensity in his question, I blinked and shook my head no. A guttural, humorless laugh was the reply. His fingers disappeared, and the hand that had been on my breast now wrapped around my ponytail. "Look at me," he said with a gentle pull. "Can't you see how wild I am for you?" There was no tease in the question.

I choked, unsure if it was lust or panic that closed my throat. I didn't have words for this, didn't want to even try to think about what response would suffice.

"Mm-mm, no, Celeste. Say it. Tell me you know I'm serious, and I'll give you what you want."

"You don't know what I want." My thick tongue slurred the words.

"You want *sex*." He spat the word.

Our eyes met in the mirror again, and I found my voice. "No. I want *you*, Ben." *Not Benjamin, not Mr. Addison. Ben. I want you, Ben.* I blinked as he gazed at me.

The scene in the mirror vanished. He pushed me to face the headboard, my hands braced to stop my fall. Before I could blink, he thrust into me so hard I wailed. His hands slid down my thighs and up again as he evened out the rhythm. "I thought this was just sex."

"Shut up," I huffed, eyes squeezed closed.

His teeth bit across my shoulder blades in hard, beautiful kisses, but he didn't say more.

Pain subsided and pleasure built again. My vision darkened, and I rocked erratically. His hands and body worked together to steady me, keep me in the rhythm, until I shook from knees to fingertips, moaning and clawing at the wall as I exploded in waves of release.

He stilled when I did, but I knew he hadn't come. I lifted my head, asking a silent question.

"Can I turn you around? I want to hold you." His voice was soft now.

I faced him. He sat in the center of the bed with me in his lap, my legs around him in a full-body embrace that had my whole being wrapped up in his. My heart thudded as I pressed my face into his hair, and we began to move.

So close... too close... oh, god, close again?

Again indeed. Another orgasm gripped me within minutes. "Jesus, Celeste." His raspy voice was faint to my ears as I came off my high.

"Mm-hmm."

We ground out a slow, lazy rhythm forever, my forehead against his shoulder, eyes closed to absorb every sensation. When my thighs were sweating from being around his hips so long, Ben held my waist and grunted. He upped the tempo, and my body swayed, completely at his command. I gasped and watched him suck more hard kisses on my bicep and down my arm. Ben's eyes were closed, his mouth on the inside of my elbow. His expression pinched, his hips jerked, and I yelped when he bit down as he came.

"Holy shit," we said together, collapsed against the pillows.

BEN

Celeste lay panting on the bed while I removed yet another condom. *At this rate, we'll need more by tomorrow.* I grinned. Hell yeah we would.

I looked at her, sprawled diagonally across the rumpled quilt, so obviously satisfied that my ego took another hit of helium. She looked up at me and smiled.

"You stink," I whispered tenderly.

Celeste bolted upright with a shriek that crumbled my straight face. "You're not so fresh either," she accused. I made a show of smelling my armpits, just to get her laughing again. Silly wasn't my normal style, but I'd do anything to hear that sound.

She climbed off the bed and caught my hand to lead me to the bathroom. My brows rose while I followed, and I was glad she didn't see. *Last night you nearly passed out when I moved to kiss you. Now we're spending the weekend together... and sharing a shower.*

I grinned again. Hell yeah we were.

"God, I'm disgusting," she muttered, so soft I barely heard as she stepped into the tub. She had a point; I suddenly felt the sticky film of sweat from the club, sex, sex, gym, and sex yet again. I wasted no time in joining her under the spray.

We moved in sync, giving each other space to rinse and wash as if we'd practiced this before, but I hadn't showered with a girl since my long-term college girlfriend. *How does this feel so natural? Shouldn't it be at least a little bit awkward, especially after what we said on the bed?*

Shit, I hadn't meant to let that much come out.

As if she heard my thoughts, Celeste blinked at me through droplets on her eyelashes. "Did you mean that?"

Every word. "Did I mean what?"

Annoyance flashed and called me on the bullshit.

"Never ask a man about what he says in the throes of passion." My lips twisted, but my sarcasm game failed. I defaulted to the lamest tactic possible: deflection. "What about you? Did *you* mean it?"

God, those eyes could talk. I smirked to read my answer mirrored on her.

Celeste hesitated, both of us clearly trying to decide how we moved past our lingering questions without wrecking this bond.

I debated telling her everything. That she fascinated me. That I wanted to figure out how to work *together* and show that idiot Rollings how much money we could make him. That she was new and different, so different than any other woman I'd ever encountered. That our connection freaked me out and had me hooked all at once.

That I cared for her more than made sense.

But before I could say a word, Celeste took control. She stepped forward, hugged my waist, and put her head on my chest. Her breathing matched mine while the water ran over us.

My thoughts exactly.

Eventually, she slipped away with a little smile and stepped out. I shut off the water and opened the curtain, grabbing the towel she'd put on the hook for me, but I froze at the sight of naked Celeste rubbing lotion on her breasts and stomach.

She caught my stare and smirked as she wrapped in a towel. "Do I stink now?"

God, that innocent voice slayed me. "Let me check." I buried my face in her neck. She giggled when I nuzzled her, so I did it again. "You smell like flowers. Flowers I want to eat."

"It's jasmine." Her arms went around my neck and made my pulse surge harder while I licked her clavicle.

"Hmm, well I like—"

A yawn hit me out of nowhere and interrupted my feeble attempt to explain without sounding like a sap that the word jasmine had just written itself on my brain. Another yawn escaped as I stepped back, and she answered with one of her own. We nodded in unspoken agreement that a nap was required.

In the bedroom, she closed the blinds and met me in the sheets. I hugged her close, her damp hair on my shoulder, and we were both dead to the world.

15

Bang, bang, bang. I jolted out of a deep sleep. *Bang, bang, bang.* "Ugh," I groaned, face buried in the pillow.

"Celeste? Are you okay? Open the door."

So much for sleep. I jolted and fell out of bed. "Sssshittt."

"Hmm?" Ben murmured. "What's—"

"My mother is here." His eyes flew open while I called out, "Mom, I'm here. I'm fine."

"Open up. I need to see you."

I stumbled to my bureau for yoga pants, then hustled to the door and squeezed out.

Mom grabbed me by the arms. "Celeste Greene, I've been calling all day!"

"Oh, Mom, I'm so sorry. I must've left my phone in my bag."

"And you've been sleeping?" She eyed me critically. "What are you up to?"

I ushered her to the couch. "Nothing. I got really busy this morning and didn't check it. I was out late. I've been kind of tired all day, so I've mostly been in bed." I sat her on the couch, perched on the edge, and prayed she didn't catch the obvious contradiction in what I'd just said.

"What happened to you?" Mom frowned at my arm.

A cold thrill shot through me when I glanced down. Black and blue marks peeked from under my sleeve and trailed to my elbow, where a bright red ring stood out against the bruise. I slapped my palm over the worst part in a pathetic attempt to hide from her.

"I, uh, fell. In the dark. Last night. Tripped over the bench in my room."

Mom clucked. "Looks bad. I hope you iced it." I nodded fast, and she looked me in the eye. "Tell me: when you fell, how, exactly, did you land on someone's mouth?"

Heat flooded my face while Mom arched her left eyebrow and pursed her lips in a look I'd seen all my life. She pushed her dark blonde hair off her forehead and waited.

"What, uh, what are you talking about?"

My own mother laughed at me. "Oh, please. I'm not that dense, sweetheart." She looked at the hall. "Do you have company now?"

My eyelids stretched wide. I was always terrible at lying to my mother. Her lips pursed again, but twitched, too. I nodded, and her smile broke. "Really?"

"I mean, it's..." I had no idea where to take that sentence. I gestured, like the dark TV held some kind of direction for my thoughts. "You know how I—"

"Yes, I do. And I know that you can't spend your life alone just because of that idiot. Anyway. I'm glad to know you're alive, and I'm very glad to see you looking flushed and happy for a change."

"Mother." I rubbed my forehead.

"That's all, I'm leaving. Let me hear from you soon,

please. You're my only child, and whether you live fourteen hundred miles or fourteen minutes away, I need to know you're safe." She tried to give me a scolding look, but it was more smile than anything else.

I threw my arms around her. "Love you, Mom."

"More than anything, baby." She kissed my cheek and let herself out.

Back in the bedroom, I found Ben by the door, fully dressed. "Wow, you are *red*," he greeted me. "She left?" I nodded. "What did you tell her?"

"I told her I'd been asleep, but this kind of ruined the story." I held up my arm, somewhat comforted by when his mouth dropped and his color drained.

"Oh, god, I'm so sorry. I had no idea—does it hurt?" He gingerly petted my elbow.

"It doesn't hurt," I promised, more interested in the care he took inspecting me than the mark itself.

Ben barely acknowledged my words while he lifted my shirt and skimmed his fingertips across my shoulders. "I feel terrible. I can't believe I bruised you."

"I think it's sexy," I admitted as he faced me.

His brows shot up. "Sexy?"

I wet my lips and affirmed. "Like you got carried away. Like you couldn't control yourself."

"*Like* I couldn't." His grin was too tempting for me to not lean in and kiss. "How did you explain it to your mom?"

I dropped onto the bed, one arm over my eyes. "How could I explain any of this? 'Oh, Mom, it's no big deal. Yes, I've got company now. Yes, we've been having wild, amazing sex since last night. Oh, and yes! Yes, he *is* the guy I'm competing with for the one decent job prospect I've found since moving home. So funny, right? Ha, ha, ha! No thanks."

He didn't speak for a long moment. "About the job."

I held up a hand. "Don't say it. I can't deal with everything all at once. Either we're doing this, or I'm thinking of that."

He knelt over me, knees by my hips and hands by my head. His lips began to slide along my neck. "Okay, forget about work. Far more interesting is this wild, amazing sex you mentioned. Hearing you say that," he kissed harder on my throat, "gives me a hell of an ego boost after all these weeks."

"Hmm, your ego's not the only thing getting a boost." I tickled his inner thigh. His laugh gusted my cheek as he lifted his head.

Icy. Withdrawn. Walled off—Ben had said that one. All words that I knew described me, even though I couldn't figure out when or how I became that person. But lying there, caged by his arms and lost in his smile, none of them fit. How could I be icy when the heat of his body melted me?

Truer and more terrifying than that was the way he made me feel unlocked. I knew what we were doing was senseless. I had vowed that no one would ever make a fool of me again, but he was opening me, and I couldn't deny it. The barriers I'd carefully built to protect myself were falling away. I had never experienced anything like this, and I had no defense to the power of what we did to each other.

He waited patiently while I pondered, but finally he kissed my neck. "Do you want to talk?"

"No, I want to kiss." I sprang to life and wrapped myself around him. What I really wanted was to embrace this unlocked sensation as long as I could. As his weight settled on me and his lips pulled on mine, that's exactly what I did.

$\sim$

An hour later, I stared at the shadows on the ceiling, perfectly content to lie there. No thoughts, no worries, no to-dos. Heavenly.

"Get up."

I lolled my head. Ben lounged on his back beside me. "I thought you said we should stay in bed."

"Yeah, but it's time to refuel. We're going to black out at this rate."

He had a point. I was lightheaded again, the sandwich long digested. "What do you want?" I asked, woozy when I sat upright.

"I want to take you out to dinner."

16

The Nashville of my childhood was dingy honky-tonk bars, seedy Printers' Alley, and a lot of time hanging out in the local mall just to have something to do. A coffee shop like Portland Brew used to be a rarity. Fine dining was steak or Italian.

Ben held the door open for me at a very hip place downtown. Across the street stood the gorgeous new Schermerhorn Symphony Center in its quiet majesty, but we could hear music blaring from the bars on Broadway two blocks away. Symphony patrons mingled on the sidewalk with hockey fans in gold and navy, on their way to Bridgestone Arena to see the Nashville Predators play.

Nashville had evolved while I was gone.

The sign above the restaurant said Etch. Inside, the staff wore all black, the kitchen was on display in the center of the venue, and diners chatted over small plates and bottles of wine. "Where's the buffet? Do kids eat free?" I whispered as we were escorted to the table.

"I couldn't get us a table at that place. Overbooked."

I absorbed the cool vibe while he ordered a bottle of

pinot noir and a starter of bruschetta. He hummed when I sat back in my chair with a sigh.

"What?" I asked, and his smile deepened. "What?" I reached for my necklace.

"I almost don't want to say it, but you look very relaxed."

"I never relax." The chain wound twice around my finger, but a laugh tumbled out.

"Mm-hmm, we established that."

"Okay, maybe I'm lacking a bit of tension at the moment," I allowed.

"And how is that going for you?"

We paused for the waiter to pour our drinks. The wine exploded on my tongue. I sipped again. "Deliciously."

"Outstanding," he said as we clinked glasses. The bruschetta arrived, and we wasted no time in devouring one each, then split the third.

"Truth? Before tonight, when was the last time you were this 'lacking tension'?"

The question was light, but I forgot to swallow for a beat as I stared at him over my glass. "What part are you asking about? The meal? The ambience? The... the..."

"Orgasms?"

I flushed. "Yes. Which did you mean?"

"Overall. When were you this at ease?"

I thought hard, took myself back long before That Day. "Thanksgiving in Connecticut. We stayed at an inn with my parents. It was quiet there. Beautiful."

"Almost a year since you've felt like this?"

The memory faded. A chill settled on my heart and hardened my voice. "No. That was two years ago. A year ago on Thanksgiving, I slept on a friend's couch while she was in Long Island. I ate Chinese food and watched *Miracle on 34th Street* by myself."

Dammit, how did he say so much without speaking? His expression didn't change, but it was obvious he knew I had just opened a window on my life for him. I met his gaze, a silent dare to pity me or query more. He did neither.

When his steady gaze was too much, I asked the first thing that came to mind. "When was your last relationship?"

He blinked as a shadow crossed his face. "Spring to early summer."

"I see. When was the last time you slept with someone?"

"Weekend before Rollings hired me, so," he paused as if adding up the time, "six weeks ago?"

I hated how much I hated hearing this. "Nice," I mumbled, picking at the remaining appetizer on my plate. "Not a surprise, I'm sure, but it's been a little longer for me."

"I suspected as much. Want to tell me how long?"

"Over a year and a half." I surgically removed a tomato from the toast.

"Celeste. Look at me." He took my fork and stroked my knuckles with his thumb. "Why did you ask if you didn't want to know?"

"Oh, please, do you think I care?" My question was all shackles and ice. Ben's brows flinched, and I swallowed the urge to wince as he withdrew. "Excuse me."

I didn't wait for a reply before striding to the restroom. There, I washed my hands and surveyed myself in the mirror. Creased forehead, mouth a thin line, eyes a little too bright to deny the hurt.

"You make it impossible for anyone to be close to you." Guess *Derrick had a point there.* My eyes got brighter. I turned away, toweled off, and opened the door.

The doorknob punched my tailbone when I stumbled backward, but I was more concerned about my stopped heart from Ben's quiet presence. He leaned against the wall outside the restroom, arms crossed.

"Yeah, I think you care," he said.

I touched my forehead and drew a shaky breath. "Scared the hell out of me. You think so, huh?"

With two steps, he had me pinned in place. He traced my jaw, his index finger coming to rest on my lifted chin. "Yes. I think you asked a question we weren't ready for. I think you're nervous about opening up to each other too fast. But I'm fairly damn certain that you care."

His words stole my breath. I tried to speak, but no sound came out.

"What was that?"

I licked my lips; he watched. "I care."

His eyes got black. Mine closed, readying for his kiss, but Ben took my hand and guided me back to the table. "If I kissed you now," he said as he pulled out my chair, "We'd never get around to dinner."

The man knew how to make a point.

We ordered, risotto for me and a pork chop for him. While we waited, I said, "I'm not ready to give you my life story, Ben. It's a lot easier to relax if I don't think past right now."

He lifted his glass. "Then here's to right now," he said, and everything was easy again.

The biggest challenge became not inhaling the delicious risotto like a pig at trough. While I clenched my arm and counted to five between bites, Ben eyed our plates and said, "I'd begun to wonder if you ate anything besides salad."

That got us talking about favorite foods. He was a burger man. I confessed to a serious weakness for barbecue and sweet cornbread. "Holy shit, you *are* a true Southerner," he laughed.

We completed the splurge and shared chocolate mousse for dessert. Halfway through, I stole the bite with whipped cream he was angling for. He glared, not a bit angry. "For that, I get to ask a question. What's your thing, Celeste?"

"My thing? Right now, it's this chocolate."

"Justifiably so, but what about in general? What's your pleasure? The thing that makes you happiest?"

I took another bite. "What's yours?"

"Music," he said without hesitation.

"Drawing."

Ben let the spoon linger in his mouth. He hummed.

"Is that shocking? I mean, I'm in design."

He set the spoon down and grinned. "No. It's surprising that you told me."

It was impossible not to smile back. "Yeah, well, don't even think of asking to see anything."

The check was laid on the table. I reached for my purse, but Ben threw a credit card onto the tray without a glance at the tab. The waiter whisked it away.

I frowned but stashed my wallet. "I can pay my own way."

He signed the slip. "Yes, I know. You'll remember that we make the same pitiful salary." He rose from his chair and helped my into my coat. "You can pay next time."

I eyed him over my shoulder. "Next time?"

"Next time, Ms. Greene," he said, lips on my ear.

Oh, even the November night couldn't cool my face after that.

We took a walk along Demonbreun Street, his arm around my shoulder. Plenty of people were out on this crisp Saturday evening. Live music drifted out of almost every bar we passed. At the river, we gazed at the Shelby Street Bridge and the lights reflecting on the water. "I can't believe this city," I said. "How different is Second Avenue now? It used to be the only place worth going."

He laced our hands. "Let's find out."

We moseyed up First Ave to stay by the river, then blocked over and headed down Second. "Oh, god, I used to play laser tag there." I laughed and pointed, and then moved my aim to a different sign. "My cousin always tried to get us to go to that Hooters. He claimed it was for the wings. He fooled no one." Ben's laugh rumbled beside me. His arm slipped around my shoulders again as we skirted tourists.

Just past Commerce Street, I stopped when I saw the familiar green columns. "Market Street Brewery closed? When?"

"Years ago."

A new pub had moved in. I sighed. "This place, oh, man. My friends and I would come here on Friday afternoons. There was no age limit until nighttime, and we thought we were so cool, teenagers hanging out in a bar. We'd order chicken fingers with honey mustard and play trivia until they kicked us out."

"Such a rebel."

I grinned and glanced up at him. "Not really. My uncle owns a bar in town. As kids, my cousin and I played hide-and-seek in the lounge during the day, when it was closed." Ben didn't answer, and my smile slipped. "What?"

He wore an intent expression, his brows and lips both curved upward. "That's..." He shook his head. "That's awesome."

"It's nothing special."

One brow went higher. "I disagree."

I understood. I'd shared part of me, a part that had nothing to do with work or who I'd become since That Day. I'd shown him something different, and I'd done it happily.

Lips pursed, brow up, I said, "I know what you're doing, Addison."

Ooh. My words darkened his eyes with that lusty fire that gave me chills. He dipped his head to my lips and kissed me in the middle of Second Avenue. "I hope you do, Celeste Greene," he whispered. "I certainly hope you do." With another kiss, he took my hand and guided me straight back to the car.

I'd been ready to fall into his arms all the way back at the bathroom at Etch. Between the PDA kiss and his arm around me, my fingers itched to be in his hair by the time we pulled into my complex. I got the key in the lock easily, but the door had barely latched behind us before I backed him against the wall and went up on tiptoes in his arms.

"Yesterday, when you asked if I wanted to come in to talk, was that an invitation for sex?" he mumbled between kisses.

"What? No." I flustered. Ben gave me a daring look, and I thought about it again. "No," I repeated. "But maybe."

"Maybe? I had to beg you for that kiss. What would you have done if I'd said yes to coming in to talk?" He pulled back, arms crossed, smirk going hard.

My pulse increased. "I don't know, Benjamin. Maybe this?"

I pushed the coat off his shoulders and stripped his shirt. His smile was gone, replaced by a stormy gaze and tight jaw when I licked the corner of his mouth, then made my way lower.

My hands and lips traveled over the smooth skin and hard muscles of his chest and arms. He tasted like he smelled—clean, spicy, and divine. I dropped to my knees and pulled his pants and boxers down. My tongue explored the deep curve of his hip and continued along his pubic bone. One of my hands slid up his thigh to caress his balls. His whole body shuddered.

I gripped his cock, stood up, and grabbed his jaw. "Look at me. I'm about to be *seriously* stupid and trust you. Are you clean?" My voice was a panicked rasp.

His gaze sharpened fast. He took my face in his hands and pressed our foreheads together. "Totally clean," he swore. I didn't move, and his erection began to fade. "Let me go get a condom. We don't have to—"

It's enough. I stretched up and kissed him until he pulsed in my palm again. Ben groaned. I pulled back, took a deep breath, and again sank to my knees.

Taking a man in my mouth had always been something of a chore. I didn't hate it; I saw it as a favor to give. But I *wanted* to taste him, to have his flavor on my tongue, to know how he liked it best. Even the sound of it, every gasp, slurp, and suck, built up my own excitement. I smiled inwardly at the wet heat between my legs, eager for him to know, too.

Ben's hands slid into my hair. He thrust gently, throbbed more the closer he got. I took him in deeper. Nails dug into his legs, I pressed my tongue flat and sucked hard. He shouted a hoarse groan, and warm, salty come spread into my mouth, his hips jerking to ride out the end of his climax.

I sat back on my knees to catch my breath. Ben sagged against the wall and rubbed his face. He opened his eyes and took a long breath.

In a flurry of motion, he kicked off his pants and caught my wrist, then nearly dragged me to the bedroom. A quick flick of his hand, and the sash of my wrap dress opened. It floated to the floor as he walked me backward and lay me down, my legs off the side of the mattress while he knelt down.

It started as kisses, but quickly became so much more. Hands, lips, and teeth found pleasure points I didn't know I had. He sucked my nipples and massaged my ass, kissed my inner thigh and squeezed the arch of my foot. When I was delirious and squirming with every touch, he kissed his way from my knee to blow a gentle stream between my legs.

"Did you like it, Ben?" I panted before he went where I knew he intended to. "The way I—"

"Did I like it? Did I *like* how you sucked my cock? Did I *like* you on your knees while I came down your throat? What do you think?"

"I think you did."

"I think *you* did, too. You're soaked, Celeste." He dragged a slow finger across my slick—okay *soaked*—skin.

I called his name, but words faded the moment his tongue flattened against me. He licked slowly, and I wailed and grabbed the sheets, glad for his steady hand on my hip. The noises that came from me were animalistic. Every time I managed to articulate an, "oh," or "fuck," he laughed, and that only made it better.

He read me precisely, changed the tempo every time I started to get close to the edge just to torment me. I was a complete mess, groaning and rocking toward his face while I tried to beg him to finish. Just when I didn't think I could take any more without release, two fingers thrust inside of me, and his lips closed around my clit.

"*Ben,*" I shrieked, blinded by an orgasm that lasted forever.

17

I have a vague recollection of waking later, naked and shivering, to see Ben on his back on the floor, one arm over his eyes. I'm not sure it registered as shock that we'd both passed out because I was half awake at best. Getting him off the floor was no small feat—the man slept as hard as he fucked—but with some sharp tugs on his arm, he fell face-first into the covers beside me.

Daylight streamed from behind the blinds when I awoke the next morning. After a moment of confusion, my senses attuned to the sizzle and aroma of bacon. Dishes clattered gently. *He cooks?*

Once I was dressed, I found him at the stove, bent over a pan. I shuffled forward to peek under his arm. "I don't remember having eggs and bacon in my fridge."

"I took your keys." He didn't look up.

His concentration was adorable, so I leaned on the counter and watched him work. He scraped the pan, brows drawn together until the moment he shut off the heat.

I applauded. "A master chef."

Only then did his expression lift. He shook his head and

reached for the pepper. "My brother says that a man needs to know how to cook a meal for a woman, and that breakfast is key." He smiled when I laughed. "It's one of the few useful things he's taught me."

I grabbed plates and poured coffee. We took the food to my little kitchen table; with the first bite still in my mouth, I hummed. "Thank your brother for me," I said around the fork. "This is excellent."

The excited look that flashed over his face was impossibly perfect, but he smoothed it fast. "I'm glad you like it."

"What do you usually do on Sundays?"

"Six hours of church."

The fork stopped halfway to my mouth.

Ben chuckled. "Kidding. Usually I run when the weather's good. Want to go with me in a bit?"

"Sounds great."

When the plates were empty and I'd poured our second cups of coffee, he chewed on his lip and gave me a strange look. I cocked my head, and he reached for his phone. He navigated for a moment, then laid it by my elbow and studied his mug.

My stomach clenched when I picked it up and saw an app of his medical report open on the screen. Last blood test: three weeks ago. Every condition or disease I could think of: NEGATIVE.

I pushed the phone away and rested my forehead on my hand. Last night flashed back, the adrenaline of the moment, the stupidity of my decision after all the worry and monthly blood tests after I learned of Derrick's *multiple* reckless indiscretions.

"You didn't have to show me," I whispered, still hidden. My heart pounded with gratitude.

"Yes, I did. I should've shown you last night, but I blanked. You trusted me. You deserve to know it was right."

It was right. Rocked with the power of those simple words, I pressed both palms to my cheeks. After a long moment, he cleared his throat. "He cheated on you, didn't he?"

"That's part of it."

Ben slid his chair beside mine. He gazed steadily at me and pushed my hair away. "I'm going to tell you some things that aren't about 'right now,' but I think you should know. The girl I dated in the spring crushed me." I caught my breath, and he hesitated. "Maybe this is too much."

I laced our fingers together and rested them on my knee. "Tell me. Did you love her?"

"I trusted her. I thought I knew her. We worked together —in a different capacity—and I thought we were a team." He exhaled and ran his free hand over his head. "She was sleeping with another guy. She stole from me and ran off."

"How much?"

"Not my money, although she was a hell of an expensive date. She stole my song."

I pursed my lips. "How poetic."

His brows danced on his forehead as the intensity of his gaze broke. "No, Celeste." He laughed softly. "Literally. I'm a songwriter. She had a band, and we were collaborating on a single and planning an album. I quit my IT job to work on it. I was so sure we were going to be big. Once the track was done, she told me she'd been fucking her bassist and took off to California. The lawsuit settled in September. It was the biggest pain in the ass I've ever known."

A string of disbelieving nonsense tumbled from my lips until finally, "Seriously?"

Disappointment shadowed his handsome features. "What makes you think I'm joking?"

I bit my lip. "No. It's just—I can't believe it."

"Which part is so unbelievable?"

For starters, try that I know exactly *how you feel.* "It's so horrible."

He let go of me and raked both hands over his scalp this time. "It was stupid on my part. Looking back, I should've gotten a hint at how flighty she was, but." He shrugged. "Should've listened to Liv. She didn't trust her." A glance at my face told him he'd lost me. "Sorry, uh, my friend, Liv."

"Say friend a little more pointedly next time."

That made him smile. "She's my ex, but also one of my best friends."

I sat back in my chair with a deep sigh. My own drama was momentarily forgotten as I processed everything Ben had said. *He knows what it's like to trust the wrong person. He needs this job. One or both of us is going to hurt again before this is over.*

"Songwriter? Really?"

Ben blinked; I flashed a tiny smile. We needed to lighten the mood or lose ourselves to worry. He rolled his eyes. "Don't tease me."

"Is that why you hum?"

"Kind of. Sometimes I'm working on a song, so I'll run it in my head. I didn't know I did it audibly until you mentioned it. Mostly I hum if I'm happy."

"You hum after we talk."

A slow smile creased his face. "What a coincidence."

We reached for each other at the same time. Ben brought me to my feet in a kiss so deep, my head bent backward. He cradled my neck, telling me without words that we were here, right now, and it was enough.

BEN

I took her to Shelby Bottoms, dismayed that she didn't know about the popular greenway. We took off in the cool midmorning sun, the trail vivid with fall color all around. I let my feet find a rhythm and got lost in thought.

If I never recounted the Ashlyn disaster again I'd be fine, but telling Celeste had been the right decision. First, it had reinforced how different the two situations were. Celeste was nothing like the flighty, volatile girl I'd been too stupid to see was playing me. Tunnel vision was always a threat whenever I worked on music; the fact that a pretty face went with it, that we had a plan for something big, had been a poison I'd drunk too willingly. Tenn Star had no such allure, and while I would've loved to see what Celeste and I could design together, there was no elixir to cloud my head this time.

Besides, now she knew we both had mistakes in our past that we'd learned from. We both knew trust was a thing not to give lightly. We were coming to this connection from a similar place.

Celeste caught my gaze when we turned around at the

pedestrian bridge. She flashed a quick smile and picked up the pace, waving for me to catch up.

Telling her was definitely the right decision.

On the home stretch, she skidded to a stop and pulled out her earbuds, hands on knees while she caught her breath. "Enough. I'm done," she wheezed.

Thank god. My legs were rubber after the weekend we'd had, but no way would I throw in the towel first. I took her hand, happy to stroll the remaining length of the path. The parking lot was in sight when Celeste froze, all the color gone from her face. Her gaze fixed on a very normal-looking middle-aged couple a few yards away. "Save me."

"What's wrong?" I looked again, expecting to see a brandished weapon or something equally sinister, but all I saw was the woman's broad grin.

"Too late," she breathed.

"Is that my baby girl?"

Shiiiiiit.

Celeste flashed a tight smile. "Hello, Mother. Hi, Daddy."

Mrs. Greene's attention snapped to me. "Well, *hello*." Mischief sparkled below her bubbly personality. After yesterday, I counted myself lucky that she wanted to give us hell, not murder me for bruising her daughter.

Celeste muttered an introduction while I clasped her mom's hand and held eye contact while we shook. "Mrs. Greene, a pleasure to meet you." I gave her my warmest pitch with just enough formality, and her smile grew wider. "Mr. Greene, sir," I said, turning to her father. His expression was unmasked surprise, so I had to guess his wife hadn't reported on her drop-in visit. Still, he shook hands with me and smiled.

Mrs. Greene spoke up. "Running, hmm? I'm making

lasagna for lunch. Why don't you join us?" She was clearly enjoying herself, and I gladly played along.

"Should we?" My lips twitched as I turned to Celeste.

Her jaw clenched. "I'm not sure. Who else is coming?"

"No one. It'll be just us four, I promise." Her mom's words made me realize I knew almost nothing about Celeste's family or friends—and she didn't know about mine, either.

"The Titans play the Broncos today, Ben. We'd love to have you," Mr. Greene said.

"I like football."

Celeste glared at all of us. "What time?" she asked like we were scheduling her execution. I swallowed a laugh.

Mrs. Greene couldn't get her smile under control. "Around two is perfect." She glanced at me again. "It's *so* nice to meet you."

Celeste hurried to hug her. "Stop gushing," she hissed, loud enough we all heard, but her mother laughed and kissed her cheek.

Once they'd gone, the glare was just for me. "Do you love lasagna that much, or is it my misery you have a taste for?"

"How could we turn her down and not look like jerks? Don't even think it," I said when I sensed a snarky comment coming. She smiled instead. "It's fine. You can use that little spiel from last night about the amazing sex as dinner conversation." She squeaked, and I laughed. "Or you could tell them the genteel version: this is new, but it's good." *So, so damn good.*

She sighed. "Alright, but you at my family home seems anti-right now."

"I promise to be noncommittal." I said, but she was right. Eventually, we had to face our complicated reality.

18

Dad whisked Ben off to watch football as soon as we arrived. Mom put me to work on the salad. She let me chop carrots for the salad for about 2.5 seconds before leaning on the counter.

I glanced at her expectant stare. "What?"

"Don't 'what' me, tell me about him!"

"He's a designer, too. We met through work," I hedged.

Her forehead creased. The excited smile faded quickly. "Wait a minute. He's not the guy you're competing with."

My hand faltered mid-chop, and I cut my eyes away. As usual, Eleanor Greene had seen right through me. This one was in record time.

I set the knife down and walked around the island to face her. All my fragile make-believes were crumbling fast. How could I have fooled myself? Mom's response was spot-on—this was crazy. Wrong.

And I knew it.

The best part of living in Nashville again was definitely the ability to rest my head on Mom's shoulder whenever I needed. I'd needed it a *lot* since I got back. She hugged me tight like always, and I whispered, "I know I'm an idiot, but, Mom, it feels so good. Great, even, except I know I shouldn't—"

"Shh, baby, baby." She held me at arm's length. "When I saw you this morning, I almost didn't recognize you, you looked so radiant. I know 'glowing' is a cliché, but it fits, and I absolutely love it. I don't think I've ever seen you like this." She squeezed me. "But I know what this job opportunity means to you. Can you keep things separate?"

I plopped on the barstool. "This job is everything, and he's really focused on winning it, too. I think we both know it comes first. I can't mess up my career again."

Mom stroked my hair. "I know how you are. You'd never let anything get in the way of your goals. You're too stubborn for that." She breathed a laugh. "You are *so* me."

My brows went up. Mom took my hands and said, "But you worry too much, far more than you should. Have confidence that things will work out. I swear, it's a better way to live."

"I have good reason to think otherwise."

Her green eyes got black. "Sweetheart, you have *no* idea." She smiled, and her gaze cleared. "Trust me."

I'd never seen this side of Mom. Her words were deep, intimate, and spoke of parts of her I didn't know. I wanted to ask, but I knew it wasn't the time.

My lips vibrated with a noisy exhale, and Mom released my hands. I resumed chopping while she went to the oven, grabbed two potholders, and said in her usual lighthearted pitch, "I'll say one more thing. He is very easy to look at."

"Oh, god, I know." In my old life, this was a conversation I'd have with a girlfriend, but it felt good to say aloud anyway.

She grinned and looked over at me. "He's even better

looking when he looks at you. He's crazy about you, Celeste."

I waved that off. "You've seen us together maybe five minutes, tops."

"I've seen all I need, including the state of your arm yesterday."

"Mother," I sighed, but her laughter was too contagious to ignore.

"Well? Was I noncommittal enough?" Ben asked on the drive back to my apartment.

I had to smile. I'd been quiet at dinner, busy telling myself we had to get this under control. He'd bantered easily with my parents, his knowledge of music and sports enough to keep them chatting through dessert. Afterward, we'd sat together on the couch to finish the football game. I caught more than one thoughtful glance from each of my parents when his hand rested on my knee.

"You were impressive," I said. "Hope it wasn't too awkward."

"Not at all. Your parents are cool. They're so chill."

"Hardly believable that I'm their offspring, huh?"

He laughed. "Your words, not mine."

"Jerk."

Another laugh. "Actually, you favor both of them a lot."

"People say that. Dad's coloring and auburn hair. Mom's bone structure and green eyes."

He pulled into my parking lot and shut off the car. "Mm-hmm, those emerald eyes. Those fucking gorgeous eyes that distract the hell out of me." His voice lowered in the way that usually gave me chills and tied my tongue.

Not that time.

"Mom knows you're my competition," I blurted, ruining his compliment.

He leaned back in his seat. "Damn. Guess I'm lucky she didn't kick me out."

"She liked you, but she knows it's complicated. *I* like you, but I know we have to be realistic."

"Maybe this is a good time to discuss what comes next. How do we handle tomorrow?"

I gave him the truth. "I absolutely can't lose focus, Ben. I can't, and neither can you. We have to go back to work."

"You can pretend this weekend didn't happen?"

Weekend. This weekend. How had it only been two days, not even 48 hours, since that moment on my balcony?

"Do you have a better suggestion?"

"Yeah. I think we should collaborate."

I swallowed hard. "After what you told me this morning?"

He flinched. "This is different."

I tasted copper as I bit my tongue. "Maybe so. Maybe it's different for both of us." I hesitated, unsure how much I could tell him. "My life fell apart after my breakup, too."

He chuckled. "I hope I didn't make it sound that dramatic," he said wryly.

Logically, I understood that he was talking about his own situation, that he was trying to bring a bit of levity to a tense moment. My wounds were too deep for that. My life *did* fall apart, and there was nothing glib about the state of my bank account.

I sat up a little straighter. "We both need the job, Benjamin, and there's only one position. We're rivals. We don't have a choice."

He gazed out the front window. "There's always a choice. There has to be another option."

"I wish there was, but this is trouble, Ben, and I—I'm not —If you saw who I really was, you'd understand." I took a breath. "It's in our best interest to focus on the project. Please respect that."

His jaw set. "At the risk of sounding like a *jerk*, that's never going to work. And I think you know it."

I bit hard on my lip. "I have to try."

Ben exhaled and rubbed his forehead. "Okay, fine, but listen to me." He leaned toward me, eyes dark. "I don't regret any of this, Celeste. And I have no desire to stop."

Our last kiss of the weekend was laced with uncertainty and salty with too much reality.

I pulled away and slipped out of his car to run upstairs. "Aw, sugar, what happened? Lovers quarrel?" My neighbors grinned at me sympathetically, but I didn't slow down until I'd slammed my door and tumbled into a ball on the couch.

I woke with a jolt before dawn, still on the couch. Sleep had come in fitful bursts, filled with replays of our last conversation and worries about facing him in that office again. The sofa cushion pockmarked my cheek, and the chenille throw was wrapped tight around me. More sleep was impossible. I struggled to unbind myself from the blanket and wound up falling hard to the floor.

Happy Monday.

Thank God for the gym's early spin class. I rode my ass off, heart hammering, sweat dripping. Anytime my thoughts wandered, I upped the tension on the flywheel and rode harder. At the end of 45 minutes, a small lake of sweat surrounded my bike.

Back at home, I hobbled into a hot shower. *This will be fine. You can go in there and get down to business. You can both focus on what you need most. It'll be fine.*

"Hey, Celeste," Sarah greeted when I entered the building. "You're early. How was your weekend?"

"Morning, Sarah. Weekend was great. Yours? How did your date with Allen end up?"

Her eyes twinkled. "So good. He kissed me!"

Oh, to have such an easy situation. He likes her. She likes him. Lucky. Despite my envy, her excitement made me smile.

She propped her chin on her fist with a dreamy expression. "We're going out again Friday, just the two of us. No drinks after work for me that night, sorry to say."

"Sorry, not sorry," I said, and she laughed. "Good luck, Sarah. I'll see you later."

I jogged up the stairs, but the three flights weren't what made my heart pound. Although the room was empty when I stepped inside, the door had barely closed behind me when it burst open again.

"I caught most of it," Ben said as he and Rollings strolled in.

"Helluva game. Titans usually don't match up against Denver very well, but yesterday was—good morning, Ms. Greene," Rollings interrupted himself. "Addison and I were just having a little check-in, so I thought I'd drop by early for a change."

A little check-in? I bristled. "Anything I need to know?"

"No, nothing for you. How's the Threads project coming? Your initial pitches went well, I heard. No questions?"

"None," I said, and Ben—no, *Mr.Addison*—agreed.

"Didn't expect so. Whelp," Rollings clapped his hands

together and looked between us. "Probably won't see y'all again today, but happy Monday." We both nodded, and he was gone.

A little check-in.

I fixed a narrow stare on my rival. Who gave a damn about the royal blue shirt and black trousers he wore, or the messy-style of his hair, or the—*shit*—faint but still-visible blush of his lips? *Thank god for lip liner.* None of it mattered when he was having secret meetings with—

"It was about the website for Garret. That's all."

No good reply came to me. "Why should I believe you?" was foolish by now. "Oh, you mean the first pitch you beat me on? Cool," sounded ludicrous, even in my head.

I looked away. *Happy fucking Monday, Mr. Addison. That would've been good.* Too bad it came to me ten minutes too late, when I was already seated in front of my computer.

The client's follow-up email requested minimal changes, and I recommitted to crushing this project. I lost myself creating code to give to life to my plans throughout the day, but when quitting time came, a terse, "Goodnight, Greene," crashed me out of the zone.

My heart dropped, guard clicking into place, shielding me as it had for over a year now. "Goodnight, Mr. Addison."

The door shut, and I was alone again.

BEN

The heavy metal door of the stairwell banged shut, and I sank down on the stairs and scrubbed my face with both hands. *I can't do this. God, I've cocked this up. Good job, Ben. You took this job to get your life back to normal, and what do you do? You let a woman flip you sideways again.*

My eyes opened slowly. "No," I said in the silence.

We'd flipped each other sideways. Of that I was sure. I could see it in her tight shoulders, in the way her eyes told me with unsaid words that this was hard for her, too. We'd both messed up, but we'd done it from day one. Celeste and I weren't meant to be enemies.

But we couldn't be friends, either.

I heaved a deep sigh and pushed myself to my feet.

Strangers it had to be.

19

When someone spends half the weekend tearing your clothes off and the other half charming your panties off, housekeeping takes a backseat. The disaster in my apartment caught up with me when I got home.

Yearning for the madness that created such a mess hit me hard. I indulged the ache for the time it took to drink a glass of water. After that, I tucked it neatly to the back of my mind and pulled out cleaning supplies. *No time to pine, unless it's Pine-Sol. Oh, god, that was awful.* I rubbed my forehead and cranked up an 80s playlist to keep my thoughts quiet.

Dishes were washed, the floor was vacuumed, the bathroom gleamed, and I sang while I worked, pleased to have a project. Bon Jovi and I were livin' on a prayer when I pushed the vacuum down the hall, into the—

Bedroom.

No rational person would interpret the chaos in there as anything but a marathon sex session. The bed was rumpled. Clothes were everywhere, complete with my bra draped over the footboard. A box of Trojans sat on the nightstand.

"Holy shit." The knot in my throat tightened when I echoed his phrase, but I swallowed it down and yanked at the sheets. When I gathered the linens, his t-shirt from the first night tumbled to the floor. My gaze fixed on it, mouth going dry.

I dropped my bundle lifted and the black fabric to my nose, bombarded by memories. Slumped on my heels, tears stung my eyes as I tried to breathe deep and wound up inhaling that delicious scent even more. *This is what you both need. You can't be anything to him anyway. Let it go.*

Finally I stood, exhausted but determined to finish my chores. At last the apartment looked like it should—like only I lived in it—but no mental pep talk could convince my heart that this was a good thing.

Tuesday was the same as Monday, so a copy of almost every day at Tenn Star so far. That night, without spin class and chores to wear me out, sleep was hard to find. I grumped around the apartment in a full-blown pity party, as my mother would say. By Wednesday, my feet dragged on the longest week ever. I'd woken to find I was out of coffee and gas, which ran me a few minutes late. Discovering that my blouse had a button missing as I stepped out of the stairwell iced the cake.

"Dammit to—oh."

The smell of gasoline on my hands, the button, and the fatigue were all forgotten when I opened the door. He was two feet from the entrance, hanging his coat on the peg. We locked eyes for the first time since I'd glared at him Monday, and his jaw clenched. "Good morning, Ms. Greene."

"Morning, Mr. Addison." I hurried around him to put my bag down. Too restless to get started, I fixed coffee, and then forgot it in the kitchen and wandered over to the windows, sweat pricking on my spine. *Did someone turn up the thermostat? I'll have to ask Sarah.* I pushed open a window and stared out at the bright autumn day.

He came and stood beside me. "How's life behind those walls this week?"

Lonely as always. "Productive."

A grunt vibrated his throat as he moved to turn away. "Outstanding. Excuse me."

"Ben."

I'd sweated, scrubbed, and worked my ass off to maintain control of myself. Three letters and a hand on his arm undid it all. He spun and moved for me, but I was already on tiptoe, my fingers burrowing into his sleeve.

His hands wove into my hair as our mouths found each other, eager to taste this kiss before it ended. My fist crushed his shirt; he pulled half my hair out of its elastic. Seconds had passed, and we were a mess.

I pushed him against the windows so he could slide down and meet me better, like the first night. He obliged, his fingers in my hair gliding to my jaw. "I'm trying, but I can't ignore you for five seconds, Celeste," he rasped between kisses. "I don't *want* to."

"You have to," I managed, then slid my tongue between his lips.

His arms tensed. The hold on my face grew firm, and Ben gently pulled us apart. My eyes opened to see that his were lusty *and* sad. "It can't be both. You can't kiss me like that and keep your walls up. That's cruel."

"I've been called worse." My words were meant to be

sarcastic; the look on his face told me it didn't sound that way. I looked down. "I'm sorry, Ben." It was a lame finish, but there was nothing else to say or do. He winced, and I backed away.

I scurried to the bathroom, sank onto the toilet seat, and hid my melted face in my icy hands. *Don't you understand I'm a bad idea? Don't you get it? I'm the ice queen. I don't care about anything but my job. I'm selfish and cold.*

I fished my phone from my trouser pocket. "Hello, Dr. Zeller-uh, April- this is Celeste Greene. I'm not able to make therapy today. I'll reschedule soon. Thanks."

He didn't blink from his monitor when I sat down, but, then again, there was nothing to say. I looked over some notes from last week's meeting, just to get my head on straight while the computer booted up.

We both jumped when his desk phone rang.

This was the first time either of our phones had rang. He fumbled for the receiver while I held my breath. "Ben Addison. Good morning, Mr. Garret—Jimmy, okay. What can I... Hold on, let me look."

My stomach churned. I fixed my eyes on the keyboard, but it was impossible not to listen to him confer with his client. Just when I started to taste breakfast again, they closed up. "Yes, I saw it. Hell of a game, yeah, Titans are on a streak, aren't they? Okay, Jimmy, talk to you soon."

Silence thundered. No clicks, no gentle squeak of a chair, and no thoughtful sighs. Total silence filled the room.

I broke it. "You understand now, right?" My voice was an entirely different sort of ragged than his had been minutes before.

He looked at me. "Are you going to hand me my ass on this project or not, Greene?"

I inhaled sharply. "You're damn right, Addison."

"Then do it." His right eye crinkled.

I wet my lips and nodded. He gave a single nod back, and we both resumed work. Before I got too swept away, I had to ask, "What's the big deal about that football game?"

His laugh set something back to equilibrium between us. "I have no idea. I wasn't really watching."

The tension lessened as the hours clicked by, but I didn't stop for lunch that day, afraid that another encounter would be just as dangerous. It was a dark sort of relief when he left without saying goodbye.

No lights were on when I got home. Because it was that kind of day, I stubbed my toe on the way to the kitchen. Forehead against the wall, I surrendered to the pain as I pounded my fist beside my face. *Dammit to hell.*

Thoughts of dinner faded. I hurried through the dark to the living room and knelt by the coffee table. With a big three-wick candle lit, I plucked the sketchpad from its spot.

Darkness and drawing: this was a new combination.

I drew without a plan and barely looked at the page. My eyes were unfocused, thoughts too, while I let the pencil go where it would. At last, I sat up and looked around. The candle had burned low enough to tell me I'd worked for quite some time, and my head was heavy with sleep. I left the book, stumbled down the hall, and barely bothered to strip to my underwear before I passed out.

It was the dead of night when my eyes flew open again, entire body clenched in pleasure. A sigh died on my lips, and I lay drenched in a cold sweat, sure that it was Ben I'd dreamed of.

He makes you come even in your dreams.

I shivered at the little shockwaves left behind from my orgasm and reveled in this dark, secret time alone with my thoughts. Here, I could be sexy. I could be warm, not some ice queen desperate for a paycheck.

With his kiss on my mind, I drifted back to sleep.

The next morning, I was so refreshed that I hit the gym before work, and then chatted with Sarah a little longer than usual. Benjamin was already at his desk when I got upstairs, but I was no fool. I avoided him with an almost scientific precision.

"You seem cheerful," he murmured when I sat down.

"Slept well, I guess."

He grunted, and I glanced over. Close inspection wasn't required to see the faint blue shadow under his eyes, the scruff on his chin. I toyed with my necklace and frowned at the desk. *He hasn't hummed once this week.*

My mood declined over the day. The project was done and perfected by quitting time, but Benjamin's energy was tired and tense, and it got to me. When Rollings dismissed us, we both moved to gather our things, in step out the door.

"Are you okay?" I had to ask.

Broad shoulders rose and fell in a deep sigh. "Yeah, Greene, I'm fine."

"Is your project finished?" I tried not to mind that he called me Greene.

"Yes."

"Do you feel—"

"I said I was fine," he barked on the first-floor landing, and his tone brought me up short. Ben paused and rubbed his scruffy face with both hands. "I apologize." He shoved the door open and stormed across the lobby, straight for the exit. I shuffled after him.

Sarah called goodnight and turned to me with raised brows. "What's with him?" I answered with a shrug, gaze still at the door. "You two are a real pair."

My attention jerked to her. "What does that mean?"

She shook her head. "You guys are always brooding. If it's not one, it's the other. Is that part of your job description?"

"Yeah, you have to minor in brooding in undergrad," I muttered, surprised by my own joke. Sarah giggled, and my lips twisted.

"I bet y'all were at the top of your classes," she said, then sobered. "It's a shame both of you won't be able to stay. How much longer do you have?"

"We have one more project, so two weeks at most." She nodded. "Thanks, Sarah. See you tomorrow."

Benjamin was long gone by the time I stepped outside and went for my car. At home, I microwaved dinner and took it to the living room. The TV was on, but I sat on the floor and picked up the sketchpad, curious what last night had yielded.

My brows walked up my forehead while I studied the page. It was a bridge.

Bridges were the first thing I'd been obsessed with drawing as a child. I've no idea why, but I remember it clearly, and I know Mom has a bunch of my bridges saved in a folder. In this one, the perspective was of someone crossing over. A path lead upward; columns and cables towered above. What lay below or ahead wasn't clear.

On this bridge, a lone traveler walked, her face to the vanishing point. It was me.

Exhaustion wrapped itself around my shoulders while I stared at the image. I pushed my half-eaten dinner away and traced the pencil lines, startled when a teardrop hit the paper. *I've been on this goddam bridge so long.*

It was one of the only things I've ever drawn that I ripped up and threw away, but I knew if I didn't, I would never get to sleep.

And tomorrow was a big day.

BEN

Idle chatter and music filled my ears. I'd thought meeting up with the guys at Bar 40 would be a good way to ease my mood and fill my mind with something other than intolerable silence for a few hours. As I glared at my untouched glass, however, I had to admit that I was terrible company.

"Excuse me, guys, but I see a couple of ladies who look thirsty."

"Go for it, Field." James laughed, reaching for a high five as my friend vacated the booth. When we were alone, he knocked on the table. "You're looking at that beer like it insulted you, but you haven't taken a single drink. Stop sulking. This job is making you fucking nuts." I twisted my mouth in silent agreement, and he nodded toward the bar. "Go with him, talk to those girls. Get your mind off things for awhile."

"Nah, man. You go. I don't feel like it." *I haven't felt like it for a long damn time, actually. This game is old. Flirting in bars with random girls you'll forget by Monday. What's the point? Distraction? And what if it doesn't distract? What if I don't want to be distracted? What if I'd rather be a cranky asshole than forget her?*

James nudged my beer. "Then drink up and relax. Shit, Ben, I'm trying to help you out."

"I know. Thanks, but really, go ahead."

He gave me another look, but I didn't flinch. "Suit yourself," he said with a shrug.

I tossed some cash on the table and left the beer untouched. With a sulk as deep as mine had gotten over this week, alcohol was a terrible idea.

The guys gave me a wave as I headed for the door. Watching them laugh and flirt with those women made me think of the dance club last Friday. My jaw clenched. *We're going to have to talk. If I win tomorrow, I might never see her again. If she wins, we're back to square one. We can't leave it like that. I'll call her—tomorrow night. After the presentations are over. We have to get through that first.*

With a plan in my head, I felt a lot saner. I drove home, determined to go to bed early and get some decent rest.

Tomorrow was a big day.

20

I used to wear Chanel No. 5 on important occasions. Since That Day, the smell of it makes me want to vomit. Its alluring scent is forever associated with the flavor and stench of regurgitated smoothie. Tragedy, really—I loved that tiny bottle that made me feel so fabulous, so New York.

After I moved home, I'd been shopping for plates at one of those discount superstores, the kind where you can buy literally everything. A deeply discounted bottle of Burberry for Women had sat on a shelf between a vase and a bottle of Suave shampoo. I couldn't resist. The fragrance had notes of jasmine, like my lotion, and I liked the idea of a new signature scent for my new life.

Friday morning, I pulled the Burberry from its box for the third time since I bought it. The first had been day one at Tenn Star; the second, last Saturday night. With spritzes on my pulse points, I took a final look in the mirror. My chignon was perfect, makeup impeccable. An emerald green blouse popped under my charcoal Kate Spade suit jacket, pointy black Dior pumps flawless and shiny on my feet. Brands meant nothing in my new life; it was almost laughable that they ever did, but this presentation warranted going all out, no question.

My electric mood as I walked into the office may account for the lightening bolt that rocked me when I saw Benjamin. He stood at his desk making notes, but he looked up when I came in.

Black tailored suit. Crisp ecru shirt with a luxurious sheen. Suspiciously familiar black tie. Hair gelled, a little spikey. *Good lord, someone needs to call maintenance about the heat in here. It's unhealthy.*

Best of all was his expression as we stared each other down. "Damn," he whispered.

I shook my head hard, adding a dramatic eye-roll. "Get to work," I said to both of us.

"I brought lunch today. Will it kill you to eat with me?" he asked while I settled in.

"Probably." My cheeky tone matched his.

"Shame." He twitched his brow, and a little smile tugged at my lips.

We buzzed around the office all morning. At noon, we met in the kitchen, unpacked our food, and proceeded to eat in silence. If I hadn't been so busy keeping my mind on the next few hours—and not on last Friday, or what this weekend might hold—the sound of our chewing might've driven me mad. As it was, I had enough to focus on.

Lunch was almost over when I saw him stir in my periphery. I tried not to look while he checked his phone and began to type, but an itch to peek flared.

"Do you have plans this weekend?" he asked, eyes fixed on the screen.

"Not sure. You?" I tried to match his too-casual tone.

He pocketed the phone and turned his attention to me. "The usual, I guess." He cocked his head. "Unfortunately."

"I see," I said, because flipping the table and straddling his lap wasn't close to a viable option.

His lips curled. "I thought I warned you about giving me that wide-eyed look."

Maybe it's more viable than you think. I snapped my mouth shut, and his brows knitted in a brief flicker of disappointment.

He rose. "Good luck, Greene."

Mr. Garret had been paternally indulgent with my presentation. Ms. Fowler, the Threads CEO, was excited and engaged. Even better, she was hip and smart, friendly but cool. Her demeanor was so similar to my former clients that I surged with confidence. If she turned me down, I might as well quit the business.

The meeting ended in smiles and handshakes. Unlike Garret, Fowler asked for the weekend to consider our designs, so Rollings wished me good weekend as I left.

Ben and I crossed paths in the stairwell, both of us coming to a stop in the middle of the flight. I tilted my head back to see him above me. He looked me over, nodded once, and moved to pass.

"I'll see you later." I said when he was one step below. The words were spicy and sweet in my mouth, enough to make me hold my breath. His footsteps stopped, but he didn't turn.

"Later."

I decided that I deserved a splurge and cruised over to an East Nashville nail salon. After a mani/pedi and a cup of green tea, I browsed the stores on the block. I emerged with a new silk scarf, earrings made by local artisans, and a little more love for my hometown. A new sketchbook called my name in paper shop, but after that, I returned to my car before I did more damage to my bank account.

The clock on the dash read 5:14. *He should be home soon.* I pushed the thought down, but it ballooned back up. With a knot in my chest, I shifted into drive. *"I'll see you later."* You *know what you meant. Do it.*

Except for job hunting and last weekend, I'd not spent much time out and about since moving home. There were plenty of neighborhoods and suburbs of Nashville that I didn't know at all, especially with the recent development. By luck or chance, though, I knew the roads of East Nashville even in the deep dusk. My aunt and uncle had lived a few blocks from Benjamin's street—they likely still did, I wasn't sure—and several of my friends lived in the area when I was a teenager. Finding his apartment was easy.

My hands trembled when I parked, so I made fists and stared up at the house. The right half was lit, the left dark. *He wants you here. Remember what he said at lunch, and let's not forget Wednesday.*

But doubts crept in the longer I sat. Maybe I'd read it wrong. Maybe he was busy or over the whole thing.

I jumped out of the car. Gulping cold air to steel myself, I paced in a little circle, hands on my head. *You're in his driveway, crazy. Congratulations, you can add "stalker" to your résumé.*

So why don't you leave?

Touché, conscience.

I lowered my hands and leaned against the car. Stalker it would be.

21

The sun's last streaks faded into twilight blue over the tree-tops while my thoughts quieted. The cold settled into my fingertips and nose. Still I waited in the peaceful silence.

Twenty minutes had passed when I checked the time. I stood up straight and rubbed my eyes, face tilted to the sky. "Fuck." *He has plans. He has friends. He's out having a Jameson, not thinking about you. He's—*

Headlights on the street slowed to turn into the drive. The blaze hit my eyes, then went dark and left me temporarily blind. An eternity squeezed into a moment before the car door thumped, and footsteps approached. The spots in my vision faded as I blinked and squinted at him.

"Hi." He stuffed his hands in his trouser pockets.

"Hi. How'd it go?"

"Okay, I guess." He might've shrugged, but it would be hard to know since his shoulders were at his ears.

"Didn't you wear a coat?" I shuffled my feet.

"Forgot it in a rush this morning. What are you doing here?"

"You know why I'm here," I whispered.

Ben shook his head. "Answer the question, please. I've crawled through the week, pretending like I didn't know you, like it meant nothing. I respected your wish to keep it professional—"

I spluttered. "You—Wednesday—"

"*You*, Wednesday," he snapped. "Every bit as much as me."

I ducked my head. "I know."

Warm fingers cupped my chin and lifted my gaze, and I trembled from that minor contact. Surely he felt my tremor, but his expression didn't change. "And now, here you stand in my driveway. I think an explanation is the least I could ask for."

My cheeks warmed. I cut my eyes away, but he pressed his thumb into my jaw and demanded my gaze on him. "I wanted to see you again," I said faintly.

"See me?"

Why had I assumed we'd be kissing by now? Did I really have to say it?

My nerve broke. "Well, um, we've not really... talked, and it's Friday. You said you didn't have plans—so I... wanted to see you."

That thumb stroked my jaw, brushed over my lips once, but his poker face held. *Come on, Benjamin. Help me out.*

"Cool." He dropped his hand, unexpectedly cheerful. "I'm hungry. Want to go eat?"

"Eat?"

"You can buy this time, if you insist. There's a good sushi place not far. Do you like sushi?"

My heart was in my throat; the heat in my core didn't know where to go. I took a slow breath. "I love sushi. If I'm buying, should I drive, too?"

The question was clearly sarcastic, but his keys dropped into his pocket. "Perfect," he said in that same cheerful tone as he disappeared into my passenger's side.

Okay.

There was no choice but to glance longingly at the house once more and get in the car—where I found Benjamin peering into my shopping bags.

"Excuse me! Those are mine, thanks." I tried to snatch them, but he twisted away.

"I'm not stealing them, Greene," he said, busy with his inspection.

"What if they're private?"

He flashed a grin, but hid it fast. "Private like medicine, or private like sex toys?"

Neither option had occurred to me. I stuttered a protest that only made him laugh. With a huff, I gave up on a reply and death-gripped his arm and growled. "If you call me Greene again."

He turned his head, the worst kind of perfect smirk on his lips. "Then what?"

My car shrank to the size of a shoebox. The fine wool of his suit coat moved against my palm, his warm skin contrasting with the cool material.

This is all a tease.

The situation became so much clearer. This was him daring me to answer his question about why I was here with truth. The realization should've irritated me, but it didn't. I took a breath and dropped my hand.

"Then we'll never get to the restaurant. Tell me which way to head."

He directed me the short distance to a cozy little spot that, if memory served, used to be a hardware store back in the day.

"Why don't you wear your new scarf?" he asked when I parked.

"I'm saving it for a special occasion." I lifted my chin, but reached in the bag and knotted it at my neck. "Happy?"

He eyed me. "Yeah, but I'm bringing this with us." Before I could protest, he was out of the car—with my new sketchbook in hand.

"No way." I hurried to catch up. "Don't even think of—"

"After you." He held open the door with a gallant sweep of his arm.

We were seated right away. I followed the hostess, but I was so busy throwing glares over my shoulder that I almost tripped on two chairs en route to the table. After the second time, he touched my spine. "Breathe, Celeste."

I threw myself into the booth, glad that he let me snatch the book before he sat. "What do you think I'm going to do with this?"

"Draw me."

"Are you going to stretch out naked on the table, *Titanic*-style?"

Oh, his laugh unwound me instantly. With a hum, I opened the book and pulled a pencil out of my bag. "Order me white wine, an eel avocado roll, and a spicy salmon roll."

I closed my eyes. When I opened them, I had my image. It was on the page by the time the wine was in front of me.

"Dare I ask to see?"

I stashed the pencil and handed the book over. With delight and a held breath, I watched while he examined it. His brows rose, then lowered, and then rose again. Finally, he looked up.

"I wasn't really going to do your portrait." I shrugged.

"Ha, yeah, I didn't expect you to. But—"

"But when I thought about you, a doorknob came to

mind." I gestured with the hand that wasn't tangled in my necklace. "Maybe it doesn't make sense—"

His gaze went back to the paper. "It does, actually. When we met. The way Rollings always bursts into our office."

"My apartment last Friday," I added, and my face heated at the quick, wicked glance he tossed me.

What I didn't say was the other part, the unlocked part. How, when I was with him, he opened things inside my heart that thrilled and scared the hell out of me. That part was my private truth, and I didn't need to share it.

He gave the book back with a look that was easy to read. I pursed my lips, but he didn't blink. I shook my head; still nothing. "Fine," I sighed at his unspoken request and tore out the page.

I waved the paper at him, just to make the imposition clear, but the message was lost when my lips curved into a smile. It was lost entirely when he snatched the sketch like a prize, and I laughed. I shook my head and put the book away, then watched from my periphery as he folded the paper and slid it into his wallet. "Why did you put it there?"

"Backup ID, in case I'm found and can't remember who I am." He picked up his glass. "What are we drinking to tonight?"

I thought about saying something like, "To remembering who we are," but when I caught his eye, saw his head cocked and the steady way he regarded me, I tucked my hair and smiled. "Here's to getting what we want."

He didn't move while I took a drink. "Oh? What *do* we want?"

I shivered at his black-coffee voice. How had I gone without it for this many days? Those few words were like getting a fix. I stood and slid into his side of the booth until our hips touched. With my head by his ear and my hand on his thigh, I whispered, "We both know what we want, Benjamin."

He didn't move, but his leg tensed. He turned to whisper back, "It's been a long week. I need more than that, Celeste."

Two sips of wine had nothing to do with the bubbles in my head or the flush on my cheeks. "I want to be back at your apartment, in your bed. I want this," I skimmed my hand closer to the growing ridge in his trousers.

"You want my cock?" he breathed in my ear.

"Mm-hmm."

"In your mouth?"

"That's one option."

Benjamin pulled back enough to meet my eyes. His were bright, lips parted over a quick breath. He at looked me, then leaned in again to murmur two words:

"Touch me."

You are who you want to be.

"I'll touch you when I'm ready." I stroked his inner thigh, and then jumped up and went to my side again.

Ben exhaled loudly. He dropped his head back against the booth with a groan, grinning when I laughed.

"Your rolls."

We jolted when the server set plates in front of us. "Wait." Ben's voice was thick. He cleared his throat. "Can you please box this to go and bring the check now?" She glanced between us, smiled, and hurried away. He looked over at me, his pupils still pinpricks. "We can eat later."

We were out of there in minutes—after I paid—and back at his place in no time. I pulled into the driveway and gripped the wheel.

"Are you ready yet?" he asked.

I turned to him. "Truth?" He quirked a brow. I leaned over and pulled on his tie. "I've been ready all afternoon."

We touched each other anywhere we could on the stumbling, sloppy trip inside and up the stairs. We kissed while he threw the takeout bag in the fridge and kept kissing into the living room.

My hair fell when he pulled out all the pins; my scarf, jacket, blouse, and skirt hit the floor soon after. I left him dressed. The glide of his suit over my bare skin was almost as delicious as his freshly-shaved face against my cheek.

He stepped away to turn on a lamp. I whined to lose contact, but the hooded gaze he walked from my boots to my eyes ended any protest. *Admit it. He's why you chose matching underwear this morning.*

Just out of reach, Ben rubbed his jaw. He opened his mouth, voice so soft and sexy that his words took a beat to sink in. "I'm pissed at you. I'm pissed at myself for the week I let you put me through. Damn you and your green eyes, your fire, your attitude. Damn you for how badly I want you."

I fidgeted, underwear and boots morphing from a sexy outfit to far too much exposure. "I said I needed to focus. We've done that so far and still chatted a little. You didn't have to completely shut me out. The only time you spoke to me, you asked me about my walls. Otherwise you didn't tease me, didn't say anything. You barely even told me goodnight." It surprised me how much hurt reflected in my tone —how much hurt I felt that I hadn't acknowledged.

He winced and pushed his hair off his face. " Celeste, you wanted—"

"I get it. I asked for the silent treatment. But is it all or nothing, Ben? Rivals or fuck buddies? God, of course we're just fuck buddies. What else would we be?"

"Wait, listen, I—"

But I sat down on the couch, my knees spread wide.

"Come on, let's get on with it. No need to chat; we both know why I'm here." Hurt made my hands cold, but I kept my chin up.

Ben regarded me a moment, then strode over, bent in half, and scooped me off the couch. I flailed, but he cradled me and marched us down the hall to his bedroom, where he calmly sat down on the bed and lay back. He rolled, tugged the sheet, and suddenly we were staring at each other under the covers.

"Hi," he said.

It was warm and Benjamin-scented in our cocoon. I bit my lips.

He continued. "You kicked my ass today, didn't you?"

"I hope so."

"How was your week?"

"Ben."

"Mine was pure hell. I had to choose between ignoring you or making a fool of myself by begging you to help me find a better way though our clusterfuck situation."

"We talked about that."

"Mm-hmm, hence my choice. I can't talk to you, Celeste Greene, without being totally fucking enchanted. Even when you're furious, you enchant the hell out of me. Yes, I want to sex you hard and watch your eyes go glassy with pleasure. Yes, I want your mouth all over my body. Yes, I think about that every few seconds. But," he twisted his lips and reached for my hand. I opened my fingers. Linking with him made me sigh. "But I can't do it all. I can't watch you smile—I can't even watch you roll your eyes at me—without needing to see it again and again."

"Ben, I—" *Don't. Don't say it. You can't make him happy. This needs to be just sex. You aren't good at personal connections.*

I swallowed hard, but the words tumbled out: "I need it too."

Right now. I meant right now. Tonight. Please, don't think I'm trying to...

Free-fall panic had my brain working hard to find the right clarification. It took a beat to register Ben's closed eyes and the way his chin dropped to his chest. "Thank you."

My plummeting heart was caught, brought back to its rightful place by the bed against my back and Ben's arms around me. Our kiss swept every excuse and caveat away as I dug my nails into his shoulders and clung to him. The longer we held each other, touched each other, my panic turned to pure pleasure.

Sweat dampened my forehead under those covers until he finally kicked them away and sat up with a ragged groan. His tie hung loose around his neck, shirttails untucked. "Let's go eat."

"*Eat*? You mean food? Seriously?"

"I don't want you to think sex is all I want from you. I think we should go eat and talk a little more."

I gaped as he climbed off the bed and began to disrobe. He slid his tie off and opened his collar. "This is a new form of bullying," I grumbled, eyes glued to the slow striptease unfolding in front of me. "You're joking, right? Don't answer that. Just get over here."

Ben laughed and set his watch on the dresser. "No, I'm not joking. The last thing I want is for you to think this is 'just sex.'" He turned from the closet and smiled in profile, then strolled back to the bed, dropping his dress shirt on the way. He stood over me and grinned again.

Good god. Hair rumpled, pants open and slung low on his hips... Ben's abs, lats, and biceps all flexed when he pulled off his undershirt. I forgot how to swallow. Drool was a very real threat.

"Sushi?"

Damn his too-casual tone. It got me every time. I screeched and reached out, hooked his belt loop, and pulled. Ben threw himself over me on the bed. "I'm being a gentleman, Ms. Greene."

"Be a gentleman later. Sex me hard now," I whispered before his earlobe was between my teeth.

"Yeah?" I thrilled at the jagged edge in his voice. He twisted and sucked on my neck. "Then I want to wear your scratch marks on my back before we're done."

We tumbled across the bed again. He wasted no time in stripping me naked and rolling me to straddle his hips. I gripped him; when his cock and the heel of my fist pressed against my clit, I moaned. Ben rocked his pelvis with a steady rhythm, and I came, hard and suddenly. My free hand caught me as I moaned and fell forward, body jerking with release.

He stilled. I lifted my head. "Oh, my god," I rasped.

"Oh, my *god*," he agreed. His hands held my face to guide me into a kiss as he sat up underneath me. "You are so fucking sexy, I can't take it."

Sweet words didn't distract from the way he still throbbed between my legs. Sweat beaded behind my knees when I lifted up, angled my hips, and lowered down on his lap.

"Yes," we groaned into each other's mouths.

I threw my head back, and Ben fell against the pillows with another moan. "Celeste, wait. Condoms. Top dresser drawer."

I forced my eyes open and looked down, mesmerized by the torment he was clearly in. His head lolled, eyes shut tight while his fists knotted in the sheets by my knees. I leaned to kiss his parted lips, and the change in angle made me gasp again. "I'm on the pill, I'm clean. I want it like this." I'd made the decision while I sat in the car. There were no regrets.

There was the exquisite sensation of him bare inside of me, though. There was also the look in his eyes when he opened them, and between the two, my thighs slid, friction-less, over him.

"You're sure?" he asked.

I sat upright again. He dug his grip into my waist as I began to ride him. The prickly tells of orgasm crept down my legs in no time, but I was too greedy and couldn't keep an even tempo. I wanted to know all the ways we could fit together, and so I kept switching from all fours to upright, from a slow grind to a sharp thrust.

The ache built inside me until sweat slicked my hair. I grabbed for his hands to brace myself and spread my knees wide. "Close... I'm close... not yet..." My face pinched with effort.

He licked his lips and puffed out a breath. "You're there, baby. Let me see you come."

My body obeyed. Instantly.

When the last blissful tingle quieted, I collapsed onto his chest and peeked up at him. "You called me baby."

A slow smile tugged at his lips. "Guess I did. But then—"

I squealed as he held me tight and flipped me to my back without pulling out. His voice went from soft to gritty: "But then, I'd do or say anything to watch you come, Ms. Greene."

Kneeling between my legs, shock waves from his thrusts rocked me hard. My ankles slid off his back so I could pull him down on top of me and rake my nails over his shoulders. I gripped his hair and scratched again. "I want to feel *you* come now, Benjamin."

Ben jerked his face away, buried in the corner of my neck to muffle the *yes* he shouted as he drove deep. We lay like that until our heavy breaths evened out. Totally spent, we rolled to our sides and stared at each other.

You're falling hard for him.

Dammit, it was true. Being with him was too easy to make sense. It was like I was hypnotized into this alluring comfort, this idea that I could really be close to him.

Don't be a fool, girl.

BEN

Auburn eyebrows knitted tight while I stroked her arm. "How can you be thinking after that?"

Her expression cleared. "I'm not."

Too blissed to call her on the obvious lie, I rolled to my back and grinned at the ceiling. "I feel like an artisan of fucking right now. That was unreal."

She giggled. "No kidding."

I sat up and guided her out of bed. "Come on. Let me be a gentleman and feed you."

Her palms slid over my chest. "Hmm, but I like artisanal Benjamin so much."

It took all my willpower to not fall back into the sheets. I kissed her softly. "If you stay with me this weekend, you can have both. Sound good?"

She didn't hesitate. "Yes."

That one word burned away the long hours of this torturous week. Last Sunday we'd moved too fast, hadn't thought things out, but we could make up for it. Her walls were down; she was smiling. She was staying. Whatever happened, we knew what we needed and had said it aloud. This time, we'd figure out how to make it work.

"Good. Let me loan you some clothes." I started to turn to the dresser, but Celeste tugged my arm, bringing me back for another sweet kiss.

You've fallen hard for her.

Wasn't that the damn truth.

22

When we were finally both dressed in sweat pants and t-shirts, Ben decided we should have wine since we'd not finished our glasses at the restaurant. He insisted I stay while he went to the liquor store.

Alone, I took the food to the coffee table, hunted napkins, and then filled the time by wandering around. The apartment's design was really quite clever, but I couldn't get over how large it was for one person. In New York, as many as six people could comfortably share this. There was another room down the hall I'd noticed, and the living room and kitchen were admirably spacious.

I kept my tour to the living room. Ben's home was comfortable and clean. Tasteful décor spoke to his personality without screaming about it. Novels, papers, and trinkets sat in the bookshelves; concert posters and landscape photos on canvas were mounted on the walls. In the corner, an iPad was docked on an impressive speaker system. I powered it on and set the tunes to shuffle. The Cure's "Friday I'm in Love" began to play, and I flashed back to childhood. Mom played this album whenever she and I cooked together. I think I had it memorized by the time I was eight.

My last two Friday nights invaded my thoughts, and the lyrics died on my lips. *Maybe we'll skip this one.* I hurried to tap fast forward, and an alt-rock song I didn't know began. At least the lyrics weren't so awkwardly applicable.

I looked around. There was a mantle above a walled-in fireplace across the room. I danced over to the collection of photos arranged there, and that itch of curiosity about his life flared up. *It's not snooping if they're on display, right?*

The first photo on the end was an older couple, clearly his parents, at what seemed to be a wedding. Next came a nature shot of a lake. I skimmed over it to study the smiling baby in the third frame, and then moved on to the fourth.

"Which one are you looking at?"

I put my hand to my heart and spun around. Ben smiled and proffered a bottle, so I gestured behind me. "The one of you in the woods with, I assume, your brother."

He stood beside me. "My brother, yeah. We hiked Mount LeConte last year."

"Is this your child you've forgotten to tell me about?" I pointed to the one beside it.

Ben laughed. "No, that's my niece." He waved the bottle toward the table, so I followed, forgetting about the rest of the photos. He poured two glasses of a California Chardonnay, and we broke apart the chopsticks. "I guess this is the part where we act like civilized adults."

I pursed my lips. "How novel. What should we talk about?"

"Tell me about you. What was it like to move to New York?"

"That's not very 'right now,' Benjamin," I scolded, but after I worked on a piece of my roll, I answered. "I moved for college, did my undergrad at Hunter. The first few nights were so lonely, I cried myself to sleep. After that, it got easier to adjust, to learn how to talk and dress so I didn't scream Southern transplant to everyone I met. I fell in love with the city, found friends and a dream job, and became a New Yorker."

"Would you move back if you could?"

I looked down in a lost attempt to hide the nerve he'd struck. "I had a life there, and thought I had everything figured out. Now that's over and," I swallowed hard and admitted the truth. "I couldn't go back. It would never be the same."

Good god, did that hurt to say aloud.

When I looked up, he had that steady stare on me, and, as usual, it helped me move on. "Have you ever lived anywhere but Nashville?" I asked.

"I was born in DC, and then lived in Arizona and Wyoming. My parents are professors, so we moved to places where they both had teaching jobs. I was a freshman when we settled here."

"Are you close with your family? You've mentioned your brother before."

Ben nodded. "We're a close enough family. He and I were always tight, though. There's a year between us; I'm the youngest of three." He gestured to the mantel. "The baby is my sister's daughter. Damn, this is fresh wasabi," he added after eating a piece of roll.

"Mm-hmm, love it. Makes me want to punch something." I dabbed a big green blob on my next bite, wrinkled my nose, and slapped his arm when the heat seared through my sinuses.

He coughed on his drink and laughed. "That was the most adorable face I've ever seen you make. I didn't know you could be cute." I slapped his arm again, and he rolled his eyes. "Cute and kicking my ass. That's more like it."

The wasabi made this kiss ever spicier than usual.

"Do you have a big family?" he asked when we sat back.

I smiled into my wine glass, a little nostalgic. "I'm an only child. There were complications with Mom's pregnancy that ended their chances with me, but my parents met through their group of friends. On top of blood relations, I have more people I call 'family.'" I made air quotes.

"By the look on your face, I assume you're close."

"I was before I left. When I was little, we were always together. My cousin and I were the only children for a long time. We were best friends and always hung out a lot—even as teenagers, when he wanted to go to Hooters and I wanted trivia, like I told you last week." Ben chuckled with me, but my smile dimmed. "Haven't seen him in years, though."

"Why?"

I shook my head. "Next question."

He hummed. "Were you in love with your ex?"

"Next question," I grumbled again, but he arched a brow. "Um, I thought I was, but that was based on seriously misguided information. He was my partner. We lived together. I thought that must've equaled love. Sad truth? I don't know what being in love means."

"I see."

I smirked. "Tell me, Mr. Way-With-Words. How does one know when they're in love?"

"God, I don't know. That's too subjective."

"Subjectively then."

Four more pieces of roll disappeared from his tray before he spoke. "At the risk of being corny, maybe you know when you realize your life isn't complete without someone. Being with her makes you your best self—your most alive you." He glanced at me and smiled. "Or him, I suppose."

My heart skipped a few beats while he muddled out that answer. I didn't want the flashback, but it winked into my thoughts anyway.

"Kandra asked if we'd said the L-word." I rolled my eyes to hide my nervous heart. "I told her to calm down. We've only been together a year, and I just moved in a few months ago."

Across the table, Derrick looked up from his copy of The New Yorker. *"Kandra's so nosy. I can't stand people who need to broadcast their relationship details. It's so juvenile."*

"Totally." I rolled my eyes again, which got me a commiserative smirk before he returned to reading.

I shook my head. "I've never been in love. I have been a fool, though." He opened his mouth, but I beat him to it. "How about you?"

"Nah."

"Oh, no you don't. Give me more."

"You haven't given me anything. You know all about my stupid mistake. All I know is that you lived with him, were cheated on, and now you've moved home—which I'm assuming is somehow related, but even then I'm not sure."

I poked at my remaining food. The whole ugly story was on the tip of my tongue, making eating impossible, but I glanced at him and hesitated. His gaze was steady but gentle, curious and teasing all at once. *If you tell him, that look will be gone. Don't ruin it.*

I cleared my throat. "What do like about me, Ben Addison?"

Right away, I saw recognition flicker. He remembered asking me this question weeks ago. Funny how it seemed like all our conversations were imprinted on my brain.

"Your ass-kicking boots. That's what I like."

"Seriously," I said after we laughed. "You have options, and that's just at work. There's no way you don't have options in your personal life, too. Why am I here?"

"You're here because you want to be, Celeste."

Whoa. That simple statement held so much truth that I startled. He hadn't asked me here, hadn't pushed or even suggested I come. *You are who you want to be.*

"Holy shit," I whispered.

Ben set our empty food trays on the coffee table and held my hand. "I can't tell you why I like chocolate better than vanilla, or why I like the color blue. It's the same with you—I just do. Easy be damned. You're smart and determined. You're an artist and a brilliant coder. That's fucking *hot*."

I wiggled my fingers against his, heart skipping around in my chest. "But I've been so cold to you."

"Yeah, but I admire that, too. I respect how serious you are about the job. Respect it—and get off on it, apparently."

"Benjamin!"

"Celeste!" He ducked and kissed my neck, prolonging our laughter. "Besides," he rumbled against my skin, "how could I resist a woman in leather pants who nearly made me come on the dance floor?"

I slid my fingers into his hair. "I'm sure I don't know what you're talking about, Mr. Addison."

He bit me. My blood was still surging when he sat back and sobered. "My brother and my best friend would punch me in the neck for admitting this, but I'm not much for random hook-ups. Maybe it's because music is my outlet, but I don't need sex for sport. Screw options, I know what I want. Since we met, I've wanted you."

Before my brain could warn us both about reality, my ears perked up. "Your music. Can I hear it?"

Ben blinked, a faint flush that looked a lot like self-consciousness on his face. "Really?" I pursed my lips, so he reached for his phone. He swiped his thumb across the screen, and the music from the speakers changed. An acoustic number began. The guitar's scratchy, sliding chords set a beautifully soulful tempo before the singer joined in with pensive lyrics in a smooth, dark rumble.

Like a cup of strong coffee.

I slumped against the couch. "Oh, my god." Forget about my core, my insides were liquid heat all over. I squeezed his hand but gazed at the coffee table, afraid that if I looked at him I might actually combust.

When the song ended, we sat in silence. "That was beautiful." It was such a pathetic thing to say, but I had no words for how hearing him made me feel.

"Seriously?"

I looked up. "Are you kidding? Ben, that was... wow. Are you in a band?"

"No, but a lot of my friends are in the business. I'm a writer. I've sold several songs to bigger artists. Recording isn't my thing."

"Why do I get the feeling you're embarrassed? Why the hell would you be?"

He scrunched his face. "I don't know. It feels like a cliché, like every Nashvillian is a musician. You're so no-nonsense. I guess I was worried you'd find it silly."

The warm and fuzzies iced over. My expression fell. "No-nonsense, right. Closed. Empty." I met his eyes. "So empty that music wouldn't move me. Yeah, I see why you'd think that."

Benjamin reached for my hand. "No, I only meant—"

But I was on my feet. "I need a shower. Do you mind?" I

stared at the wall past his shoulder. He didn't answer, so I disappeared down the hall and into the bathroom.

The water couldn't be hot enough. My skin was pink from the start, but cold still clung to me. "Dammit," I sighed as a shiver ran through me.

I shivered again, but this time due to the draft as the door opened. Before I dared to lift my head, strong arms wrapped around my abdomen and brought me against his naked body. A beat passed, and then another and another. With every breath we took, it became harder to keep from melting into him. I wanted to cry. I wanted to kiss him. I just didn't want to be so fucking empty anymore.

Tears slipped down my cheeks with that thought, and I pictured the bridge I'd drawn. "Dammit," I sighed again in a shaky whisper.

"Dammit," he agreed, lips at my ear. "Just when I'd seen you smile, heard you laugh, watched you take what you want like I've not seen in the whole time I've known you, you put words in my mouth and run away. What's with you and hiding in bathrooms, anyway?"

A little laugh hiccupped through my sniffles. "Pure coincidence, I swear." I squeezed my eyes closed. "Ben?"

He hugged me tighter. "Yeah?"

"I loved your song."

His hum echoed in my ribcage. "Nonsense."

Another tease—another push. I get it.

I nodded slowly. "Complete nonsense. As nonsensical as waiting in your driveway."

"As spending another weekend together."

"Mm-hmm." I turned my head. "Benjamin. What are you doing to me?"

He cocked his head, reached slowly to fill one hand with

shower gel, and started to wash me. "I could ask you the same thing."

"No, really," I started, but he squeezed my shoulders.

"No, *really*."

I knew I should remind us both of the distance that needed to be honored, but I also knew the soapy glide of his touch melted my knotted muscles and unleashed blazing hot fire inside me. I knew we'd already blown each other's minds once tonight—and I knew, as his sudsy caress attended to my tight nipples, and I reached around and gripped his cock where it pressed into my tailbone, that we were going to do it again.

"I *am* no-nonsense," I said, but the steady slide of my fist along his length changed the message. "I'm empty, Benjamin. You have to understand."

Oh, his laugh. "I can fix that right now."

"Seriously, I'm—*mm, god*—I'm not like this."

"Like what? Fuck, Celeste, do you want it or not? I'm dying here."

With my nod, he bent at the knees and pushed himself in. I pressed my forehead into the tile wall and cried out. "You were saying?" he asked, grinding slow.

I've never been this wild, this needy, this sexy. "I'm not this person," I mumbled.

He sucked on my neck and laughed again, voice pure gravel. "You can be as stubborn as you want. You can bull-shit about being *closed* and *empty*"—he thrust extra hard on those words—"but you can't begin to hide what I do to you. You are most definitely this person. With your back arched and your ass pressed into me, you do wicked things to me."

My vision went dark. I spiraled fast into intense concentration on how he struck the perfect spot inside of me, the tickle of his fingers, the bite of his kiss. With other men, especially Derrick, my favorite position had always been me on top. With Ben, it didn't matter. If he screwed me sideways, I'd get off from it.

I bit my lip and braced against the wall, legs spread wider as I went up on tiptoe. "More," I hiccuped. My tongue was thick, thoughts foggy, but I loved the talking. I shook all over, and his hands went to my hips to steady me.

He pulled me closer to his pelvis—he was so long, so *deep*. "How much more can you take?"

"All of it—as hard as you can."

"Don't talk like that," he warned through his teeth, then clamped his mouth on my shoulder in what would certainly be another black-and-blue bite. I howled at the beautiful pain. "Celeste—I can't last..."

"Tell me to come." I could barely talk. Hell, I could barely breathe.

There was a half-second pause in this perfect torture, in which Ben sucked a deep breath. "No." His words were staccato, just like the rhythm of his hips. "If you're going to tease me, make me wait this long, I think I'll come so hard you forget the word empty, and leave you in the torment you've got me in now." He pinned my breasts to the tile with the weight of his body and licked my ear. "Is that what you want, Celeste? Or are you going to come for me, just for me, *only* for me, right...fucking...now?"

My hand slammed into the wall, and I shattered. He grabbed my wrist and squeezed gently, wrapped the other arm around my ribs, and didn't let up. His moan joined mine as he let go, and my body spasmed again from the force of his orgasm.

The water, lukewarm now, ran over my face, but my throat was dusty when I croaked, "You bullied me into an orgasm."

His laugh tickled my spine. Ben nuzzled my neck, kissing softly where he'd bitten so hard. "Just a suggestion," he murmured, and I smiled.

My body was so damn exhausted that I could barely walk, but endorphins took the edge off as we washed up. In the bedroom, we fell into the rumpled sheets, my head on his chest.

He yawned. "I am spent. What was that all about? You were crazy—you had me out of my mind. Did I hurt you?"

"It felt good. I like the bruises. And I like you crazy."

Silence fell. Just as my eyes closed, I heard, "Oh, I didn't tell you." But Ben dozed off without saying more.

So much for drowsy. *Tell me what? Is it good? Bad? Urgent?* I nudged him, but only got sleepy sounds. I pressed my teeth into his shoulder, and then bit a little harder.

"Celeste," he whispered and pulled me closer.

My stomach dipped. I'd never heard my name with that kind of reverence before. It was a dangerously beautiful sound. I lay my head on his shoulder and gazed at him in the dark, the unfinished thought forgotten.

"Benjamin."

That was a dangerously beautiful sound, too.

23

Sun streamed into the bedroom when my eyes opened again. Ben was sound asleep, and I snuggled into his side and gazed at him.

You're going to do something stupid before this is done.

I frowned, wishing that I didn't talk to myself so much. My inner voice was edgy, and I didn't feel edgy when I was with him.

Ben yawned. Dark lashes fluttered as he flipped to his side. "Hey."

"Good morning. Sleep well?" He nodded at my question, but his eyelids drooped again, and my heart melted. He was so damn peaceful with that dreamy smile. On top of that, he still smelled like our shower and radiated a cozy warmth. My fingertip skimmed his forehead, down along his scruffy jaw. He hummed muffled sounds of contentment when I traced circles on his chest. I stared at my hand and marveled at the way he responded to my touch. *Where does this power come from? Since when can you make a man do everything from sigh to curse a blue streak?*

And just how long do you think it will last?

I imagined standing on a bubble. The false reality of "right now" was beautiful but thin, barely substance in the face of the direness of my real reality. But until that bubble popped, I didn't want to do anything but enjoy every moment—and every touch.

His eyes opened, so I tapped his chest and dropped my hand. His brows drew together in a sleepy scowl. "If I go back to sleep, will you keep doing that?"

"Wake up, lazy." I tapped again, and he rolled on top of me. Our lips met with a collective hum, but I flinched when he flexed his hips against mine. "I'm kind of, um, tender this morning. We were too wild last night, sorry."

He sat up fast with a frown. "I knew it was too much. Are you—"

"I'm fine. I just need a break."

"Sure. We'll see how you feel later." He rolled off and stretched out beside me.

I don't know why I was so embarrassed, but I rolled my eyes and looked away. "What if there is no later? Then I've ruined everything."

"If there is no later? Then I guess this is how the world ends. I'd be okay with that, so long as you promise to kiss me while it happens."

"*Ugh.*" I groaned and stamped my feet on the mattress. "Seriously? Is it the songwriter in you that makes you say such stupidly perfect things? You've got a panty-dropping line for everything, you jerk."

Ben's eyes went wide, but one look at each other and we both lost it. He chuckled, and I burst into giggles that sounded nothing like my usual laugh. These were light and airy, like I was exhaling bubbles.

In that moment, that perfect "right now," I guess maybe I was.

A short while later, I cradled a cup of coffee and sat across from him on a barstool at the kitchen island, my feet hooked on the rungs. Drinking was a challenge with my lips still tugged into a smile.

"What?" I asked when Ben shook his head.

"Nothing. You just look really happy right now."

My cheeks warmed, but the smile held on. "I am... right now."

His brow creased suddenly, eyes lifted to the corner, grin widening. "Did you bite me while I was asleep?"

"Maybe."

"Vampire much?"

I wiggled my brows and sipped. "Isn't it obvious?"

"Mm-hmm, you are pretty good at sucking."

"Benjamin!"

"Celeste!"

Oh, my god. Ben rounded the island and hugged me from behind, his forehead against my neck as we laughed together. My chest tightened with so much more than humor. That warm tightness pulsed from my toes to my hair, and I let it claim me.

We quieted, and I looked back at him. "I was trying to wake you. You started to tell me something, but then drifted off. 'I didn't tell you' is a cryptic way to finish the evening."

His eyes glinted; he still wore that playful smile. "All the ways to finish that thought. I didn't tell you..."

"I have a wife and three children in Alaska," I said with a grin.

"Or I'm in debt to the mob, and they're going to break my legs if I don't pay up."

"Or Threads hired me on the spot. You're out, Ms. Greene."

He scolded me with his look and stroked my cheek. "Not now," he murmured, and I breathed deep and nodded. "I didn't tell you that I'm having a party tonight. You're going to meet my friends."

It took me a beat to realize this wasn't a joke. "A party? Seriously?"

"One of my buddies and his band just released an album, so we're celebrating. You're squeaking again."

I shook my head. "It's too much, too soon."

"Recall that I met your parents last weekend."

"That's only two people."

His brow wrinkled. "They're your parents. They're at the pinnacle of important people to meet."

"I don't know, Ben." I frowned.

"Aw, but I've told everyone about you."

My squeak made him laugh this time. "You haven't. Please tell me you haven't."

"No, I haven't." He hesitated, a ghost of smile on his lips. "James knows about you, though."

"Who is James, and what does he know?"

Ben caressed my cheek again. It was a thoughtful kind of gesture, easy to lean into. "My brother doesn't know a lot, but he's been curious about my rival since the job started." I pursed my lips, and he rolled his eyes. "Look, I want you to come, but don't if you're uncomfortable. My friends are great, and I think you'll have fun. If you *seriously* don't want to, I understand."

Of course I agreed to go. Nerves lost to curiosity, but more than that, I didn't want to break the bubble to spend another night alone.

When we'd eaten breakfast, Ben declared that since we

spent so many hours cooped up at the office, we should get some fresh air. We swung by my place to get clothes, before heading to a state park. The vibrant spectacle of foliage on last weekend's run was a little dimmer today, but there was still plenty of fall color on display as we hiked. The fallen leaves created a sweet-scented carpet and absorbed the sound of our footsteps.

"You're quiet," Ben said when we settled on a rock to eat lunch. "Everything okay?"

His hip was beside mine. Our shoulders leaned into each other. He held a turkey sandwich I'd made at my apartment. We were sharing an apple. The beautiful morning winked through my mind.

"I'm great," I said, but his eyes widened at the thin croak of my words. I cleared my throat and flashed a smile. "Everything is great."

Right now.

Ben scrunched his face, clearly skeptical, but nodded. "Tell me something."

"What?"

"Anything."

I thought. "Sarah said you fell out of the sexy tree."

He coughed on his sandwich. "*What?*"

I giggled until tears wet my cheeks. "Don't say anything. I think she'd die if she knew I told you that. Oh, god, your face right now." I lost it again.

"I think she knows I'm in-interested in you." The strange stumble in his words made me tilt my head. Ben shrugged. "She gives me looks like she can tell."

"Her expressions say a lot." I wondered if I should be nervous about the idea that Sarah suspected us, but it was too much effort. "She cracked me up at dinner last week when Joe bought my drink."

One brow lifted. "*He* thinks you *are* the sexy tree, whatever the hell that means. I heard him talking to Kevin on the way in Monday morning."

I wrinkled my nose. "Creepy. What did he say?"

"He thinks you're shy." My heart fluttered at the grumbled scorn in his voice. Once again, Ben Addison seemed to know me so well.

"Does he now?"

Ben's hand slid to my jaw to turn my face. "Did you tease him, Ms. Greene? Make him think you're a shy little thing?"

That cardiac flutter kicked up triple time at the tease in his voice. "I guess I just didn't want to stand out in the cold talking to him."

Oh, his smirk. "You stood in the cold to talk to me."

I hadn't thought of that. Why it had me trembling after the million moments since then, I couldn't say. Ben scanned my eyes and pressed a soft, wet kiss on my lower lip. "I almost snapped when he offered you a ride home," he murmured.

I grabbed his jacket before he could pull away. "How do you think I felt about Alison and her friend that night? About the idea of you going home with them? I..." I swallowed hard and finished the thought with my look.

Ben used one hand to push the food aside and laid me back on the rock. "Goddam, I want you right now," he rasped before his tongue was in my mouth.

After we finally got around to finishing eating, we chatted the whole hike back about easy, fun things like favorites and dislikes. In the car, we discussed the job. Not Tenn Star or the office, but rather coding and design. We swapped details about sites we'd done, platforms we preferred versus ones we didn't, and our creative process. It was exhilarating. I'd not talked shop since my firm in New York, and our conversation told me we had a lot in common in our approach—but a lot we could learn from each other, too.

It turned me on. Badly.

So badly that he'd barely shut his apartment door when I pushed him into it and jumped into his arms. He gripped my ass and pulled me even closer before we began to walk backward. We were still kissing when I tumbled down to sit on a step. He leaned into me, and his woodsy scent and the firm pull of his lips negated any discomfort from the stair pressed into my shoulder blades.

I opened one eye to see his hands planted on either side of me, most of his weight in his palms. "You can't be comfortable," I mumbled.

"Oh, I'm very comfortable." He grinned, but then paused, his forehead on mine. "Still sore?"

"Nope, full recovery."

"We'll take it slow, just in case." Ben's gaze was on my lips. He swallowed hard and met my eyes. "I want to believe I can do that," he admitted. "But if I get you in the bedroom..."

"Get to work, Mr. Addison." I leaned forward and whispered, "Maybe you could start with your mouth."

We were in the bedroom in seconds.

24

When we'd recovered from my "full recovery," Ben insisted he didn't need help prepping for the party. He went to the grocery and tidied up, and I took my time getting ready. First I blew out my hair, and then dressed in a mauve skirt, black-and-white striped boat-neck shirt, black tights and, of course, my Prada boots. Ages ago, this was a favorite going-out look; now, as I slipped in my new earrings, it made the bubble I stood on shimmer.

Ben was in the shower. I didn't know what to do with myself, so I paced around the room and practiced introductions. "Hi, I'm Celeste. Benjamin and I..." My whisper trailed off, adding to the knot in my stomach. With a deep exhale, I rummaged in my bag for my phone.

Me: Checking in so you don't beat down my door—I'm not home.

Mom: Thank you and??? Where are you, young lady?

Me: No comment. Just not home. Safe.

I could picture her face.

Mom: Happy?

Me: We'll talk later.

Mom: You canceled therapy. Why?

"Shit," I whispered.

Me. Busy week. I'm fine, promise.

Mom: Hmm. Ok. Tell Benjamin we say hello. Love you, Twink.

I spun around at Ben's footsteps in the doorway. He was dressed in dark, fitted jeans and a white button-down. In the middle of my ogling, he disappeared into the closet and reemerged in a brown and blue color-block sweater and oxblood shoes, too.

It was that same lowered-lid tour from toes to eyes that he'd done the week—and the night—before, but this time, it was both of us. This time, when he met my gaze, he smiled.

"James texted. He'll be here any minute." Ben crossed the room to take my hand and guide me into the hall. "He's going to hit on you."

I stopped. "Excuse me?"

Ben eyed me again. "Especially since you look that damn good." He chuckled. "Ignore him. It's a tradition between us that goes back to high school."

I spluttered, but the doorbell rang. He dropped my hand and jogged toward the stairs. Still muddling his nonchalant warning, I perched on the stool in the kitchen. The rumble of relaxed male voices drifted up, followed a moment later by Ben and a man who could only be his brother. He was a bit fairer, but the similarity in the nose and jaw, not to mention those striking gray eyes, was unmistakable.

Ben stepped forward while his brother's smile began to grow. "Celeste, this is my brother, James. James, meet Celeste." He leaned against the island, the picture of attentive.

I slid off the stool to accept James's extended hand.

Instead of a shake, he lifted my knuckles to his lips. "Enchanted," he purred. I raised a brow, but he kissed my hand again. "Celeste is a fitting name for a woman as heavenly as you."

Ben groaned a laugh.

I disengaged my fingers. "I never heard that one before. At least you're original."

"Don't encourage him," Ben said.

James's eyes flared. "I'm more than happy to continue. But first, I have to ask: why are you and I having what's obviously a destined meeting of two souls in my brother's kitchen?"

Ben rolled his eyes and went to get the door again. James watched him go, and then turned back to me. "We can get out of here right now, if you want," he whispered.

He winked, and I couldn't contain my laughter anymore. The glint in his eyes had let me know all along that he was teasing, but James Addison *did* have a lot of charm.

His face relaxed into a real smile. "Let's get a drink," he said in a much more natural pitch than that flirty purr. He motioned for me to join him at the counter, poured a glass of wine when I pointed, and opened a beer for himself. We held up our glasses. "It's nice to meet you, Celeste, but I'm perfectly serious the moment you realize that you're far, far too good for Benjamin."

"You'll step in and save me?"

"In a heartbeat," he said cheerfully.

"Benjamin warned me you might make such an offer. He said it was tradition."

"Nonsense. I've waited for you all my life." He didn't blink or hesitate in the least, and I laughed again. James flashed another grin and shrugged. "Here's to tradition."

"And not asking more," I added.

"And definitely that." He tapped the bottle against my cup.

We took up residence on the stools. James was also a programmer, which began a lengthy conversation about work. He had an office job, but mostly he wanted to talk ideas and compare skill sets. His sights were set on making a million-dollar app, and he offered to cut me in. I couldn't tell if he was joking and didn't dare ask, so I smiled and toasted him without commenting. Our chat didn't arouse me like my talk with Ben earlier, but it absolutely loosened my tongue and eased my nerves.

Voices began to float in from the living room while we prattled on. Soon, people appeared in the kitchen, headed for the makeshift bar.

"Let's go mingle." James stood and offered me his arm.

I looked at his angled elbow. "Sounds good," I said, then went to the door. He laughed as he caught up.

Half a dozen people were in the living room when we walked through. Ben's voice came from the stairwell: "James is bullshitting her in the kitchen. Oh, wait, there they are. Celeste?"

"*Celeste*?"

James and I turned. Ben moved toward me, but I saw no one except the man beside him. My hand clapped over my mouth.

"Celeste?" he asked, and I realized it was he who'd spoken. "Oh, my *god*, no way." His face creased into that familiar smile that had spelled trouble so many times in the past. I choked on my laughter, throat tight as Nick Field folded me into a bear hug. "No way," he laughed again. "How long has it been?"

"Too many years." I stepped away and wiped my eyes, still grinning as we turned to the brothers.

They traded a look. "I was about to say, 'meet Nick,' but clearly..." Ben let the thought finish itself. He swallowed hard.

"Well, this is awkward." James almost vibrated with amusement.

His mirth made me cast another glance at Ben. My eyes widened at the increasingly ill look on his face, but my giddy smile wouldn't quit. "No, not at all! Nick is my cousin —the one I told you about."

"Oh, god, what did you say?"

"I told him you were my favorite."

"She told me your ass was always trying to go to Hooters in high school." Ben's apprehension had melted into a smile. He crossed his arms. "Surprising absolutely no one."

My cousin grinned and shrugged. "I started young," he acknowledged before turning back to me. "You dare call me your favorite cousin? Mom said you moved home back in the spring—*and* that you were supposed to come to our show last month." Nick's hazel eyes narrowed playfully behind his black-framed glasses. "Why the hell am I only seeing you now?"

"You were going to that show?" Ben blurted.

My head swiveled fast. "Uh, I was, yeah. And, I'm sorry, Nicky." I bit my lip. "Things have been kind of rough. I've been busy trying to get my feet underneath me."

Nick hummed with a twist of his mouth. He glanced between Ben and me. "Yeah, it must be hard getting your feet underneath you with this guy around. You probably find yourself on your back a lot, huh?"

I squeaked; Ben didn't even blink as he punched Nick on the arm.

"Fuck, dude," Nick laughed, rubbing his sleeve.

"You asked for that, you bastard," Ben said, but he could

barely conceal his own laughter. He glanced at my flaming face and lost the battle. James was already in pieces.

Nick pushed his hand through his shaggy hair. "Aw, I'm sorry, Celeste. Just joking."

"Go get a drink, Nicholas," I snipped. "Make it straight dish soap to wash out your mouth. Then come over here, and we'll catch up."

All three of them laughed again, and my embarrassment faded fast. Nick promised to find the Palmolive and chase it with bourbon as he retreated to the kitchen with James.

Alone for the moment, Ben stepped closer. He pointed across the room. "There's at least one photo with your cousin in it on my mantle."

"Really? I didn't get past the one of you and James."

"We've been friends for years. I know your aunt and uncle. Hell, I might've met your parents before. Holy shit."

"Holy shit," I agreed. "You were at his show?"

"I played that show. It was him, Jack, Dave and Kira—they'll be here soon—and me. God, what would I have done if you'd been there?"

I wasn't sure if I regretted not going to the show, or if I was glad to have avoided him seeing me out with my parents on a Saturday. I *was* sure I was tempted to kiss him in the middle of this party, but his text chime brought us out of the moment.

Nick and James reappeared, wearing looks that made me hold my tongue. Ben hissed a breath and glared at them. "What'd you do?"

Nick held up his palms, but James said, "She texted me."

"She said she was busy tonight. What the hell did you tell her?" Ben.

"Might've mentioned you had a date," James hedged, so I let my eyes drift to Ben's phone.

Liv: I'm there with bells on in fifteen, punk. Can't believe you didn't tell me!

He caught my snoop. "Give us a sec." The guys wandered away. "I think I mentioned Liv last week?" He flashed a half-smile.

"Girlfriend."

"*Ex*-girlfriend. Friend," he insisted.

"Now you say, 'you'll love her, I'm sure,'" I prompted.

Ben sighed. "No, probably not at first. She can be a little abrupt, but it's fine. I—shit, Dave's here. I'll be back." He moved to go, but when he looked up from his phone, his eyes caught on my necklace around my finger. "Screw it, he'll wait."

My hand dropped when he pressed me to the wall and bent his head to my ear. "I'm so damn glad you're with me tonight." Warm lips dusted a sweet kiss on my temple before he turned and hurried away.

I found Nick and James on the couch and accepted their invitation to sit. They were easy to talk to. I quickly settled in, and soon was laughing so hard my sides hurt. When our drinks were empty, James offered to refill my wine while Nick caught me up on family news. The fresh Solo cup was at my mouth when a shadow fell on us.

Nick's attention slid upward with an expectant smirk. "Hey, Liv," he murmured.

"Well, hey, boys. James, you said I needed to meet some-one. Might this be her?"

The breezy tone didn't match the critical gaze locked on me. The girl cocked her head, hands on hips, so I stood and forced her to take a step back. She was tall, a good head and shoulders over me, with the figure and coloring of an Italian bombshell and a greaser-chic style. The dark brown hair on the crown of her head blended into vibrant purple pigtails.

An obscure band t-shirt, shredded jeans, and Timberlands added up to hip and beautiful on her.

She rolled her lips; the purple MAC matte matched her braids almost perfectly. "You're Ben's new girlfriend?"

Girlfriend. I swallowed hard, but lifted my chin. "Do I know you?"

Her brows rose. "I'm Olivia, and if Benjamin has a new girl, I'm the one who makes sure she's okay."

I let my brow arch, too. "Hmm, that's cute. Too bad the third degree vibe doesn't work on me."

We eyed each other for a tense moment, but then her shoulders dropped. She stepped back with a small smile. "You don't take any shit, huh? That's cool. Good to meet you."

"Same," I said, not sure I meant it. She plopped on the floor in front of us, and I sat down.

"So what's up?" she asked the guys, and instantly became part of our little group.

We chatted on. The room filled up with pockets of people, but the tempo of the party changed when the band arrived. Four men ascended the stairs, three with guitars on their backs, and everyone applauded. "That's Cellar Door," James said, but I'd caught the gist.

"Are they famous?" I asked as the fanfare ebbed.

James shook his head. "They own a studio. The album will hopefully draw clients with a similar sound. It's business."

Business or not, it was exciting to me.

Liv scuttled away to say hello to someone, and Jack Spencer, Cellar Door's lead singer and guitarist, walked up. He waved off congratulations about the album, but stayed to chat with Nick and James.

I glanced toward the kitchen to see Ben with two

strangers—and Liv beside him. I never was good at taking my eyes off Benjamin if I had the chance to stare. Too bad for me that *she* noticed. She caught my gaze, then turned away and propped her forearm on Ben's shoulder. He dipped his head, but he didn't need to go far. She was so tall, she easily put her violet lips to his ear. Whatever she said made Ben's attention jerk to me. He blinked, and then rolled his eyes. Liv grinned, and they nodded to the other two and stepped away to whisper together.

I tried very, very hard not to care.

BEN

Liv put her arm on my shoulder while we chatted with some of Jack's friends we didn't know well. "Your girl's staring at us," she whispered.

I whipped around to see Celeste's hard gaze, her lips set in a line. *Thanks a lot, Liv.* My elbow to her ribs made her grin. She excused us from our companions and drifted a few paces away, tugging my sleeve. I moved to return to Celeste, but her words stopped me.

"I don't like her, Benjamin."

Cold alarm swept through me. Liv was bold and sometimes brash, but she had the biggest heart—and she knew how to read people well. She'd hated Ashlyn, hadn't trusted her from the moment they met.

I swallowed hard. "No?"

"No." She looked into my eyes, surprising me with the bittersweet expression there. Her lips curled into a sad smile. "She's fucking perfect for you, Ben. She fits in with the guys, she's smart, and she takes zero bullshit." Liv blinked and tossed her hair, but her voice was soft. "Can't believe this moment has come, but go for it, tiger. All the best."

My pulse pounded at the enormity of the moment. Liv and I were never jealous when one of us was seeing someone, but we were very protective of each other. This was her letting go, giving her blessing to our bond being usurped by a new one.

One with Celeste. *Holy shit.*

She smirked when I continued to gape. "Come on, boy, it was bound to happen. But for old time's sake—" She put her hands on my shoulders—"I'll give her a little more to think about," she breathed in my ear.

That broke the moment. I groaned and shoved her shoulder. Her Timberlands clomped on the hardwood when she stumbled and shouted a laugh, trying to keep her Solo cup aloft. "Dickhead, don't make me spill my drink."

"Then don't play games."

Celeste clearly worked hard to keep the jealousy off her face when we walked up. I caught her gaze as often as I could, and every time I did, she smiled a little more. After a few minutes of Liv and I chatting in her circle, she seemed to relax.

"Y'all jamming tonight?" I asked Jack. He agreed and excused himself to round up his band, who set up by the fireplace while everyone else found seats.

Nick dropped down on the couch beside his cousin, but then he caught my pointed stare. *Move it, Field. Don't make me ask.*

He got the message. With a laugh, he slid to the floor beside Liv and let me take his seat. Celeste studied her hands while everyone watched us. I draped my arm around her shoulder.

"Aww, how cute," James drawled.

"Shut it, bro." I pulled her closer. "Hey," I whispered.

Cellar Door captured everyone else's attention when they began to play, but she cut her eyes up. "Hey."

"Did James steal you away?"

"Mm-hmm. We're sneaking out at the third song. Have it all planned. It'll be about the same time you and Liv hook up in the bathroom."

"Ouch." I stroked her cheek, a laugh rumbling in my chest. Liv's blessing had me walking on air. "And after she said you fit so well in our group."

Celeste's expression told me that she understood this was a high compliment and a big deal, but her hopeful look fell as a shadow crossed her features. She crooked a smile but didn't reply. This wasn't a time to talk, so I sat back and turned our attention to the band, my finger tapping lightly on her shoulder as we got lost in the music.

25

"It's time for a drink," Jack said after they'd played awhile. "Ben? Take over?"

I startled from a musical trance when Ben stirred. "Nah," he said, but everyone cheered him on. He raised a brow at me, then crossed to Jack and accepted his guitar. Ben sat on the chair. "Stop that," he scolded the fresh round of applause. "What should I play?"

"Hallelujah," someone called, and I wondered why *my* adrenaline spiked.

Ben nodded and began to strum and sing. I knew I blushed from the second he opened his mouth, but there wasn't a thing to do about it. That black coffee voice, those hands gliding over the guitar. I was a wreck, could see and hear nothing but him.

The assault on my senses got worse when he did one of his own songs next, because the depth of feeling in his voice was even more potent. I worried briefly that I might actually come just sitting there. He looked at me when the strings quieted, but I barely managed to crook my lips before Jack returned. My agony subsided while a quick shuffled ensued.

Ben and Nick disappeared down the hall, returned with two guitars, and sat with the band.

A sing-along began. The joy in the room was palpable, the energy light and fun and completely lovely, but something heavy began to tug at my heart that kept me from joining. I looked down to where James sat with Liv, both of them shouting lyrics. I looked at my cousin as he laughed and played.

I looked at Ben.

My blood pounded like I'd run ten miles. *I can see you, Ben Addison.* For all the times he'd made me feel seen, now the tables turned, and those moments of itchy curiosity came together and made perfect sense.

What I saw was this. Benjamin Addison wasn't a bully or a jerk; he was sure of himself. And why shouldn't he be? He was a good man who lived a life he loved. His apartment was full of friends, beautiful music poured out of him, and he was talented in a whole host of ways. He needed the job, but that was only a small part of his world.

What I saw broke my heart.

This isn't yours.

Why can't it be? Don't I deserve to be happy? How broken am I?

Maybe a lot more than I'd ever realized.

"Celeste isn't singing." I startled when the music stopped, and Nick pointed his pick at me. "You should sing."

Ben flashed a sly grin. "'Play, 'Born to Run.' That'll make her sing."

I shook my head. "This time, make it—"

"'Thunder Road.'"

My words were echoed from the floor. I looked down to find Olivia side-eyeing me. She grinned when our gazes met. I pursed my lips, but it made her laugh. Our joint request began, so I smiled and sang along.

"Thunder Road" is one of those classic rock songs you have no choice but to belt at the top of your lungs. With close to twenty people doing so, this version was so raucous that the musicians were sweating by the time it ended. "Shit, I'm done," Jack laughed, and his bandmates agreed.

"One more?" Ben asked Nick.

Nick pointed at me again. "What should we do?"

"'New York City's Killing Me.' It's my favorite song," I added, eyes on Ben.

He grinned while Nick hummed an approval and said, "Nice and bluesy. Okay, for the ex-Yankee."

The Ray LaMontagne number had become my theme over the past year. It was my crying song, a funeral tune to New York. Ben sang it and changed everything. In his mouth, the lyrics weren't a lament. They were good riddance to a closed era of my life.

But then he got to That Line, the one about Nashville and the woman of his dreams.

Oh, god. Oh, god, oh god, ohgod.

Ben nailed me to the couch with his steely gaze. My thoughts, pulse, breath, all short-circuited, but I wasn't the only one who noticed. Several whoops floated up around the room, which made him drop his attention to the guitar as he continued to sing. I clutched my necklace, unable do anything but ache through the rest of the number. At least I pulled myself together in time to add to the thunderous applause at the end.

"Great choice!"

A girl sat beside me with a smile. "Great choice," she repeated.

Still recovering, it took me a beat to answer. "Thanks. That song means a lot to me."

"Cool." She nodded and stuck out her hand. "I'm Kira Ireland." We shook, and I introduced myself. "You and Ben are cute together. I didn't know he had someone new."

My stomach clenched all over again, but she was so friendly, so completely without judgment or evaluation, that it was easy to warm to her. "How do you know Ben?" I asked to shift topics but keep her talking.

"We met through Jack."

"I think he mentioned you. Are you a musician, too?"

A blush tinged her cheeks, turning her complexion a warm honey-brown as she smoothed the braid that twined around her hairline. "Technically, I'm a hairdresser, but, yeah, I sing a little." She looked around, and I followed her gaze. We found Ben and Jack laughing with a third man. Kira gestured. "That's David. He's my partner—uh, my singing partner," she clarified, and the way she'd almost sighed his name did make the detail necessary. I was about to inquire more when a pair of shredded jeans blocked our line of sight.

Olivia took the cushion beside Kira. "Your turn to play," she said, but Kira waved her off. "Come on," she whined with a grin, completely different than the girl I'd met. "Do 'Fake Empire,' puh-leese?"

"The party's ending, Liv," Kira said, then bit her lip. "But we're at open mic at Bluebird tomorrow, if you want to come."

Liv clapped gleefully as Nick and James walked up. They took seats on the floor and made us a crowd. "Y'all playing Bluebird?" Nick asked, and then nodded to me. "Good last request, cuz."

"You guys were awesome. I remember you were in a

band in high school. It's cool you kept it up. Are you a professional musician?"

Liv coughed, and Nick's brows arched. "Ah, no. I'm an audio engineer at a recording studio. I didn't 'keep it up'— music is life."

I winced. "Sorry. I'm an asshole." We both ignored Liv's second cough.

He shrugged. "You've been gone a long time. The only things I know about your life come from Mom's reports."

"Great. Now I'm a bigger asshole." I sighed, suddenly confronted with how absent I'd been.

"*Was* an asshole," he teased. "Now that you're back, we'll fix that fast."

"I'd love to. I really want to see you more."

"Definitely. Especially since you're with Ben, we'll see each other a lot."

Time out.

I twisted my necklace. "Um, or you could call me. You have my number now. Maybe we don't plan too far ahead."

Four pairs of eyes settled on me, but I only looked at Nick. His gaze narrowed. "Why?"

"Ben and I aren't..." I waved my hand. "Technically not... well, it's complicated."

"What's complicated? Seems simple to me. You care about each other. Who cares about technical?"

"You don't understand."

"It sounds like *you* don't," Olivia butted in. I glared. She puffed out her lips. "Are you really going to bullshit with 'it's complicated' when he geeks on you that bad?"

"Liv," Kira murmured.

"My situation isn't your business," I snapped.

"It's none of our business," James said, and we all turned to him. He nodded at me. "But my brother doesn't sing his ass off for any girl, Celeste. Not that I can blame him with a girl like you." The others groaned at the line, but James got serious again. "He's been through it this year. He looks so happy around you. Hell, you guys look so happy together. That's awesome, right?"

"Celeste?" Liv's voice was saccharine. "I told Ben you seemed cool, but my claws will come out if I even think that you're going to screw him over like that bitch did. So, fair warning: my business or not, do not hurt our Benjamin."

Enough. I gritted my teeth. "Piss off. Save your attitude for someone else. And don't ever try to give me an ultimatum again, because you have certainly mistaken me for someone who gives a fuck about what you think." I forgot to apologize to the rest of them as I jumped up and strode straight to the bathroom.

Here we are again. With a flip of the lock, all I'd been holding back broke loose inside me. I gripped my hair, my complexion white and red in the mirror. *This has gone too far. We should've stopped last Sunday. It would've been safer. Smarter.*

Tears burned, and I clenched my teeth.

You just paid rent, so it's salads for lunch and dinner again. Benjamin has his friends to look out for him. You have you. You made this life. You chose to be the career-driven ice queen. He'll see it soon enough anyway. He'll know I'm not worth all this drama.

That part hurt the most.

Screw bathrooms. I turned out the light and slipped across the hall to the bedroom. The party's volume had faded considerably, but I locked the door before going to my bag.

With the new sketchbook in hand, I stepped out of my boots, flopped down on the bed, and drew a circle. Inside was a party of shadow people without faces. Outside was blank space.

My bubble.

I'd begun to add music notes above the revelers when a soft knock interrupted. "Celeste?" I stashed the book and opened up. Ben frowned, brows drawn. "Are you alright? Nick and James said you seemed upset. Did something happen?"

"No."

He studied me but nodded without inquiry. "Everyone's gone, and I've got it mostly cleaned up. I wanted to check on you."

I followed him into the now-empty living room. The furniture was still arranged for a party, but the place was clean. "Fast work."

"You've been hiding awhile," he said, and I looked at the clock to see that an hour had slipped by.

We dropped down onto the couch. I pressed my palms between my knees. "You want my truth, don't you?" He hummed a yes, so I turned toward him. "I feel safe with you, Ben, but I know that's dangerous."

His jaw clenched. "Why? Do you think I'm going to hurt you?"

"I know you are." His eyes flashed, but I continued. "We're going to hurt each other. We're pretending like there's no problem here, but we both know that's stupid."

"Did I miss something? Do something wrong?"

"No." I sighed. "I shouldn't have brought this up now. I'm sorry I said anything."

"I always want your truth, Celeste, but I don't know how to answer. I want you happy, and I want you to trust me." After a pause, Ben picked up my hand and laced it into his. "Can I give you *my* truth?" I nodded, and he rubbed my knuckles. "I know we need to figure out what happens next. I know we have to stop living in the right now. But," he hesitated, "I want to finish tonight first."

I knew by the tone of his voice what that meant. He knew my answer by the look in my eyes.

We jumped each other; there's not another way to put it. Good thing the coffee table had been pushed to the wall, because we tumbled off the couch in a wild scramble of hands and kisses. Ben was all over me. Tonight his touch was strong, almost greedy, but as always he knew exactly what I wanted—what I needed—and turned me into a gasping mess, writhing on the floor beneath him.

"You sang for me," I mumbled while he pulled off my shirt. *Mm-hmm*, he answered. "You sang my song."

"Did you like it? You looked intense while I played. Very serious."

My head lolled. I lifted my hips, let him strip my skirt and tights while I smiled dreamily. "Very hot," I whispered. "Very, very, wet." I didn't need to say it—he could feel it.

"For me?" he asked against my mouth. "Because I sang for you?" I hummed a yes that turned into a moan when those fingers thrust inside of me. They pulsed, but his kiss disappeared. I opened my eyes to see his brilliant grin. "Oh, baby, do you know how that makes me feel?"

"Like you're making me feel?" My hips twisted for more of what he gave.

He laughed. "I hope so."

I curled up for another kiss. Sucking on his lip kept me from thrashing at the perfect rhythm of his fingers. I gripped his hair and remembered to breathe hard through my nose, just to hold the kiss until the last possible second. Until his fingers pulsed heavily, and his thumb was *there, right there*—

"The best, the best," I cried through the pleasure.

"Every time."

We couldn't stop. There was no end to what we wanted from each other, no bottom to the depth of desire to taste, to touch, to melt together. I knelt for him while he sat on the couch. He had me with my hands braced on the mantle while the photo frames clattered and fell. It still wasn't enough. He carried me to the bedroom, kicked my bag to the floor to put me in the chair, and dropped his head between my legs.

When my moans and spasms quieted, Ben sat up, clasped my wrists, and kissed my palms. "Celeste," he rasped in the darkness. "Celeste, I'm—I'm never going to hurt you. I swear."

In the dark, I had an answer. "I swear it, too." *Because I won't let you.* And then I was up, our sweat-slicked bodies wrapped together tight as we fell to the bed.

He sat against the pillows, held my hips and let me ride him, slow and exhausted and still so perfect. Our breaths were dusty, rattling sounds in the room. My body spiraled once more toward an explosion, but my heart twisted tight, too. "Benjamin, it's too much... *please*," was the last thing I screamed for him.

"It's not." He guided me to help him finish. "It's... so... *right*," he groaned as he thrust hard into me.

I collapsed against his shoulder. As the haze of pleasure receded, that twist in my heart sharpened, and I knew the truth. I wasn't falling for him. It was done, and it was deep.

And it could break me.

26

I woke in the same position as the day before, snuggled into his side with him on his back, but everything was different. Ben's eyes were open, the room was dim from a cloudy day, and I was anything but comfortable.

"Morning," he said when I stirred.

"Hi." My throat was parched.

He gave me a playful look. "I'd talk about last night, but it would sound like a cliché." I nodded. "Fucking incredible," he chuckled.

I nodded again, but a sour taste crept into my mouth. Ben scanned my expression. His smile dimmed, and he took a quick breath. "I know. Right now is over, and we have to face it. I thought maybe we could go to the gym, clear our heads a little. Then we'll come back and talk."

I sat up. "Sure." I went for my bag.

There is no substitute for absolute knowledge. Know yourself. Know your business. Damn that little poster and its too-fitting sentiment.

I sweated hard at the gym. Cardio, weights, the works.

Exhausted already from the weekend, now I was tight and purged, too. I was sharp. I was ice.

I was sick.

~

He let me shower first, knew without asking that I didn't want him to join me. I dressed and packed my bag while he took his turn, then dropped it by the couch on the way to the kitchen. The ice had set deep in my veins. It made routine tasks like finding cereal laborious, but I assembled breakfast and got coffee brewing by the time he emerged.

He walked in and looked at the spread. "Thanks. You didn't have to do that."

"Yeah, well, it's not scrambled eggs." But, god, I wished it was—wished we could go back to last Sunday, to yesterday, to anywhere but where we were.

We sat and ate. Well, sort of. I stirred my raisin bran until it was mush, and he took about two bites before focusing on the coffee. After ten minutes of this farce, we traded a glance and dumped the food, then went and sat on the couch.

Ben didn't hesitate. "Let's figure this out. We can't go through another week like the last one. How do we move forward?"

My palms grew sweaty inside my sleeves. "One of two things will happen tomorrow. If Ms. Fowler chose me, we're back at square with this competition. If she chose you, I'm out on my ass and trying to start life over again."

"I think she'll pick you. She practically said as much Friday."

I couldn't be excited. "Whoever she picks, the situation is

no basis for a personal relationship. You have to know that's true."

"I know." He rubbed his jaw. "This is what I'm thinking. Collaborate on the last project, crush it, and leave Rollings looking like a moron when we pitch the same idea at our separate meetings."

My eyes pinched shut. "I'd love to do that, but there's budget for one, Ben. Rollings won't suddenly find another salary just because we throw the contest in his face."

"I'm willing to take a pay cut to work with you. James really wants us to make an app, and I've got a few songs in the works—"

I shook my head. "It's too big a risk, Ben. What if Rollings fires us? What if they don't realize it's the same pitch and pick you? And, we're forgetting, I haven't won the last round yet. We don't even know that tomorrow isn't my last day."

He slouched, and I exhaled, comforted that at least he saw my point. "Maybe I should quit," he mused, gaze on the coffee table.

"Quit?" I yelped. "Come on. You can't do that any more than I can."

That thoughtful stare remained unfixed. "I could. I could talk to..." He trailed off.

"Benjamin, seriously. I know you need this job. You can*not* walk away. I can't believe you'd even suggest that. I could never let you. It's not worth it."

"I don't agree. I think it might be."

I exhaled a long, shaky breath. This was the part where I had to be fair. That he would even offer to quit twisted my insides. *It's not worth it. I'm not worth it.*

Before the words were out, Ben brightened. "I could talk

to Mr. Garret. He's had me working on a side project this week. Maybe he could hire me freelance for now."

"He's had you *what*?"

"Jimmy's got a side business selling antique chairs. He contracted me to do a site for... that. What's wrong?"

Bile turned my stomach inside out. My fingers and toes were numb. "You're doing another project for Mr. Garret?"

"On the side," he insisted.

I rasped a sandpaper laugh. "Garret and Rollings are buddies. You might as well have just told me Rollings hired you for a side gig. Are you kidding me? That probably *is* the final project, and they slipped it to you early to give you the leg up."

Ben scrambled to sit up straight. "No, no, I swear it's not. Rollings doesn't know."

"My ass Rollings doesn't know." The snarl in my voice knocked us both silent. I clutched my hair. "This isn't happening. Please don't tell me you sold me out, Ben. Please, god, don't tell me this is happening again."

"Again?" Panic flashed in his eyes. He gripped my shoulders. "I never sold you out, ever. Fuck, Celeste, you have to believe me. I swear to anything you want me to, you're still in the contest. Jimmy asked Rollings to have me do another page for the company site on Monday. He called me Wednesday about the side project and said not to tell Rollings. He didn't want him to think he was trying to poach me."

Another rough laugh spilled out. "Because he knows Rollings is going to hire you."

"*No.*"

Ben practically shouted in my face, but I pushed him away and jumped to my feet. Vile memories mingled with the sickening present until I crumpled to my knees and looked up at him.

For a moment, it wasn't Benjamin I saw. The floors weren't hardwood; they were carpet. It was May, not November. And this was an apartment in a high-rise in lower Manhattan.

Derrick wore his boxers That Day. They were all he bothered to put on while his afternoon guests dressed and clacked their Jimmy Choos out the door. When silence fell, he sat on the couch in front of my pathetic heap on the living room floor and sighed. Not a sad sigh; this was the sound of a man faced with something he'd rather not address.

First came the explanation about the job, about how my inexperience and his career equated to a position far beneath my current employment. He didn't explain why he didn't tell me it was an assistant role. Instead he said, "I guess we need to address the obvious truth. I think we both know this relationship isn't working. I have needs, Celeste, which you don't care to fulfill. You're always so focused on your job, your image. Clients and friends are where you put your energy. At first I thought you were sweet, but that's part of the image. You're so cold and closed —you make it impossible for people to really be close to you. When the flash is gone, all you want is to draw at the dinner table. I need passion. I need to feel a fire, in my career and my bedroom. You need something different. I respect that—I hope you can respect my needs, too."

Benjamin's gray eyes were tormented, but he didn't move. At last, I spoke. "Whatever. You sold me out, you didn't sell me out, we'll see. Either way, we're fooling ourselves. We're talking about the job, about what choices we have. We're pretending like it's the only issue, but the truth—my truth—is more than that." A lot of effort went into drawing enough breath to say, "Choices don't change who I am, Benjamin."

The color drained from his face. "Who are you, Celeste?"

"Not who I want to be, that's for damn sure." He cocked his head at my bitter words, clearly not understanding. "I told you way back, I'm empty, Benjamin. No tease, no shower talk, I'm a failure at personal relationships. I make it impossible for people to be close to me." The words that came out of my mouth echoed in Derrick's voice in my head. I dropped my gaze.

"What are you talking about? None of that is true."

My eyes burned with unshed tears. "I wish it wasn't. I don't know when I became this person, but if we drag this out until you really know me, you'd see."

"That's the biggest load of bullshit I ever heard. I really know you now. I know you're proud, determined, and not empty in the least. Hell, you're so full of fire and life that it scares you sometimes." I gulped, and his tone softened. "I also know that you and I are already close, and it's more than sex. There's no way you'll convince me that somehow that would all just evaporate. No way."

Everything he said was so tempting, such a beautiful mistake. I longed for escape, for darkness and my bed—for a place to hide from life again. I closed my eyes as a substitute and shuddered. "We're standing on sand, and we both know it. There's nothing here to build on."

I opened my eyes. The tendons in his neck constricted. "Say what you're saying."

"This can't work," I croaked.

Ben froze. I hid my face behind my palms. Finally, he spoke. "This is over? We're finished?" Still hidden, I nodded. "Fucking hell, Celeste, I cannot believe this shit." His volume amped up, but his voice was raw.

"Please don't curse at me. You have to understand—it makes sense."

"Nothing you've said makes sense. How can you say that? How can you not see how good we are together, how right? Don't tell me you don't feel it, too. Ending this is stupid, Celeste, *don't do it*."

"You have no idea—"

"No idea? No idea of what? That you clearly had the rug pulled out from under you by some prick in New York? Yeah, I really don't. You won't tell me anything, but I don't give a fuck. All I know is I have every idea that I make you happy, and you know it. I have every idea that nobody, *nobody* has ever made me feel like you do, and I'm pretty sure that you feel that too. You've said I'm crazy more than once, but are you listening to yourself?"

I lifted my wet face from my hands and struggled for a proper breath. "I can't do it, Ben," I whimpered. His eyes were too much to handle, so I looked at the ceiling. Tears trickled down and pooled in my ears. "It's safer if I'm alone."

His high, hoarse pitch only twisted me further when he pleaded, "Don't do this, Celeste."

"I'm sorry if I hurt you," I said in the world's most pathetic waver.

His eyes fluttered shut on a heavy sigh. "God, what do I say now?" He gripped his hair with both hands. "How do I beg you not to do this? Trust me about the job. Trust that you don't want to walk away. Let me change your mind. Let's just talk, think about our choices."

It took a lot to shake my head. When I did, more tears fell.

He groaned. "Please?"

It was all I had to deny him again.

Another ragged sigh. "Well then, I guess you should

leave." His gaze flicked across my face. "I can see your walls are back up already, despite those tears." I flinched at the direct assessment. "Let yourself out."

I collapsed in a ball and bit my tongue so hard I tasted copper. Benjamin stood and gave me one more look, then turned and walked down the hall. A door clicked shut. A second later, there was a thunderous crash of things being thrown to the floor, and a stream of muffled, hot expletives. I heaved a single sob, then clamped down on my tongue again and got up, grabbed my things with shaking hands, and stumbled down the stairs to my car.

Thank heaven for the Bible Belt. Traffic was almost nonexistent at midmorning on a Sunday. Fortunate, considering I have no idea how fast I drove, and I'm pretty sure I ran at least one red light on the way home.

The next morning, I would realize that I parked in two spaces at my complex before stumbling up the stairs, through my apartment, and into the bedroom, where I fell facedown onto the mattress. It was then that I lost it, hidden in the quilt as sobs racked my body so hard my ribs hurt and my teeth chattered. The linens were soaked with hot, messy tears, but the empty room had no answer when I kept asking what the hell I had done.

BEN

My phone rang on the coffee table. I reached for it without bothering to rise from the couch. The volume must've been on max, or else my drunken haze was to blame for the headache it was giving me. "Shut up," I grumbled as I fumbled to answer Nick's call.

"We're all going to Dave and Kira's set at Bluebird tonight. You and Celeste want to join?"

I rubbed my bloodshot eyes and adjusted the phone. "No."

Nick laughed. "Jesus, dude, keep it in your pants for a couple hours and be there."

"No, I mean—no."

His laughter died. "What's wrong with you? You sound drunk."

The Jameson bottle hit the floor and clattered to its side. I didn't care. "She's gone, Nick. She's—*fuck*—she left." I fell back on the couch and groaned.

"Gone?"

"She left me." Christ, just saying the words aloud

opened up the gaping wound in my chest. The Jameson did nothing to numb this pain.

"I've got you, buddy. Hang on."

I grunted. "I don't want to go out. I know you and James are going to tell me move on, more fish in the sea, all that bullshit like you did last time—"

His dry laugh cut me off. "No, dumbass. This is different. I'm coming over."

27

I cried myself to sleep, woke up, and wept again. By the time it got dark, the sobs were gone and the shaking had stopped, so I dragged myself into a shower and sat under the water to gather my wits.

The madness was over. Sexy Celeste was a fun character to play, but now it was time for a good dose of reality. I'd known all along that reality meant I was better off alone. Alone, but this time, I could stay in control. The decision had been mine. I'd chosen to protect myself and my future, so what possible good would it do to let heartache undermine all that? I still had the job for the time being, and I could continue with my plan for getting life back on the rails. This pain, this fresh bout of emptiness, was all for nothing if I didn't keep moving forward.

I rose from the tub and breathed deep. *It's over. It was great, it was wild, it was fun, but it's over. You have to think about you.*

The first thing to do was pull myself together. Forcing a routine seemed like the best way, so I laid out my clothes for the week and packed lunch for the first three days. I considered dinner, but had zero appetite. Instead, I drank a giant glass of wine and stared mindlessly at the television for a couple of hours. As I brushed my teeth for bed, I decided that I'd done well with the evening.

If only my heart would quit the throbbing pain that persisted with every beat and get on board with the idea of normal, I'd be fine.

My heart still throbbed while I dressed for work the next day, like someone had struck my chest with a hammer. By the time I parked in the office lot, I was sweating at the thought of sitting across from him. All those hours, those smiles and quietly funny comments, tumbled around in my memory while I gripped the steering wheel with clammy palms. "Stop it," I hissed and gave my head a strong shake. *Know yourself.*

Cool autumn air helped on a slow walk across the parking lot, but it's hard to move fast when your legs are jelly. Inside, Sarah gave me highlights of her date on Friday. I'm sure she was happy, but I have no idea what she said. I also have no idea if I answered her coherently before drifting to the elevator; no way could I climb stairs in this condition.

I was perched in the desk chair at nine sharp, staring at the vacant seat across from me and listening to my choppy breath in the silent office. Where was Rollings? I needed a new project, anything to distract me, so I powered up the computer and checked email. My attention caught on a message from "kfowler," subject line: *Threads Website Contract.*

I'd won the client. Ms. Fowler loved my design and was ready to contract me today.

I pounded my fist on the desk and hastily typed out an acceptance and thank-you reply, and then got busy deleting junk messages. When I looked up again, it was 10:00, and I was still alone. Rollings's extension went straight to voice-mail, so I called Sarah.

"Ohmygod Celeste," she exclaimed in a whisper before I could utter a word. "You missed everything. Let's go get coffee."

Downstairs, Sarah was fit to burst. She gave me screaming eyes and waved to the door, almost forgetting her coat in her rush. The story bubbled out as soon as we started toward the Starbucks at the end of the block. "About nine-thirty, Ben walked into the office wearing a hoodie and jeans, so right away I knew something was off. I teased him about being late, but he didn't answer, just said, 'Please ask Rollings to come down.' That's the only he said to me the whole time. Hang on. Hi, can I have a white chocolate mocha, please? What for you, Celeste? I'll buy."

"Grande skinny latte. Thanks. So he was dressed..."

"Like he'd slept in his clothes. Unshaved, too. Still super cute." She giggled, and I had to smile. "Anyway, I called Rollings. He came down all frowns and asked what was wrong. Ben stood there a minute, kind of getting himself together, I think, and then looked at Rollings. Now, Celeste, understand that I'm just repeating what I heard. He said, 'I quit. I won't play your, uh, *effing* game anymore. You're an idiot, Rollings. If you knew anything, you'd have hired us as a team. We would've made you a fortune together. Since it has to be one, give her the job. I'm out.' And then, with Rollings standing there all red and puffy, he turned and walked out the door." She sipped her drink and nodded to punctuate the story.

The latte turned my palm red while stared at her, slack-jawed. "Shut your mouth," I gasped. "He didn't."

"I swear he did. And between you and me? I bet he was a hundred percent right. I mean, I don't even know what all it takes to do what you do, but you two are so much alike, I'm sure you'd have made a perfect team."

Oh, my heart. The pain in my chest went from dull to icepick when I heard that truth, but what could I say? I held the office door open for her as we stepped back in. She gave me a secret smile, then slipped behind her desk and grabbed the ringing phone. My thoughts raced on the way back to the third floor.

Rollings stepped into our—*my*—office about twenty minutes later. He smiled, but his tension was evident. "Well, well, Ms. Greene. We've had a very interesting morning. I have good news all around for you. First thing is, Ms. Fowler chose your proposal. Second, and maybe most surprisingly, you have the job here, if you want it. Mr. Addison declined the position and, to be honest, I feel better about you anyway. I'd be mighty pleased if you'd like to join our little family permanently. Do you need time to think?"

No mention of Garret or his antique furniture. I should've trusted you on that one, Ben.

"You feel better about me?" I asked before I could think about it. He twisted his mouth, and I refocused. "I don't need to think, Mr. Rollings. I'd love to accept the position. Thank you so much."

"Great, great. You'll be getting some prospective clients coming in over the week, but the last one that was going to be y'alls together will come in today. It's a new bar down-town, run by a nice young man who's friends with my son.

The two-week deadline is still ideal, but you may set the routines as long as you let the clients know. Oh, and I've got time this afternoon for us to discuss your salary and finally get you some keys. Welcome to Tenn Star, sweetheart. Hate that you're all alone up here, but in the new fiscal cycle you and I will hire and fill out the department together, okay?"

"Perfect." My cheeks ached from a bittersweet grin. Rollings gave me his toothy smile and left.

I strolled to the break area, tried to decide if I had earned this job or landed it by default, and wondered if it mattered either way. I had what I needed: a reboot for my career. With this job, I would have a routine and a good income. I could soon get a better place and finally be in control of my life again. I gave myself a hug and hopped up and down, but the pain and emptiness weighed on me like shackles. I couldn't even muster the excitement to text Mom. Instead, I wandered around and willed the next job to come in fast.

The following weeks split me in two. At work, I zeroed in on projects. Three came in over the week after that first lonely morning. Between client meetings, drafting sample pages, and revisions, I had enough work to officially be swamped for the first time in ages. I stayed at the office late most nights, and even a little on Saturday, because it gave me purpose. Because, between the lines—the lines of code, the lines of goals and deadlines—I was nothing, and fading fast.

If I didn't have a specific task in front of me, all I could think of was Ben. Every time I thought about him, my throat burned and my stomach turned to jelly. Dark, hateful regret would leave me doubled over, hugging my insides, unable to let go. The only remedy was to minimize coherent thoughts in my down time. I skipped meals and drank my dinner, stared blankly at the walls and silent TV, roamed around my apartment, and slept fitfully. I didn't even think of rescheduling therapy. What the hell would I say to her? She couldn't make it better. One night I tried to draw, but that, too, turned into gazing at a blank page until I slashed a giant X and shoved the book deep in the shelf.

Two Celestes emerged. One was in hyper-focus, all sharp angles and tight organization. The other was a ghost of a person with no definition or purpose. *If you know yourself, which one is really you?* I asked this question a lot. The answer was never more than *neither* before I returned to work or staring at walls.

The blurry passage of time was familiar but different— better, I guess—since at least I had Tenn Star. My days were bookended by Sarah's morning gossip and Rollings's nightly check-ins. They gave me structure as I survived one week, and then another.

28

I begged off drinks the first Friday post-Ben, but Sarah wouldn't hear of it for a second week in a row. She insisted we celebrate my position on staff, which is how I found myself surrounded by colleagues at The Flipside again.

"Celeste, have you lost weight? You look thin," Sarah said as we walked in. I mumbled a vague negative, although my clothes had in fact seemed looser when I'd gotten dressed that morning. She gave me a tsk. "I'm the one who has to start my diet Monday. No carbs, one glass of wine per week, until I'm down five pounds, I swear."

I shook my head. She was curvy, sure, but Sarah was adorable. "Sarah, seriously, you don't need it."

She patted her tummy. "*You* don't. What are you doing, anyway? Exercise or diet?"

"Nothing," I said, and the subject was closed. I dropped into the chair beside her. The seat opposite was instantly filled by—who else? —Joe.

He grinned. "Hey, you. It's been a while."

"Jameson and IPA," I said to the waitress. "Oh. Hi, Joe."

He whistled low and chuckled. "You know what they say

about girls who drink whiskey, right?" I squinted at him, and he waved his hand. "Don't worry, it's a good thing."

"Ah."

Joe tried again when the round was delivered. "Here's to Celeste! Congratulations on your victory, and welcome to the team!"

"My 'victory'? What does that mean?" We clinked glasses before I knocked back the shot, chased it with a swill of beer, and lifted a brow.

He faltered. "Well, just—we all knew about the competition. We're glad you won. Ben was alright, but um, well. Welcome to the team."

He's being nice. Don't take it out on him. I forced my lips into a smile, and his shoulders lowered. "Thanks." I took another drink. *But don't you dare brag to your boys about me again, or my ass-kicking boots will have your name on them, Joe, baby.*

The evening rolled on with several more whiskeys and a few more beers. Near the end of dinner, Allison and Janet began discussing the holidays, and I realized Thanksgiving was this coming Thursday. I listened as they talked travel and turkey.

"This time of year flies by. Halloween feels like yesterday, but it was weeks ago," Sarah said.

"Oh lord, Halloween was crazy. Lily and I still laugh about that." Allison shook her head.

Joe cleared his throat. "Laugh?" he echoed, and she smiled at him.

"Laugh about what?" I asked.

"Oh, uh, we were determined to make it a night to remember." She giggled nervously and looked between Joe and me. "Our choices might not have been the most professional."

"You mean when you were trying to fuck Benjamin?"

The table fell silent.

Allison's face grew red at my question; Joe's did, too. Everyone else either studied their phones or visibly perked up.

"I beg your pardon," Allison said. "We just had a little fun with him."

"Mm-hmm."

She glared and tossed her hair, flicking a disdainful look over me. "But then, I don't think I've had as much to drink as you have, so maybe I'm more careful with my words."

"You probably are," I agreed with a nod that made my head swim.

I held her stare while she dealt out one huff, and then another. "And anyway, what's it to you? Thought y'all were rivals. You're thrilled he's gone, right?"

"You presume a lot."

Phones and decorum had been totally abandoned. The whole table bounced their attention back to Allison.

"*You* do, saying we—we tried to—"

"Fuck. Him. That's what I said." At my words, she squirmed and made a lemon face. "What? You don't like the F-word?" I grinned—I was out of my damn mind. Joe coughed, so I grinned at him, too. "Watch out for girls who drink whiskey," I whispered loudly.

"It's incredibly vulgar." Allison captured our attention again. "And anyway, we were *just having fun.*"

I cut her off with a laugh. "Semantics."

She pounded her fist on the table, and I got the distinct impression that she wished it was my face. "I wasn't going to say it, but I'm not sure you're one to pass judgment. You threw yourself at him on that dance floor. I saw you. And the way you ran off with him after was hardly subtle, either."

I'd begun to giggle, and, once I did, I was lost to it. "Oh, don't get righteous on me now. Damn, girl, I thought we were having fun." I downed my latest Jameson and coughed through my laughter.

"You're drunk," was Allison's final shot at me.

I hummed and glanced around, laughing again to see almost everyone hiding smiles behind raised drinks. Only Joe looked at me like I'd grown another head.

"'Scuse me, *y'all*, but I think I'd better call it a night b'fore I offend anyone else. 'S been fun," I slurred. I nearly dropped my bag as I rose on wobbly legs.

Sarah popped up, too. "I'll walk you out." She took my elbow while everyone called goodbye.

I knew the moment I stood that Allison was wrong. I wasn't drunk. I was *wasted*. Blurry vision and a lurching stomach made the walk across the restaurant eternal. Sarah clucked that I should've eaten dinner, but I couldn't respond. Walking was challenge enough.

She held the door open. Even the cold night air did little to sober me as I rubbed my eyes and looked to Sarah. "I can't drive. Will you call me a cab, please?"

"Celeste, you seem really unsteady. Is there someone who could come get you? I'm not sure a cab is the best idea," she said gently.

I swayed backward and grabbed the porch rail when she released my elbow. "You're so nice." Tears began to well up. "I'm sorry I was mean to Allison."

Sarah laughed. "Yeah, but you weren't wrong. Joe was after you on Halloween, and Allison and Lily wanted Ben, but the three of them..." I tilted my head, and she giggled again. "Um, they wound up making out at the bar. I'm not sure what happened after."

"Seriously? Good for Joe." The tears threatened to spill with my laugh.

Sarah hesitated before she blurted, "Celeste? You and Ben, were you, well, you know—"

"Shh. Shh." I shook my head and almost fell over from it. "Don't say that. Shh."

Her expression asked questions, but she didn't speak more. It was too late, though. The alcohol flooded the dams I'd built inside me, and an urge to weep for days wrapped around my heart.

My vision blurred again, but I battled for control a little longer. "Sarah, I need my Mom. Can you call her, please? I should sit." I groped in my purse to give her my phone and then stumbled to the bench by the door.

Sarah's footsteps approached. "She'll be here in twenty. Move over." Before I could lift my heavy head, her hip was beside mine.

"I can wait alone. Go back inside."

Sarah snorted and zipped her coat. "Right. Like I'd leave you out here in the dark, drunk as a skunk."

I chuckled at the euphemism, but said, "No, really, I can handle myself. Go have fun."

She turned, and I met her gaze. "I'm not leaving you, Celeste." Her patient tone left no room for argument, and another dam holding me together cracked.

Fresh tears stung, but I crooked my lips. "Thank you."

While we stared into the night, an ancient memory floated through the muck of my brain. Out of nowhere, I began to talk:

"Once, I was at a party in Brooklyn with my girlfriends. Amy had just broken up with some guy. She drank her feelings so bad, there was no way we could get the subway home. We only had twenty dollars—this was pre-Uber—so we hailed a gypsy cab, and I put on the biggest Southern accent and told him I was a country music star. I don't know if he believed it, but he took us all the way to the Upper West Side for the twenty."

Sarah laughed. "That sounds like a TV show."

"It felt like it." Those old times, memories of too much alcohol and too many random clubs, things I'd defined as my life, they all seemed so far away now. My friends had moved on.

So had I.

The only problem was, I was still nowhere.

I looked up at the moon. "I thought I knew what life was supposed to be," I whispered to myself. "Now, I have no idea."

"Someday, I'm going to have to hear that Southern accent of yours."

I think I smiled. "Over my dead body."

She laughed again just as the headlights of Eleanor's SUV swung up to the curb. Sarah got to her feet and helped me up. The world spun, and I fell hard back to the bench. "Come on, sweetie. You gotta get home," she coaxed. I blinked blearily at her, and she flashed a sympathetic smile. "Girl, you're a wreck."

Didn't I know it.

"What's all this?" Mom appeared just as I got my feet under me. Sarah stepped aside right away, murmuring goodnight to us both.

I faced my mother. She crossed her arms, but I reached for her. "Mom, I need help." I almost sat down again, but her arms were around me, her lavender and patchouli scent in my nose. We staggered to the passenger's side, me leaning heavily on her small but sturdy fram. Slumped in her car, I pressed my cheek to the cold window, my hot tears and ragged breath fogging the glass.

It was a short drive to her house—I didn't have the wherewithal to ask her to take me to my place—but the drive wasn't a minute too long. I tumbled out when she parked and promptly vomited in her hydrangea bushes.

Mom sighed a mild expletive and lifted my hair away from my face, her soft hand rubbing my back. "Oh, baby. Why are you such a mess? I haven't heard from you lately. What's going on?"

Loud sobs exploded from me, and I vomited again and again until there was nothing left but tears. When she was sure I'd finished heaving, Mom handed me a tissue and guided me inside. We limped together to the bathroom, where I sank to the tile floor. A cold cloth against my forehead brought on a bout of fresh, grateful weeping.

"Mommy," I burbled. "I'm sorry."

"Why are you sorry?"

"I fucked up, Mom. I'm sorry I'm such a mess. I really fucked up."

"Oh, Celeste, don't use that kind of language with me. What have you done?" She sat down beside me, our backs to the tub.

"I got the job. I didn't tell you. I got it because Ben quit." She didn't respond. "But Ben quit because I told him we wouldn't work out. I ended it. And the next day he quit. And I haven't seen him since."

"When?"

"Two weeks ago." I sniveled.

"Two weeks and you didn't tell me any of this? Celeste, why do you do this? Why wouldn't you have told me?"

"I didn't know how. I've been fu—messed up, Mommy. I didn't know how to say it. I knew you'd be disappointed."

"That you got a job?"

"That I pushed him away." My voiced hitched. I was in pieces.

"And tell me, dear daughter," Eleanor tucked my hair behind my ear, "why I'd be disappointed in that?" Her tone was patient; I knew what she was doing, even through the alcohol.

"Because I ruined it."

"Why would it disappoint your mom if you broke up with someone?"

I sniffled again and wept, "Because it was right, he and I. And I pushed him away because I didn't trust him. How could I believe it was real, that he really cared about me?"

"How could you think he didn't?"

I couldn't answer. The last thing I remember about that night was breaking into uncontrollable sobs on the bathroom floor while my mom held me tight.

29

I must've passed out, because the next thing I knew, I woke in the guestroom with daylight on my face and an aspirin by the bed. Water helped my dusty throat, but my head throbbed and abs ached as I hobbled to the bathroom for a shower.

It was pretty clear I interrupted a serious conversation when I walked into the kitchen. Mom and Dad looked up with creased brows while I poured a cup of coffee and joined them at the table. "Morning," I mumbled.

"Morning, love," Dad said. "How do you feel? Would you like some toast?"

My heart swelled, even though the rest of me felt like yesterday's garbage. Despite the years I'd lived away, my bond with my parents had always been strong. I loved being babied by them. Their love and support meant everything.

I tried to decline food with a wrinkled nose, but caved at Dad's frown. Mom spoke while he went to the fridge. "How *do* you feel?"

I knew she didn't mean my hangover. I lowered my eyes. "I'm—"

"If the word fine comes out of your mouth, young lady, so help me, I might have a meltdown."

Her clipped tone made me jump. "Mom, I—"

"You're always fine. You were fine when we texted weeks ago—*the last time I heard from you* before last night. You were also fine when you broke up with Derrick, moved in with one friend, then another, and then took that sublease before calling to tell me you were moving home. You were fine with taking time off from your job to regroup after the failed interview, but then you never told us why you didn't go back when the money ran out."

I winced. I'd forgotten all the lies I'd told about why my world fell apart.

Mom leaned forward and covered my hand with hers. "You're not fine, Celeste. Whatever happened, whatever this is, it's time to admit it. Your father and I have our trip to Paris next week. I can't leave with you like this."

Dad's hand rested on my shoulder. I whipped my gaze from one parent to another, briefly panicked before my chin wobbled and I gave up.

"I tried to be okay. I tried to be strong like you. I wanted to handle it on my own, but I can't. Everything is such a mess."

Mom's hand flew to her mouth. Dad's arms wrapped around my shoulders, and I buried my face in his bicep to hide my tears. He held me until I quieted, then kissed the top of my head and knelt in front of me. Without words, his kind blue eyes told me, *it's about time you admitted it.* I wept a laugh. "Thanks a lot, Daddy," I said, surprised at the drawl I heard in my own words. He winked.

Mom gripped my hand again. "I called Monica once we put you in bed last night. She called back this morning.

April will see you today at three, no time limit on the session."

I took a long, slow breath. "I think that's a good idea."

My therapist wore jeans and a Clemson sweatshirt when we met at her office that afternoon. She pulled up to find me seated on the steps with Mom, who kissed my cheek and promised to pick me up whenever I was ready. I stood and faced April Zeller, marveling at how much younger she looked with her light brown hair loose and wavy around her face.

"You didn't have to do this," I said when she crooked me a smile.

"No, I didn't. But then, neither did you."

She ushered me inside and went to her desk while I perched on the brown suede couch and gazed at the wall. When she sat in her usual chair, her cat-eye glasses were on again, notepad in hand. The oddly comforting familiarity broke me out of my trance.

"So. Let's start over, shall we?" She crossed her legs and sat back in the chair, temple propped on her fist. "Tell me everything."

I fidgeted, took off my jacket, curled my feet on the couch, and then realized that was rude. She smiled and told me to take my shoes off and be comfortable, so I did. I considered a million starting places, but finally exhaled and nodded.

"I moved to New York when I was eighteen."

From there, I told her everything: college, Derrick, falling apart and moving back, Ben, all the way to last night. It took an hour.

A second hour was filled with her thoughts, my tears, and a lot of analysis on the toll That Day had taken on me. I left utterly exhausted, with another appointment scheduled Monday night.

Mom drove me back to her house, where I crawled into the guest bed. She moved to leave, but I grasped her hand. "Wait."

She sat on the edge of the bed, so I swallowed and said, "I lied to you about what happened in New York."

I told it all over again. Mom listened intently until I finished with, "He broke my heart, Mom. We never even said I love you, and he still broke me. I couldn't tell you. I didn't want you to be disappointed."

She grabbed me and pulled me close. "I am never disappointed in you," she whispered fiercely. Her shoulders trembled as her grip tightened. "Oh, baby girl, I understand more than you know." I looked up, curious. "There was a man I knew a long time ago. He was a smart choice. Good job, on his way up in life. I was young—too young—and I thought that was how things were supposed to be. I was wrong."

"But you met Dad, and you realized—"

Her expression cut me off. "It wasn't nearly as easy as all that." She scanned my face and smiled. "You've got enough on your mind today. Your eyes are peaked. Get some sleep and worry about you. Someday soon, we'll have a cup of coffee together, and I'll tell you everything."

I wanted to insist, but my eyelids were lead. Wrung out and hung over were a draining combination. Mom kissed my forehead as I drifted off and slept until dawn the next day.

∾

Sunday afternoon, still in that bed, my eyes followed the ceiling fan around and around while I replayed the words April had been telling me since our first session: *You are who you want to be. No one but you can define that. Trust your instincts. You know what's right for you.*

I was finally starting to believe her.

Insights and affirmations all pointed to action. I reached for my phone, scrolled through the contacts, and dialed.

"Hello?"

"Nick?"

"Celeste?"

"Yeah," I croaked, tongue thick from hours of silence.

"Are you sick?"

"Mm-hmm."

"What's up?"

"I need Ben's number. You probably know why."

Nick went silent. Finally, "Of course I know, and I'm not sure you should have his number."

"Why?" My chest tightened. "Is he seeing someone else?"

His harsh laugh made me jump. "Hmm, no. Honestly? I can't believe you could be so cold. One night you two are so cute together it's stupid, and the next morning you walk out." He took a breath and softened his tone. "What happened, cuz?"

"I messed up so bad," I whimpered.

"Yeah, no shit." At least his tone was gentle.

"Nick," I begged, battered by his truths. "I'm sorry. Please, help me. I have to talk to him. Please."

Nick groaned. "I can't believe I'm in the middle of relationship drama. This isn't my jam. I'll text it to you, but do not make this worse." The line went dead, and my messages dinged.

I touched the digits that, I realized, I'd had memorized all along. The dial tone droned while I watched the fan blades again and planned a quick voicemail, something simple and—

"Yes?"

His voice was as gorgeous as I remembered, but loaded with tension. It still made my insides clench. "Hi."

"Yes?" Same tight tone.

"Benjamin, we need to talk."

"No, we don't."

"Then I need to talk. Can we meet up?"

"No. If you have something to say, tell me now. I can't—I don't want to see you."

Those words cut deep, but they were fair. I propped up against the pillows and brought the blanket to my chin. "Okay, I'll do this on the phone if you want. Benjamin, I'm so sorry." My voice cracked, but I soldiered on. "I know it's my fault, but I want to try and explain, if you'll let me." He didn't speak, but he didn't hang up. "I'm broken, Ben."

"I don't want to hear that old—"

I cut him off. "Not empty; broken."

"I'm listening," he said, half a shade softer.

"You knew I was cheated on, but it wasn't that simple. We lived together for two years. I thought we shared a life. I thought we were what a couple was supposed to be. He was —is—in real estate with a high-end firm. His company revamped their online image and recruited an in-house Webmaster. I thought it'd be worth leaving my job for such a prestigious position."

I gave him the outline of that disaster, ending when I walked into the bedroom. It was the third time in a day I'd told the story, and I was surprised how saying it aloud could make me feel angry *and* absolved.

"Once his, um, lovers left, he told me he'd been unhappy —cheating—a long time. He told me the life we'd built, the life I thought was what we both wanted, was a sham. Beneath the image of success, I was so cold, so obsessed with work, so empty. He was miserable. I wasn't good enough for the job, and I wasn't a good enough partner to keep him happy. That's basically what he told me.

"I believed him, Ben. In my mind, we lived the right kind of life, growing our careers and having fun with our friends. I see now how little that is to build a relationship on, but I thought I knew how things were. I'm starting to understand how badly he manipulated me, but I believed that I should've known he wasn't happy, that I was empty and horrible. And, yeah. It broke me."

I took a breath to recall what April had given me as a mantra to break through that wall of shame and pain. *The definition of manipulation is unfair control. Derrick put the blame of his infidelity on you to control the situation. If you continue to believe his lies, if you let his deceits shape you, he continues to exert power over you. He moved on, but you're living under his shadow until you define yourself.*

"Jesus, Celeste," Ben murmured. "I—"

"Please let me finish." Tears rolled down my cheeks. "Then I met you. I went from so alone to, god, so..." I broke down, held the phone away, and wept into a tissue until I recomposed. "Sorry, um," I sniffled, "you were right. Nobody ever made me feel as good, as adored as you did." He inhaled deeply, but I kept going. "But do you see why I couldn't trust it? Why I couldn't let a personal relationship upend my life again? You were right about Mr. Garret. I should've known you wouldn't betray me, but it was more than the job. I was terrified I'd push you away when you saw the 'real' me."

I wiped my eyes with the soggy tissue. "That's my truth, all of it. I'm not empty, Ben, and I know that because you helped me see it. With you, I was so much more than I ever knew I could be. More confident, bold—alive. Thank you for showing me a better me."

It was a long, heavy, silence before he exhaled. "I don't know what to say."

"Don't say anything. I didn't tell you this for pity, or in the stupid hope that it would somehow fix the mess I made. I thought you deserved to know. Maybe you won't hate me so much."

"Oh, god, Celeste," he groaned. "I don't hate you. Don't you know I—"

But he broke off and didn't finish.

"Are you working?" I asked when the silence was too much.

"Hmm? Uh, yeah. Garret hired me to run his sites. I work from home. James has big plans he wants to work on, too. Oh, and I wrote a song. That was more than you asked, sorry."

"No, I like the details. Congrats on the song, and good luck to you and James." I caressed the phone. My heart throbbed again, but this was a pain I could bear.

"Thanks. Look, I'd better go."

"Do you miss me?" I clapped a hand on my mouth too late, but—

"Every day."

Silence. We'd said too much.

"Take care of yourself, Ben," I whispered.

"You too, Celeste." He ended the call.

$\sim$

Did I mention I love my parents? Mom knocked with a grilled cheese sandwich and tomato soup half an hour later. She sat on the side of the bed. "You're scrawny. What's that about?"

"I don't eat," I admitted, mouth full of sandwich. She laughed; so did I.

"You look a little brighter at least. Feeling better?"

"Some. I called Ben."

"That's good. Do you think you'll see him?"

I stirred the soup and shook my head. "No. But maybe that's better." She narrowed her eyes, so I redirected. "Did you know he's friends with Nick?"

"Our Nick?" She furrowed her brows, then lifted them. "He did seem familiar. I bet I met him at that holiday show... four years ago? Younger then, of course—does he have a brother?" I nodded, and she pursed her lips.

"What?"

"He flirted with me."

I had to set the tray aside as I giggled until tears rolled down my cheeks. "No, he didn't," I gasped.

"Is it that unbelievable?"

"Not at all. You're gorgeous and he's... James. What did Daddy say?"

Mom waved. "Never mind that. He didn't have anything to worry about."

I grinned again, but then swallowed hard. "Mom? I don't know how to thank you for everything."

"Hush. You have no idea how much good it does my soul to have you close again. I'm only glad you let us be here for you. You're my life, Celeste."

I put my head in her lap, and she stroked my hair. "I was always close, Mom. I lived far away, but we've always been close."

She sighed contently. "I couldn't agree more."

BEN

With you, I was so much more...alive...a better me.

Her ragged, thoughtful words haunted me. I couldn't remember precisely what I'd rambled about true love on the couch that night, but I was certain that was the gist.

I'll kill that bastard right now if you want, but come back. You don't have to fix a damn thing. I'm done, Celeste. You're everything.

If I wrote lyrics that corny, I'd never make a dime.

Nick texted he was coming over later. I whiled away the hours in what had become my favorite position over the past few weeks: sprawled on the couch, one foot on the floor, staring blankly at the fireplace.

At least this time, I had something new to think about.

30

I walked into the office Monday morning with a white chocolate mocha in my hand. Tossing a sheepish smile to Sarah, I marched straight to Allison's desk. She looked up, clearly surprised when I set the drink in front of her. "To make amends. I was unacceptably rude," I said. "I shouldn't have made you so uncomfortable. I hope you can accept my apology."

Allison sipped and stood with a little smile. "Apology accepted, Celeste." She extended her hand, and we shook on it.

Just before I pushed open the stairwell door, a voice spoke behind me. "You look a lot healthier than the last time I saw you."

I turned to see Sarah's teasing smile as she leaned her elbows on the high counter of her desk.

"Pretty sure if it weren't for you, I'd still be passed out on that bench. You're the best, Sarah."

She waved me off. "What are friends for?"

I bit my lip and nodded, echoing Mom. "I couldn't agree more."

The vise-grip that I'd given the job lately relaxed a bit, and it felt right. No working late that night; my second appointment with April was scheduled right after six. In this session, I reported on my conversations with Allison, Ben, and Nick. Then I opened up about Derrick and Amy.

"Does it upset you that he's with her?" she asked.

"It worries me. Why would she trust him?"

She repeated her question. She did that a lot when I avoided answering.

"No," I admitted. "It did when I heard about it, but then Ben—" I blushed. "Um, I guess it doesn't feel like part of my life anymore."

April nodded. "Because it doesn't need to be."

She made me repeat my mantras: I wasn't to blame, I deserved to be happy, and I defined me. Saying those things aloud and having a professional affirm them helped more than I imagined it would. At the end of the hour, she reminded me to eat, and I left feeling another tiny bit better.

The days went fast on that short holiday week. I went to the gym Tuesday and Wednesday. Sore muscles reminded me to be stronger, but mostly it was just better than wall gazing. Tenn Star closed early Wednesday, and I spent the night with my parents. We ate chili and watched *Miracle on 34th Street* like we had every year when I was a child. Something about the innocence of the tradition filled me with a sense of renewal. The year was almost over, but a new phase of my life had finally begun.

31

I hadn't been home for any holiday since junior year of college. Last Thanksgiving, like I told Ben, I got drunk on wine and ate cheap lo mein alone on a friend's couch in Queens. This year, people and laughter surrounded me.

There are five families in my parents' group. No grandkids yet, but when Mom put me on door duty, I had my hands full. Aunts, uncles, cousins—everyone wanted to welcome me home, and not a one asked about New York or old what's-his-name. The barrage of hugs and familiarity left me smiling and dizzy, but what stole my breath most was how easily I found my place in this world again.

The last to arrive, Aunt Jen shoved a stack of dishes at Uncle Alex to throw her arms around me in a weepy embrace. "More beautiful than ever," she said with her hands on my face. "Oh, and you're the spitting image of both your parents."

"Mom," Nick chuckled behind her, also loaded with Tupperware. "I'm freezing. Get inside." She kissed my cheek and took Nick's burden.

"Hey, cuz," I murmured, but before I could twist my necklace, he pulled me close.

"That's favorite cousin," Nick said, his arm slung around my shoulders.

We went inside to see the aunts assembled in the kitchen. The uncles and younger cousins were in the rec room downstairs. Music played through the house speakers. Nick left me in the kitchen with another squeeze, and I was immediately busy helping out and listening to gossip.

Today, the only bubbles were in the champagne.

I filled glasses with ice water and sweet tea, marveling at the precision with which the feast was rolled out. Each family had brought something, and the sidebar in the dining room turned into a buffet of gorgeous dishes. Mom's turkey sat center stage, sliced in uniform perfection and surrounded by garnish. While plates were distributed, she leaned against the wall with a gleam in her eye, and I wondered how she got so good at this kind of thing. I doubted I'd ever be "grown up" enough to execute such an event.

The beauty of the spread was only secondary to its deliciousness. Those people could *cook*. The aunts had laughed at my skinny jeans, and by the time I was scraping sweet potatoes off my plate with a slice of cornbread, I understood why. I hadn't even seen that many calories in the last month.

When I finally put my fork down, Mom smirked at me. "Go get some yoga pants from my dresser."

I jogged upstairs to change and returned to a bustle of activity that rivaled 5th Avenue. "Can I help?" I asked anyone who might hear.

Uncle Brian laughed and jammed a cling-covered dish into the fridge. "Almost done, kiddo. Get your coat; it's time for football."

I hadn't played football since before I wore a bra, but the "turkey bowl" was a blast. I was on Dad's team, although sides were quickly disregarded. Everyone ran after whoever had the ball, and then cheered whenever a touchdown was made. When cold and dying light sent us indoors again, we all gathered in the living room. Dad built a fire and poured wine, and Jen found enough takers to start a game of Trivial Pursuit. I smiled at the scene and went to the kitchen for a drink.

"Seriously? Why didn't—you just ask if you wanted pie, Nicholas?"

Mom's voice stopped me in the doorway. Three different desserts sat on the counter, but Nick leaned against the island a good distance away. Both glanced at me but quickly looked elsewhere when I walked in.

"I just wanted water," I said, under the distinct impression I'd interrupted.

The cupboard's hinge squeaked. The fridge groaned and hissed to dispense ice and water. My swallows reverberated in the silence so loudly that I finished half a glass and gave up. Nick smiled when I frowned at him, but Mom avoided my gaze by rummaging in her box of specialty servingware. *Okay.* I beat a quick retreat to the living room.

They were behind me moments after I'd settled on the couch. Not a hint of tension came from either of them, so I let it go. The couch drew me into a cozy coma, far more appealing than any worries. A steady drone of voices and the popping fire had my eyelids heavy fast. My head lolled, and I hugged a pillow to my cheek while Mom threw a blanket over me.

"She looks so peaceful," someone—Monica, maybe —murmured.

"Thank God." Mom.

Dreams and reality blurred as my nap stretched on. There was nowhere to be, nothing to think about. There was only the peacefulness of this day, and I let it claim me. The smell of coffee snuck in. Someone said something about music. I think Dad threw another log on the fire, but a draft made me shiver. I sighed and pulled the blanket higher. The hum of the room changed. I slept on.

Someone stroked my hair, and I purred at the pleasant tickle. Those fingers tucked a strand behind my ear and skimmed slowly down my cheek while I struggled to wake. It wasn't my mother, of that I was sure. My eyes opened.

The fire crackled. No one spoke.

Benjamin cocked his head at my rapid blinks while I tried to confirm it was really him, and not a dream. "Hi."

Nope, really him. No one else could do those kinds of things to my insides with two letters, but I was still dopey with sleep. "What?" I jolted away from his hand and immediately regretted it. "Why?"

He stood straight, shoulders tight. "I'm here to play a few songs with Nick."

Nick clapped a hand on his back. "Let's tune up," he said, and they turned away.

"Mom?" I caught her eyes, as if she could explain this.

She gave a mask of a smile. "Would you help me serve dessert, Twink— uh, Celeste?" That smile turned wicked as she dropped my nickname, but I was too flustered to care. I stumbled to my feet and followed her obediently.

In the hall, she whirled and grabbed my arm. "Are you okay?"

"I don't know!"

"Nick told me in the kitchen about an hour ago."

"Well, that explains that." Mom's eyebrows wiggled at me, and I exhaled. "What else did he tell you?"

She put both hands on me now. "He said Ben came to play. He said that Ben asked if he could come, but that's supposed to be a secret."

I clutched her fingers. "Oh, god." I broke into a smile that clearly surprised us both. "Seriously?"

She chuckled. "That's my girl. Go freshen up, then help me."

The face in the bathroom mirror was flushed with sleep, but pretty. Pink cheeks lit up my green eyes and made them glitter. I smoothed my ponytail and noticed the tendril behind my ear that he'd put there. With a swipe of balm on my lips, I took a deep breath and went to face the literal music.

When your mother owns a pastry shop, there's no point in describing desserts beyond one word: incredible. She'd gone traditional with apple pie, coconut cake, and pumpkin mousse, but it was a given that everyone would want everything. I walked into the kitchen to see the pre-nap spread had been divvied out onto a village of crystal dessert plates. Matching coffee cups stood at the ready.

"How do you do this?" I wondered while she buzzed around.

Eleanor stopped, dropped her head back, and grinned. "I've been practicing for over thirty years. God, that's hard to believe." She put plates in my hand. "It all started with pot candy and coffee cake."

"What's pot candy? Like, a cast iron or—Mother!" I squeaked when she began to laugh at me. "You're not serious!"

She winked. "It was a huge hit. Now, scoot."

All thoughts of my mother's illicit confections vanished while I shuttled plates and mugs into the living room. The guys jammed. They began to play a couple of holiday tunes while I served, but I couldn't look at either of them. I wasn't ready to process that he was actually here.

Mom put a final plate in my hand. "Give it to Ben. I have Nick's."

"No, I," I stuttered, but she pushed the crystal, no room for discussion.

"Jingle Bells" stopped when we entered. "Thanks, Elle." Nick eagerly accepted Mom's offering. To Ben he said, "You are in luck. Aunt Elle is a pastry chef."

Ben looked at Mom with lifted brows. "It looks amazing, Mrs. Greene."

"Enjoy, Benjamin. We're happy you're here."

Gray eyes settled on me. "I'm glad to be here."

Mute, I handed over the plate, but it was a long moment before I could bring myself to go sit on the couch.

The concert continued, and now that all I had to do was watch, *good god*. I was wrecked as badly as the first time I heard him play. A tiny part of me said I should be ashamed for the throbbing heat between my legs—*Your parents are right there. These people changed your diapers*—but no mental scolding could stop me. If anything, the wrongness of it made me a little worse off, drunk on the secret.

At least, I hoped it was a secret, and that my face didn't give me completely away.

After "Can't Buy Me Love" by the Beatles, they set the instruments aside to finish dessert, and I took the opportunity to breathe again. My focus on Benjamin eased as I looked around at all the happy faces.

Mom was snuggled on the floor in the crook of Dad's arm, feeding him bites of pie. She gazed up at him with a soft smile and proffered the fork, and my heart lurched. They were so perfect for each other, still so deeply in love. *How does someone get that lucky?*

I turned my head and found Ben's gaze on me. *So damn lucky.*

"Want to do one more?" Nick asked, capturing his attention.

"I don't have to," Ben said, but their audience perked up. He and Nick traded another look.

My cousin laughed. "Okay, guys, one more. In case you didn't notice, Ben, uh, knows Celeste." I almost throttled him for the sly glances that hit me from all sides. Ben studied the guitar. "I wanted him to do his new number, but he claims it's not ready, so anyway—"

"Anyway, one more song," Ben interrupted, clearly ready to get on with it. He cocked his head at me and hit a chord. "If you want."

I could only nod, already braced for impact.

"Okay, then, for the ex-Yankee."

Forget New York City, just kill me now. Bluesy, raw, and sexy as hell, Ben tortured me with the most perfect rendition of my song. Tunnel vision hit me hard and took away everything but him and that guitar.

When he got to That Line, the one about the woman of his dreams, a thought took hold that turned me cold. I shook my head to get rid of it, palmed my throat to swallow it down. *It's not an option. You're just drowsy and confused. You're not really in—*

"Lovely," my mother murmured, and I jolted to realize the song had ended. Ben lifted his head, smiled at the applause that I had the sense to join, and cased his guitar. Jen fetched him a glass of water while conversation restarted.

The guys conferred. My cousin nodded toward me, but Ben shook his head. *He came to play. He's not going to cross*

*this room and carry you off, and you are not going to think That
Thing anymore. Don't be crazy.*

Dad started to collect plates and cups, a subtle signal
that the party should wind down. Plans for the next get-
together were discussed, and compliments on the food and
party were passed around one more time. I stood and
moved to give goodbye hugs when jackets began to appear.

I didn't hug him. We didn't even look at each other while
I promised Nick I'd text soon. By the time I had the nerve to
glance over, he'd followed the Fields outside, and I had
another hug to give.

Mom chased after Monica with a bowl in her hand as
Dad shut the front door. We traded a smile, and he hugged
me tight. "My little girl," he said into the top of my hair. "You
had a good day?"

"Wonderful. Did you?" My voice was muffled in his sweater.

He squeezed me again, then stepped back. "Absolutely.
But I sure could use a bourbon." We chuckled and went to
the kitchen.

Mom burst through the back door with a gust of cold air
just as we clinked glasses. Dad cocked his head at her bright
eyes and flushed cheeks. "What's up, beautiful?"

Her lashes fluttered at the endearment, but she turned
to me. "You should go outside, Celeste. Now."

"He calls you beautiful and you kick me out?"

"No," she laughed and wrapped her arms around Dad.
"Someone's waiting for you." Her eyebrows were at her
hairline.

"Shit—oh, I mean, really?" I bumbled, but they just
smiled. With a hard exhale, I scurried to get my coat and
hat. Adrenaline knotted my fingers and tangled my feet as
Mom and Dad all but pushed me outside.

BEN

I leaned against my bumper, coat pulled tight, but I wasn't cold in the least. The cozy scene I'd just left had warmed me inside and out. Mrs. Greene's smile when she found me in her driveway, fiddling with my phone and trying to get the nerve to text Celeste, fueled that flame. While I waited, I closed my eyes and replayed the last few hours.

Nick and I made this plan after she called me, but my pulse had been in my ears when I walked into that house again. The scene that greeted me was practically a Norman Rockwell vision of family Thanksgiving. Friendly faces smiled hello, a fire popped, and, in the corner of the couch, slept the most beautiful girl I'd ever known.

She was lovelier than ever. Her face was placid with sleep as it lolled on the pillow, so sweet and innocent. I thought of the four mornings of my life I'd woken next to her. *Sleep beside me forever. I give no fucks how corny I sound.* It would've scared me how much I needed her if it didn't terrify me how much I couldn't bear to be without her.

Despite everyone's not-so-subtle gazes and the hushed silence that fell, I had to swallow a moan when I pushed her silky hair behind her ear. Her shock upon waking made me want to cringe, but it was a fair reaction. When she started carrying desserts into the room, I forgot about tuning up and watched her, mesmerized by her energy—and by her ass in those yoga pants.

She was tense, yes, but Celeste had changed. She radiated a new, quiet confidence. Not a chin-up barrier, just a soft kind of yeah that was so damn sexy, I couldn't handle it.

Moan that yeah for me, gorgeous. Let me hear it loud. I'll admit, the thought occurred to me more than once—especially while I played her song.

Her parents were right there, you pervert.

Didn't stop me.

The back door opened, and I jolted out of my thoughts and snapped to attention. Panic hit me hard when I realized I had no idea what to say.

32

The porch lamp cast a yellow pool on the driveway, but I had to step out of it in order to find him against his car. Even in the half-light, I could read the tension in his stance, the set of his jaw. My heart hammered, but I stepped toe-to-toe with him. "Benjamin."

"Celeste."

And then, silence. We stared at each other; we looked at the ground; we jammed our hands in pockets, and then took them out again. We probably looked like two bad actors playing at awkward. Ben caught my eye and flashed a look that said what we both knew: *This is weird.*

"Thanks for," we said at the same time, then traded not-quite-a-smile.

"Thanks for coming outside," Ben said when I gestured. "I won't keep you, but I didn't think of how public it would be with your family here today."

Keep me. Keep me as long as you want. "You know I don't mind standing in the cold to talk to you, Benjamin." The throaty pitch of my voice surprised me. Ben's lashes touched his cheek in a slow blink, but he only nodded. "Did you come to see me?"

"Of course." He gave me a once-over. "You look different."

"Probably the twenty pounds of food I ingested."

The right side of his mouth curled. "Hmm, no, not that," he said, but then inhaled and shook his head. "Of course I came to see you. After you called, I needed to."

Say it. You have to know. "For closure?"

He tilted his head, a ghost of smile in his expression. "I'm not sure. I hope not."

I balled my hands into fists to keep from collapsing with relief. "Thank you for my song. It was perfect."

His pleased face flickered, but, typically, smoothed fast. "I practiced this time. Messed with the arrangement a little."

"You practiced?" His single nod made me bite my tongue and check my melted heart. "Of course you did. You played it for a roomful of strangers."

Ben's eyes went wide, his lips parted. He stepped forward. I lifted my face to meet his gaze, but we didn't touch. "I played it for *you*."

Breathing equaled his scent in my nose, so I wasn't sure if I should sip or gulp air. "For me?"

"Mm-hmm." Ben held me with his gaze and nothing more for another long, silent moment before he stepped back. "I should go."

"Should you?" Dammit, my voice was thin.

"Yeah. Thanks again, and please thank your parents for hosting. Goodnight, Celeste."

"Ben?" His hand was on the car door when I spoke, but he turned his head. "If it's not closure... call me or something?"

A pause. Then, "James wants you to call him."

I almost choked on my spit. "*James*? James wants—"

Damn that smirk and all the times it had derailed me. "He wants to talk to you about an idea for an app. Jesus, you didn't seriously think I meant for a date, did you?"

My mouth moved like a fish gulping water. "Uh—app?" *Use your words, honey.*

"Mm-hmm. He says we need your skills if we're going to do this right and make a lot of money."

I reached for my necklace. "What do you think?"

He eyed me and stepped closer again. "I told you day one that we should've collaborated. Without you, I think there's no point even trying." Ben hesitated. "Your hat is crooked." He reached to straighten it, and the simple gesture made me sick with longing. "Think about it, okay? Goodnight, Celeste."

I stood and stared after him until silence filled my ears.

Mom and Dad looked up when I returned to the kitchen, picked up my bourbon, and sipped. "He said he needed to see me, told me about a job, and then left," I said, to them or myself I'm not sure. "It was weird."

Dad leaned on the island beside me and clinked his glass with mine. "Of course he did."

"But he didn't say anything, not really. Why come here, play me a song, and then goodnight?"

I looked up from the glass when Dad laughed. "Oh, Twink, what did you want him to say? He doesn't know how you feel, he's in your parents' driveway. He's certainly not going to tell you the truth."

"The truth?"

"Mm-hmm, that he's in love with you."

The floor dropped out from under me. I clutched the counter. "Why would you say that?"

He looked over at Mom. "Because he looks at you like I've looked at your mother since the moment I met her. He looks at you like there's no one else in the room—the room, the next room, the next house—just him and you."

Mom's cheeks turned a dark rose. She moved closer, and he rested his hands on her shoulders. I would've melted at their cuteness, but I was still busy searching for solid ground. "You guys don't understand. It was never like that with us."

Mom snorted. "Celeste, it was *always* like that with you and him."

Just when I'd put a tile or two underneath me, the floor was gone again. I opened my mouth to argue with her, with my aching heart, with anyone who'd listen, but Mom waved her hand.

"Whether you two see each other again or not, whether you tell each other how you both really feel—don't interrupt, because I already know what you'll say—doesn't change the truth. What will be will be. For now, don't fret too much."

I shut my mouth with a *humph* and drained my drink. She eyed me sharply and added, "Or drink too much. My hydrangeas aren't up for it."

I ducked my head. "I promise."

Dad put the liquor away and set a glass of water in front of me. "We better go pack. Sure you don't mind driving us to the airport?"

"Not at all," I said for the hundredth time, and they kissed me goodnight.

I sat on a stool while they made their way upstairs. Soon, their footsteps and muffled music from the stereo drifted down. The peaceful house quieted my thoughts and brought me back to the equilibrium I'd been working on lately. Drowsy and content, I meandered to my bedroom and pulled back the sheets. Just before I flipped off the light, I reached for my phone to set an alarm—and saw I had a text.

Ben: Softer. That's what looked different.

My heart started to pound all over again. He'd sent the message a while ago, probably right after he got home. I wondered if it was too late to reply, but typed anyway.

Me: I'm trying to be.

I switched off the light and flopped against the pillow with a huff. *He's not going to text back. He's asleep and—*

Ben: Happy?

Me: More like healing.

Ben: You should be happy.

"I deserve to be happy." I whispered my mantra, but having him say it twisted my heart in ways I didn't want to think about more today.

Me: U 2.

Ben: Thx. Why do they call you Twink?

"Ugh," I groaned, then typed it. Ben sent back an "LOL" that made me smile.

Me: Twink=twinkle=stars, etc.=Celeste. Also was a character in a show I loved as a kid.

Ben: F*ing adorable. Can't believe you really told me.

Me: Yeah, yeah. Go to bed, Benjamin.

Ben: I'm in bed, bossy.

I caught my breath at the heat I couldn't control. It was too easy to envision him on his back, phone in hand, probably smirking at calling me bossy, in his underwear...

I started a hundred different replies, but nothing seemed right. I'd just typed, "TAKE ME, I'M YOURS," laughed, and deleted it, when another chime made me jump.

Ben: Did you fall asleep?

Me: Yeah.

Ben: You know I can see you typing, right?

Shit. Busted.

Me: Must've been a glitch.

I knew, knew in my heart, that he was grinning. I also knew he was calling me on my bullshit.

Ben: #TooWeird

Me: #GoToSleep

Ben: Who's bossy now? G'night, Ms. Greene.

I could've stayed up all night analyzing this exchange. I didn't. I put the phone down and fell asleep with a smile on my face.

33

"Come on, genius." I sighed and glared, then reached for the eraser. "Who forgets the e in Shakespeare?"

Sunday morning was perfectly Zen. I'd been at my kitchen table for over an hour. A second cup of coffee cooled by my elbow, and a book I'd found at home sat in front of my sketchpad. The book was a collection of watercolors of various sites in Paris. Mom had given it to me as a child. They had been too complex to replicate at first, but I'd drawn every image again and again until I improved. Today, my subject was the storefront of Shakespeare & Co., the world-famous bookstore and a favorite haunt of my parents when they lived there before I was born. Their flight had left on time Friday, and I pictured them there now. I fixed the sign and added in their silhouettes.

By the time the coffee was gone, I sat back and looked at the page. "Not bad." I declared, the highest praise I'd ever give my work, then closed the books and went for my sneakers.

It had been a good weekend. I'd been alone but not idle since leaving Mom and Dad at the airport. Christmas shopping, gym, a Netflix movie—no vacant floating for this girl. I'd been inspired to draw this morning. Now, I wanted fresh air, and knew the perfect place to get it.

Shelby Bottoms was a different kind of beautiful so late in November. The bursting color from the first of the month had been replaced by a dull yellow and hint of winter's gray-brown, but the day was bright blue, and my feet pounded a strong cadence for three miles before I turned around.

Less than a mile. That's all that remained between my car, a perfect morning, and me. But as I approached a trail outlet, a couple emerged just ahead and changed my run into the Worst Idea Ever.

Yes, couple. Benjamin jogged easily alongside a tall, curvy brunette with a suspiciously familiar purple ponytail.

My feet became bricks as I continued to limp along. What else could I do? A sinkhole to swallow me would've been a convenient escape, but I'm not that lucky. *Breathe. Think. You have to get out of this.*

In retrospect, I admit that my course of action wasn't the brightest, but I was in fight or flight mode. I figured going slow spelled disaster and a certain encounter. The path ended in a few yards, and I couldn't bear to trail behind, watching them finish. She'd hold up a hand to high-five. He'd hug her instead, flash one of his irresistible smiles. The thought made me shudder. They wouldn't notice a random jogger run past, right? Seemed logical to me.

I skirted them on her side at an all-out run, my head bent low. For a moment, I thought I'd slipped by unseen.

For a moment.

A firm hand wrapped around my bicep and pulled me off balance. I stumbled backward and crashed into an equally firm chest. "Easy," he murmured while I found my feet. "You're in a hurry."

I turned around. *Dammit.* No one should look that beautiful when they're working out. His hair was damp at the corners, a ruddy flush from the cold on his cheeks. I swallowed hard. "I was just finishing up. Guess I didn't see you."

"Didn't you?"

My core throbbed at the familiar, teasing tone, but reality couldn't be ignored. "Yes, I did, actually. But you looked busy." I jutted my chin toward Olivia. She stood several feet away, intent on her phone.

Benjamin followed my gaze and smiled. "Nick and James got sick of me. She said I needed to get out of the house. I don't think running was what she had in mind. Come say hello."

I did everything I could to keep the dread off my face. "I don't think that's a good idea."

"I do." He grasped my wrist. I wanted to dig my heels in, but he guided me to where she stood.

Olivia had a brow up before we were within speaking distance, and I mentally armored myself. "How the hell are you running that fast?" she said in greeting. "We've done, like, a billion miles out here—"

"Three," Ben murmured.

"—And I'm ready to chug a beer and nap until Wednesday. This is the last time I let you pick what we do, Addison." She glared at him, then flashed me a commiserative eye-roll.

I tried not to gape. Where was the snark? Why wasn't she tearing my hair out?

As if she read my mind, Liv flicked her gaze over me and smirked. "Chill, girl. We're cool."

"We are?"

"Sure." She shrugged. "Not much point in beating you up when you already did it to yourself."

"Dammit, Liv." Ben's bark was fierce, but she laughed him off and shoved his shoulder.

He didn't see it coming. His feet didn't plant in time, causing him to stumble sideways, straight into me. I gripped his arms and pushed back to keep us from falling over. My cheek crashed into his chest as he got his feet untangled, one knee between my legs, his hands on my waist.

Oh, good god.

I couldn't keep my eyes open as his scent, his warmth, invaded every part of my being. It was all I had not to moan or break into tears. Ben held me long after we stabilized, seconds probably, but they felt like years. He drew a quick, shuddering breath, squeezed me gently, and stepped away.

Liv wore a Cheshire-Cat grin. "You're welcome," she said, gaze flicking to both of us.

My face heated even more, but Ben chuckled and pushed his hair away. "Yeah, I owe you a beer for that one." He glanced at my deer-in-headlights look and started to speak, but Liv beat him to it.

"Why don't you come get a beer with us? We can go to Southern Grist since it's close. You in?"

I don't remember saying yes, but we stayed in step to the end of the trail. Minutes later, sweaty and still tingling, I took a long pull of a delicious IPA in a bustling taproom. Liv and Ben chatted about music and local brews, but I barely spoke. *Is this a dream? Nightmare?* Whatever I called it, it was nice. Liv barely glanced my way, but her attitude was totally relaxed, and their jokes made me laugh. No need for my walls, apparently.

Ben glanced my way a lot. He frowned when I drained my glass and refused a second round, but I didn't want to press my luck.

Back at home, I'd just emerged from the shower when my texts chimed.

Ben: Glad you came w/ us.

Me: Thanks for the beer.

Ben: Did you really think I wouldn't see you?

Me: Dunno. Didn't want to bother you 2.

I bit my lip and went for it.

Me: Nick said you guys got back together.

Ben: WTF?!?!?! Bullshit... right??

Me: Yeah, bullshit. Just teasing.

Ben: Ha. Ha. Tell Joe I said hi.

I squeaked and lay down on the bed.

Me: Will do. (You=JERK)

He sent a smile, but the next message made my heart flip.

Ben: *Srsly, you know there's no one else I even THINK about, right?

Me: I like that.

Ben: I'm glad.

I stared at the screen, considered the implications—and then reminded myself of reality. I hadn't asked to reconcile, and he hadn't offered. A few smiley texts didn't mean all was well.

Me: But it won't be true very long.

Ben: Why??

Me: I can't stop you from thinking about someone new.

Ben: Completely UNtrue.

Three nights later, I threw my hand in the air. "But it *is* true, right? He's a gorgeous guy with tons of friends. He's going to meet another woman."

"Has he contacted you again?"

I leaned back on the brown suede cushion. "Yes," I admitted. "Um, every day."

April's brows lifted. "And what's the nature of the conversation?"

"Work stuff. Questions, mostly. Nothing deep. Ugh, what does he want?"

She pulled off her glasses and smiled. "As you know, Celeste, I take notes during our sessions." I nodded. "Would you like to guess how much of our conversations are somehow related to Benjamin?"

My cheeks heated. I hugged my knees. "Probably a hell of a lot."

She chuckled. "That's a fair estimate."

"Because—because he—I—" I waved again and gave up the excuse.

"What he wants isn't the question we should address. What you want is what matters, and you should have the confidence to ask for whatever that is. Have you articulated it yet?"

I clasped my hands between my knees and stared at her with a tiny shake of my head. She repeated herself.

"Well, I guess maybe we could be friends? He's friends with Liv, so..." I trailed off at her expression.

"Celeste, you must be able to say for sure what you want, and it's pretty clear that friendship isn't a truthful answer. Until you're honest with yourself, it's useless to speculate about his feelings. Do you want to try again?"

I didn't. I wasn't ready to say aloud that scary thought that had grown in my heart with every text he sent. I promised I'd work on it. With a recitation of my mantras, we closed the session.

Questions about whether Rollings still did his goodnight routine and why my parents picked Paris for vacation were definitely not what I wanted from Benjamin. I resolved to slow down my replies to his messages so he'd get the hint.

Of course he didn't text me once the next day.

By the time I got home, I'd checked my phone too many damn times not to be pissed at myself for it. Why that prompted me to text Nick for James's number, I have no idea. Maybe it was my way of taking a little control of the situation.

"Please tell me this is about pleasure, not business," James said as soon as I said hello.

I snorted. "Business. I was told to call. You know I have a full-time job, right?"

Now he snorted. "Yeah, and that's cool. Your boss sounds like a good old boy, but I thought maybe you'd want to expand your horizons."

"I'm listening."

"I've got plans, and between our talk at the party and my brother's reports of your work, I'm prepared to cut you in. Do you really know six coding languages?"

"Mmm, proficient in four, but yes."

"Get over here for a meeting Saturday afternoon. I'll text you the address."

"Great, see you then." I hung up and put the phone by my bed, determined not to check it again.

At midnight, my ringtone jerked me awake in a panic. "Hello?"

"Shit, you were asleep. I'm sorry."

"Ben? Hi." I yawned.

"Hey." His throaty voice made me shiver. "Sorry I woke you."

"It's a work night." I rolled to my belly and cradled the phone on my shoulder. "Why are you up so late?"

"I've been at the recording studio all day. Cellar Door demoed my song."

"Nick said it wasn't finished."

He paused. "It's finished."

I lifted my head when my heart skipped a beat. "Yeah? What's it called?"

He was driving; the hum of the car filled my ears until finally he said, "'Hard Truth.'"

My face fell into the pillow with a muffled groan I hoped he didn't hear. "I know a little about that," I whispered.

"I know."

"What's your hard truth, Benjamin?" I flexed my hips into the mattress, just drowsy enough to make me bold, just bold enough to tease him.

It worked. There was a telltale grit to his words when he said, "I called to hear your voice. And."

"And?"

"And listening to you all sleepy like this turns me on."

I flipped to my back and caressed my stomach. "Your voice always turns me on," I confessed.

I'd been here so many times before. Darkness made time and reality irrelevant and left me free to explore myself. But now he shared my secret space, and I wondered if he had any idea how much that meant, or how much I wanted him here with me.

Ben laughed. "Oh, really?"

"Yeah, really. Come over and I'll prove it."

My eyes opened as everything froze. I thought of April's instructions to articulate what I wanted. *Guess I just did.*

"Prove it? How?"

Heat unfurled between my legs. Every nerve in my body stood on end. "However you like."

"That could lead to trouble. I'd want to know precisely how turned on you are. I'd have no choice but find out for myself, and once I did—"

Both of us sucked in deep breaths. "Come over, Benjamin."

"I can't."

My palm flattened over my pounding heart. "What?"

"I can't. If I can't have you, I can't *have* you, dammit." His tone had cleared and gotten louder. "I shouldn't have called. I'm sorry."

"No, just—"

"I've got to let you go," he almost pleaded.

"You really don't," I begged right back. Wide awake and cold all over, I sat up. "Wait, Ben. Wait."

Silence—but still the hum of the engine.

"We can't go on like this," I said at last. "I can't take it."

He exhaled loudly. "Neither can I. Let's talk. Dinner tomorrow at six? Café Margot okay?"

"Sounds good."

We hung up, and I curled into a ball and closed my eyes. Stinging rejection and questions about what tomorrow would bring turned my dreams into distorted memories of our time together. It was something of a relief when the alarm went off.

34

"Yowza, look at you! Hot date?" Sarah greeted when I walked into the office.

I winced and looked down. Black leggings, my beloved Prada boots, and a winter-white one-shoulder sweater that hit my thighs had seemed like a good work-to-dinner choice for a Friday. Now, I wasn't so sure. "Plans, yeah. Is it that obvious?"

Sara's aquamarine eyes flicked over me. "Yep. Luckily, you have the floor to yourself for a few more weeks." I agreed and tried to hitch up the neckline of my sweater. She laughed, and I headed for the stairs with a wave.

Rollings and I had finally hired a little team that would start in January. I'd officially be the head of Tenn Star's online department. We desperately needed people to maintain the sites for our clients if we wanted to keep them, and there was simply no way I could create and run everything.

I thought of my appointment with James while I settled in with a cup of coffee. That made me think of the party, which made me think of hiking and talking work on that perfect Saturday with him.

By midmorning, thoughts of Ben seemed destined to ruin my productivity. My biggest accomplishment was the empty coffee cup. I was plodding along when Rollings popped in.

"Morning, Ms. Greene! How's the Threads update coming?"

"Going alright." *For a good old boy, he's not so bad as a boss.*

"Glad to hear. Listen, got a little rush job for you. A prospective client, car dealership, called earlier. They need a rehaul to their current site ASAP. They have a big sale in two weeks and want to get it revamped by the end of next week. The owner sent over a detailed outline of their needs and goals. I said we'd try to have a initial proposal tomorrow morning. Can you do it?"

You bastard, I hope you choke on a doughnut... Stop that. Focus.

I mentally calculated. A review of the current site and the specs for revisions, time to plan, then draft. At my most rushed, that was a full day's work for the homepage alone. If I started at lunch, I might be done by—eight? Nine? Ten??

Know your business. This is the job you essentially sold your soul for. You're not the only one who can fill this chair.

"I'll do my best." I gritted my teeth into a smile and barely made it until the door shut behind him before sinking my face into my hands. So much for daydreaming. I finished the updates before lunch, ate at my desk, and took a look at the new project.

"Fuck."

The word bounced around the room. This website looked like it was designed ten years ago. By a student. In high school. I looked at the client's requests, which boiled down to, "We know it sucks. Help," and picked up my phone.

"Hey," I said when he answered. "I just got a massive job dumped in my lap that's supposed to be done by tomorrow morning. I don't think I can make it tonight."

Ben hummed. "Sorry to hear that."

"Tomorrow?" I asked.

"I'm supposed have a meeting with James, but I can cancel."

I chuckled. "*I've* got a meeting with James. We talked last night."

"Awesome," he murmured, but I sighed.

"Sorry, Ben. Guess I'll see you there."

"It's okay."

We both knew it wasn't.

I slogged on through the next few hours, but my heart wasn't in it. At four, Rollings appeared again with his usual grin. "Thought I'd check in, see how it's coming."

I looked at the screen, and then at him. Rollings moseyed over to lean on my desk while my pulse climbed into my throat. "Actually, Mr. Rollings, I don't think I can finish tonight."

His brows went up. "No?"

Breathe. Know. "No, sir. This is a huge task. I'm essentially starting from scratch, and they have more than one goal for the site. I'd like to meet with them before continuing this draft, get a better feel of the style and specifics of what they're envisioning. I can come in tomorrow morning if you need, but honestly I could sit here all night and would probably just be spinning my wheels, if you know what I mean."

I twisted my necklace, braced to hear something like, "No problem. Just clean out your desk and we'll mail your check," but Rollings nodded.

"You know what, Ms. Greene? Good for you. I've never

known you to say no to a deadline, but even I thought this one might be much. These folks want your skills? They can wait until Monday. Do what you can, and take off when you need. I'll give them a call before I head home."

Warm, sweet relief coursed through me so hard, I sagged in my chair. "Thank you so much, Mr. Rollings," I whispered with a face-aching grin.

He blinked and straightened his tie as his ears went pink. "Of course, sweetheart. Have a good one."

I went back to the screen. Rollings was at the door when his chuckle made me look up again. "Don't let Joe see you dressed like that. It'll break his heart," he said over his shoulder.

"Mr. Rollings," I gasped, eliciting another chortle.

"Oh, honey, I hear all the gossip in this place." He winked, and then shut the door.

I shook my head, set an alarm for 5:45, and turned back to my notes.

BEN

"Oh, my *god*!"

"Hello, Sarah. How's it going?"

Thank god she was still there, and the building was still unlocked. Sarah already had her coat and keys laid across the desk, but she sat down when I approached.

Her smile made her eyes disappear. "I'm good, Ben. How are you?"

"Alright, I guess." I glanced around. "Rollings still here?"

"Nope, went home about an hour ago. Most everybody's gone, actually."

She propped her chin in her hand and waited for me to say what we both knew I would. "Celeste's working late though, hmm?"

I smiled when her eyes disappeared again. She was cute. Too young and, well, not Celeste, but cute. Bantering with her had been a highlight of this place.

"Nope." Her dreamy sigh almost made me miss the message. "She should be down anytime. Told Rollings she couldn't work late tonight."

"Really?" I muttered. "Good for her."

Sarah nodded. "Totally. Who wants to sacrifice a hot date for work on a Friday—or ever?"

I looked at her sharply. Her eyes were wide, lips bitten into a line. "Hot date? She said that?"

Sarah emitted a high-pitched giggle. "Hmm, no, she said she had plans. Her outfit says hot date, though."

My brows arched as her gaze swept over me. She giggled again, face crimson, and I laughed and shook my head. I jerked my thumb to the stairs. "Will you bust me if I go up? Just to make sure she doesn't need any help with the website, of course."

Sarah stood, put her elbows on the desk, and drew an X over her heart. "I won't tell a soul."

I leaned so we were face to face, winked, and said, "You are a rock star, Sarah Rose," then turned and ran for the stairs.

35

"Come on, come on." I drummed my fingers on the desk. The server had been slow all day, but now I was ready to pull my hair out. Finally, the file saved and the window closed, and I lunged to shut off the monitor. The clock read 6:00. If I'd left fifteen minutes ago as planned, I'd be halfway to Ben's and a half step closer to getting some answers.

I slashed a coat of lipstick on, grabbed my purse and coat, and ran for the door. I reached for the knob, but the door sprang open before I could touch it. My hand stayed suspended in midair as I faced...

Benjamin Addison.

No suit this time. He was casual in a dark plaid shirt and chinos, but the set in his jaw and the glint in his eye took me right back to our first meeting.

"Apologies if I scared you," he said with a curl of his lips.

My eyes filled with tears that I blinked away. "You didn't scare me. But I certainly didn't expect someone else to be here."

"You look like you're on your way out. Thought you had to work late."

I tossed my hair. "Yeah, well, I had something more important to do."

Oh, he liked that. His eyes flashed as he said, "I figured since you couldn't leave, maybe I should come to you. Back to the beginning."

His words sharpened me up. I scowled and turned into the office. "Come to me, really? Funny thing to say after last night." I dumped my stuff and spun to him, pointed and said, "That was some serious bullshit, Addison. You baited me."

He strode into the room, slamming the door. "Are you yelling at me?"

"Yep, sure am. Pissed as hell, too."

Storm clouds gathered in his expression. "Don't. Don't you dare."

"Oh, I dare. I deserve an answer. And I want to know what's up with the random texts, too. Since when did you become such a hedgy bastard?"

"What?" he barked. "Hedgy?"

"You heard." I threw my shoulders back, and he stalked toe-to-toe with me. *Good. Anything is better than nothing.*

"And what, exactly, would you have me do? You walked out on me. What the hell can I say to you after that?"

I flinched. "I told you—"

"I know. But I can't push you anymore, can't suggest, can't begin to know what you want." His ire wavered. "I can't seem to stay away, either."

Both of our lips parted, and we drew in the other's breath. "I don't want you to stay away," I whispered. "I know myself better now, Benjamin. Never perfect, but better."

He stepped away and nodded. "I know. I can see how much brighter you are. Your walls are gone."

I exhaled and wandered to the empty space of the office

that would soon be full of new desks. The carpet was clean, brand-new still, and I dropped to sit cross-legged on the floor.

Ben stood over me. "I thought you were pissed."

"So pissed," I snapped, but I was tired of this already. *So tired of fighting everything.* I drew up the last of my ire by recalling the sting of his rejection last night and glared up at him, but I think he knew how much effort it took. "You always knew how to push me. You knew what I needed, even when I wasn't sure. I should've trusted that more, I know. Now, when I am actually sure, you reject me."

He shifted his weight. "I told you already: sometimes I have to save myself. And I can't—I'm not sure where you are with this."

My glare relaxed. "I'm right here, Ben."

All his edges softened. "So you are. Here, pissed, and distractingly beautiful. Classic Celeste."

My cheeks heated. "Definitely here and pissed."

He sat down beside me. I hid my face, but he was close enough to smell and feel. "Definitely beautiful. And, as always, completely enchanting." Ben dragged his finger from my earlobe to my shoulder. His lips touched my neck, and I shuddered. He hummed. "Should I stop?"

"No." I shuddered again. My head bowed lower. He kissed, a little wetter, a little longer.

"Still pissed?" he whispered. I nodded, so his lips pressed on my neck again. Good god, his mouth was too much. He tasted me with slow, savory kisses that spoke of unhurried exploration, a lifetime to enjoy it.

A lifetime.

"You're melting." He shifted behind me, legs beside my hips, chest to my back. "And it is still so... fucking... hot."

Ben cuffed my arm to pull me closer, and a gasping

moan fell from my lips. "Shh," he soothed, his nose where his mouth had been. "You're mad, remember? So very angry at me, right?"

"Right."

He laughed in my ear, then touched his forehead to my hair and hugged me. I was completely cradled in him. "Do you really think that every part of me didn't want to come to you last night?"

I lifted my head. "Why didn't you?"

Ben was silent. He kissed me again, this time at the L of my neck and shoulder, and turned my face to see him. "Truth?" His tone made me open my eyes.

"Truth."

He sighed. "This is going to come out wrong, but... When we met, you fascinated me. You decided so quickly we should be enemies, but that was impossible. As soon as we started talking, I felt our connection. I wanted to tear your walls down and see who you really were.

"Then you let me. And that ruined everything." He smirked.

I frowned and turned to face him better, but he shushed me before I could speak. "Straight shot, no hedging," he whispered. "When you called, you said—you said I made you a better you." I nodded, and he squinted. "Do you remember what I said on the couch? Your best self? Your most alive you?"

I. Stopped. Breathing.

He scanned my face and chuckled humorlessly. "You remember. It's okay, I knew you didn't mean it like that." Ben drew back, pushed his hair away, and met my eyes. "But I do. I mean it exactly like that. And I didn't come to you last night because I can't do the right now with you anymore. Maybe I never really did."

He caressed my cheek and dusted his thumb over my lips. Gray eyes went liquid. "I'm so in love with you it's killing me, Celeste Greene. That's my hard truth, and I can't pretend otherwise."

That Thought, the one that had scared me since it first took hold, laid out in no uncertain terms. A tear slid down my cheek as I forced myself to submit to his gaze. There was no hiding from this moment. There was only his confession and my poor heart.

He waited me out, but when I spoke, my tongue, like my brain, was tied. "Ben, I—I don't—" I trailed off and sucked a ragged breath.

The look of defeat that shuttered his face made me realize what I'd said. My eyes went wide, and I reached for him. "No, I—"

"You don't." He drew away.

I gripped his shirt with one hand, hair with the other, and refused all his attempts to retreat. My voice was still broken when I whimpered, "I don't understand how we know that."

A light flared in his eyes, but it didn't change his expression. "How *we* know what?"

With a sniffle, I tried again. "How we know we're in love when we only had a few days together."

Now he held me too, both hands on my cheeks to bring us nose-to-nose. "Did I hear you say we're in love? Did you just say that?"

I tilted my face and pressed a kiss salty with tears to his lips. "Mm-hmm." I sighed and kissed again. His grip and his lips softened. "I want to be with you, Ben. I love you, Ben."

Whoa.

I lifted my gaze to his, and he broke into a brilliant grin.

His laugh gusted my lips. "Holy shit," he said before he sealed his mouth to mine in a kiss that stole my breath.

You are who want to be. I want to be Celeste Greene, wizard coder and designer, daughter, and friend. I want to be Celeste Greene, in love with Benjamin Addison. I even want to be Celeste Greene, proud resident of Nashville, Tennessee.

The fear around those wants, those definitions of me, unshackled from my heart and stripped the last barrier between us. I melted into his arms, into his *love*, right there on the floor, certain that Ben Addison and I would redefine what it meant for two people to be close.

"Should we leave?" I asked when his lips moved across my jaw, his hand over my sweater.

He laughed in my ear again. "No, we should play out every single fantasy I ever had in this place."

"Benjamin," I gasped as he pulled me to my feet. "NSFW."

He swung me into his arms. I squeaked, and he grinned. "Ms. Greene, I don't work here."

ACKNOWLEDGMENTS

Sitting here overflowing with gratitude, but I'm supposed to keep it to a page. I'll try for two...

To my quirky, fantastic family, who all raised their eyebrows to learn I was writing steamy romances but supported me anyway. You all are my touchstones in this crazy world, no matter if we live 10 minutes or 1,000 miles apart.

To my grandmothers, who taught me to shine in such different ways. I miss you every day.

To Michael. You first taught me the exhilaration of falling in love. Our romance might've ended, but you showed me how big my heart could be. Thank you for encouraging me through so many hours of writing and rambling about plot holes and new ideas.

To Eva, who believed in Celeste and Ben. This book wouldn't be what it is without you. To Avery! Thanks for your enormous patience as I muddled through my visions for a book cover. Your talent has given me stunning artwork and a killer logo.

To Saranii, my biggest fan. To Brooke and Summer, my dear friends who cheer me on.

To my readers and writing community on Twitter! Y'all inspire me and give me life when the road is dark and long. Bonnie and Lily, thank you infinitely for your feedback and for fangirling over Ben. Extra special love for my partners in writing and silliness, Sarah and DeAndre. Thanking you two for your impact would require many more pages and leave everyone feeling awkward at my gushing. You know it's true.

And thank you, readers. I write for you. If you smiled, laughed, loved, or felt lighter even a little as you read, then I count the novel a huge success.

Thank you all so much from the bottom of my sparkling heart. —Skye

ABOUT THE AUTHOR

Skye McDonald is the author of the Anti-Belle books, a contemporary romance series set in her hometown of Nashville, Tennessee. As an English teacher, a die-hard romantic, and a huge fan of Nashville's hip new vibe, Skye's Anti-Belle series are standalone novels about sassy GRITS (Girls Raised In the South) learning to love themselves before they can claim their happily ever after. (Spoiler: they always do!) Her first book, *Not Suitable for Work*, won the 2017 Linda Howard Award of Excellence in the Romantic Sensual and Sizzling category.

When she isn't lost in a love scene or grading student essays, Skye can be found cheering for the University of Tennessee (go Vols!), exploring Brooklyn with her adorable Corgi, or heading off on some new adventure. She'd love for you to connect with her on Twitter and Instagram @WriterSkyeMcD.

COMING SOON!

Off the Record (Anti-Belle #2)

Nemesis (Anti-Belle #3)

EXCERPT FROM OFF THE RECORD (ANTI-BELLE BOOK 2: NICK)

Nick Field is a ladies' man with a life full of music, friends, and good times. Mel Thomas works 24/7 as the media manager to America's newest heartthrob. Ten years ago, Nick and Mel were high school sweethearts. Reunited by chance, what should've been ancient history reignites into a passionate present. Too bad there's no future in it.

Sneak peek

Nick

"Field!"

"Yeah, boss?" I didn't need to look up to know who was shouting.

Rick Alvin appeared in the control room. "Showtime, Nicky. Follow me." He jerked his thumb behind him toward the commotion echoing down the hall.

The lobby was so packed, we had to squeeze through a wall of shoulders to join the fray. Every employee of InSight Studio ringed the room's perimeter. I took my place and looked around at my colleagues. Their faces wore various states of awe at the dozen-plus reporters popping flashes and shouting questions to the men in the center of it all.

Well, to one of the men. The guy in the suit was irrelevant; the guy in the black harem sweatpants, long white tunic, and aviator sunglasses was Jesse Storms, the man of the moment.

Six weeks ago, Jesse Storms won the most popular of the reality/talent TV competitions. Everything about his image was brilliantly marketed to make the country fall in love with him. Even this return to Nashville to record his debut album was great spin.

Three weeks ago, I didn't know any of this shit. I was grinding along on a project when Rick brought me into his office and said we got the Jesse Storms contract.

I replied with, "Cool. Who?"

My boss called me a dumbass and told me to do my homework. Then he said, "Nick, you're the best damn engineer I've got. It's time to move you up. Storms's label wants authenticity to the Nashville feel, and Storms must have a hell of a lawyer, because he's somehow gotten more control over recording than a debut artist should have. You're the executive producer on this project, son." He pushed a check across the desk and smirked. "You do this right, have it wrapped by the end of August and make sure it doesn't sound like total garbage, and you'll be second in command around here. How's that sound?"

"Partial garbage, end of August, and I—holy—" My words broke off when I glanced at the check.

Rick grinned. "You've more than earned it." Clearing his throat, he motioned me out the door. "Don't screw up."

～

The next morning, I had the soundboard ready, the mics checked, and the backup band busy rehearsing when the interoffice phone shrilled.

"A white Suburban just pulled up—I think Mr. Storms is here," our receptionist gasped into the phone.

"Cool. Show him back." I took a quick breath and headed into the lounge just as the door opposite me opened. Jesse walked in.

He shook my hand and gestured behind him. "This is the crew." He stopped and looked around. "Where's Melody?"

Melody. The name tickled the hair on my neck and made me forget every single name I'd just committed to memory.

One of his guys said, "I think she was talking to the receptionist." He jogged to the hallway calling, "Hey, Miss Twitter! You're wanted in the lounge."

I scratched my neck to make the tingling stop. "Did you say Melody?" *Shut up. There's no way it's her. Focus.*

"Yeah. She's a hell of a writer, and the best damn girl-friend a guy like me could ask for." Jesse shrugged like we shared a joke.

The tingling started to close my throat. "Writer?"

But the guy reappeared, and the woman who followed him in confirmed every ounce of adrenaline coursing through my system. My pulse beat in my ears and muted the scene as her ocean-blue eyes landed on me.

Suddenly I was eighteen again, rocked by nostalgia and memories that had been locked away for a decade.

His girlfriend. Jesus, I didn't see this coming.

Melody

Nick. How did I not see this coming?

There are over a million people who live in Nashville. Of those million-plus, there were maybe three who would really remember me. Of those three, there was one I wanted —no, needed—to never see again. One I needed to remain ancient history. One I hadn't let myself think about in over ten years.

I'd been back in town for 48 hours and had seen no one outside of the crew and my father. What the hell were the odds that he would be the first person I encountered?

And why did he have to look so damn *good*?